SUN CROSSED

ZODIAC WOLVES #3

ELIZABETH BRIGGS

SUN CROSSED (ZODIAC WOLVES #3)

Copyright © 2022 by Elizabeth Briggs

This is a work of fiction. Names, characters, businesses, places, events and incidents are either the products of the author's imagination or used in a fictitious manner. Any resemblance to actual persons, living or dead, or actual events is purely coincidental.

Cover designed by Natasha Snow

Cover photo by Wander Aguiar

ISBN (paperback) 978-1-948456-43-2

ISBN (ebook) 978-1-948456-30-2

CHAPTER ONE

FOR MOST OF MY LIFE, the moon's cool light had been a comfort—a reminder that I wasn't alone and maybe, just maybe, someone was watching over me. Now the full moon shining overhead seemed to mock me with every step I took across the empty beach. It peeked out between the dark clouds, casting an ominous light across the lone house standing before me, the only thing I could see in the distance other than sand and waves.

It seemed impossible that only minutes earlier I'd been somewhere else entirely, where the sun had shone while battle waged on all around me. Shifters from different packs had fought one another in the forest while the Sun Witches closed in on us, casting their deadly magic. Magic that had taken down the man I loved, seconds before I was whisked away to this strange place by the mysterious Moon Witches. I'd begged them to take me back, but they'd refused, leaving me here on the beach with nothing but my grief and the slight chance that I might be able to save Kaden with their help. That small flicker of hope was the one thing that kept me moving forward.

Cold raindrops soaked my clothes and sent a chill through my bones as I approached the wrap-around porch. The house looked like something out of an old movie, a two-story Victorian with faded yellow and white paint, complete with spindles and spires. The front door was solid dark wood with stained glass windows depicting the moon in its different phases.

I stopped outside it, gathering my strength and resolve. Celeste, the Moon Witch High Priestess, waited behind that door with the answers I'd been searching for ever since I'd found out about my heritage. I needed them if I was going to save Kaden, but my emotions were still roiling in my gut after what I'd just been through, all clashing together and making it hard to think straight. I drew in a breath and wiped rain and tears off my face. I didn't have the luxury of grieving Kaden right now, and if I stepped inside the house, maybe I'd never have to truly grieve him at all.

I reached up to touch the door and it creaked open before me, revealing an entryway with a rug covered in an elaborate star pattern. The first thing I noticed was the flickering light dancing across the walls, illuminating the house from many candles on trays and dishes. No electricity—had the storm knocked out the power? The second thing I noticed was that the moon and stars theme continued throughout the house through knick-knacks and pillows, in paintings hanging on the walls, and carved into the dark wood of the furniture.

Celeste appeared through a doorway, pale as a ghost with her long, silvery-white hair, and motioned for me to follow her. She'd discarded her black and silver robe along with the moon crown and now wore a simple blue long-sleeve dress. "Come to the kitchen, let me get you something to drink. We have a lot to talk about, and I find it's best to do that over a hot cup of cocoa."

Her voice was cool, calm, and inviting, but most of all, it promised answers—and a way to save the man I loved. As I followed her, it quickly became apparent that the house was well-maintained but clearly trapped in the past, though it was a mishmash of different eras. I was no expert, but some of the furniture looked Victorian or even Medieval, while others had an Art Deco style, though a few pieces were more modern. The kitchen was just as unusual as the rest of the house, with a beautiful star tile across the floor and an old-fashioned wood-burning stove that seemed straight out of a history book.

"Please, sit down," Celeste said, motioning to the round breakfast table on one side of the room, underneath a half-circle of windows overlooking the beach and the stormy night sky.

I sat in one of the chairs and watched Celeste move around the kitchen. I couldn't pinpoint her age, despite the white hair. Her face put her in her forties perhaps, but her eyes were time-less. She grabbed a kettle and filled it with water, then put it on the stove. She twitched her fingers, and suddenly a flame licked at the bottom of the kettle. I gasped out loud, and Celeste looked over at me with a small smile. I'd only ever seen the Sun Witches use their magic for important things like rituals and combat, not small things like lighting stoves. I wondered if the Sun Witches used their magic like this in private too.

I shook myself out of that train of thought as Celeste went to the pantry and brought out a startlingly modern box of hot chocolate packages. She poured one into a mug and stirred hot water into it, then slid it in front of me. I noticed she didn't make anything for herself, just sat opposite me with a little smile on her face.

I wrapped my hands around the mug, its warmth instantly making me realize I was cold, almost to the bone, and not just from the rain. *Shock,* my mind provided. *You're in shock.* I took a tentative sip of the hot chocolate, and it settled in my stomach and pushed back some of the unease I felt from sitting in this outdated kitchen with a strange Moon Witch. Unfortunately, it didn't help with any of the pain I felt related to Kaden or how I'd left him, but at least I could concentrate a bit better to ask Celeste some questions. This was my opportunity and I needed to take it, despite the crushing weight of the grief pounding through me.

"You must have questions," Celeste said. "I will do my best to answer as many as I can."

"Am I a prisoner?" I asked. My voice sounded rough, and I cleared my throat.

"No, of course not." She looked horrified by the very idea. "Why would you think such a thing?"

"You kidnapped me and brought me to a strange place without any warning," I muttered. "Usually when that happens I end up inside a cell."

She touched her throat as if alarmed. "That has happened before?"

"More than I care to admit." I glanced outside as lightning flashed across the beach. "Where are we?"

"This is my house," Celeste said. "I promise you'll be safe here. You're my guest, not a prisoner."

"That doesn't answer the question."

Celeste tilted her head and gazed out the windows. "It's a tricky question to answer. This area is called Lunatera. The Moon Witches have been hiding here for decades to escape the attention of the Sun Witches."

"But where?" I pressed, growing impatient and annoyed. "Back in Oregon it was still daytime, but here it's night. It was a new moon there, but somehow the moon is full now. That should be impossible."

Celeste's eyes rested upon me again, and she still wore that little smile. I couldn't tell if it was kind, or sad, or pitying. "The moon is full because we're in an alternate realm ruled by the moon goddess, Selene. Here time stands still and it is always night."

I swallowed the cocoa I'd been sipping, nearly choking on it. "I'm sorry, what? An alternate realm?"

"Yes, this place does not exist in your world. Only those blessed by Selene can journey here, which is how we've stayed hidden and safe all this time. The Sun Witches cannot find this place, and they have no power in this realm."

I shook my head, finding all of this hard to accept, though it did explain why no one knew how to contact them. "How do I get back to Kaden and my pack?"

Celeste laced together her hands and rested them on the table. "Time moves differently here. Unlike on Earth, it does not march forward in a straight line, so we can return you to the moment when we took you. Once you're ready, that is."

"Ready?" I let out a small huff. "What does that mean? Why can't we go back now?"

Celeste began shaking her head before I even finished the sentence. "If we send you back now, you will be taken by the Sun Witches, and your cause will be lost. You're not powerful enough to fight them yet, but we will train you to use your magic properly so you can stand a chance against them."

The tiny bit of hope she gave me stole my breath away. "And Kaden? Will I be able to save him too?"

Sadness made Celeste's eyes crinkle, and her smile faded away. "I don't know for sure, but yes, there is a small chance you can save Kaden as well."

I didn't listen to the word 'small.' All I heard was yes. There was a way to save Kaden, a chance he wasn't dead. That was all I cared about. I closed my eyes and breathed in the warm smell of chocolate, focusing on that flickering hope inside me. I'd wanted so long to learn how to use my magic, and now I would do it for Kaden, no matter what it took. But that thought only brought more questions.

"Why me?" I asked. "Why not one of the other Ophi-uchus? Or Kaden? I'm pretty sure they all have more magic than I do."

Celeste straightened her back as if bracing herself for something. "You're my daughter, Ayla."

My mouth fell open as the mug slipped from my fingers and clattered against the table, sloshing cocoa from the rim. I barely noticed, too busy scanning Celeste up and down with wide eyes, trying to understand what she'd just said. *This is my mother?* Somehow I found it harder to believe than the idea we were in a magical moon realm. My hands shook so bad I had to clutch them tight in my lap to make them stop. *Mother.* After all these years, she was sitting in front of me, and she was nothing like I'd expected.

"But—" I wanted to say a hundred things, but what came out was, "but your hair is white!"

Celeste let out a laugh that seemed almost startled out of her. "Yes, it is. Your hair should be white too, but when you were a baby I used a spell to change it to hide you better. No one would ever look twice at a red-haired little girl and think she had Moon Witch blood."

My hand jerked up to touch my hair. I'd always thought I'd inherited my red hair from my mother, but that was another lie. The thought sent a wave of crushing despair through me.

"I can change it back for you, if you'd like," Celeste said.

"No," I said with perhaps a bit too much venom. I tucked my hair behind my ear, almost protectively. Even if it was fake, it was a part of my identity now, something I'd lived with my entire life.

How much of my identity is built on a lie?

"Of course," she said quickly. "It does look lovely on you, especially with your eyes. You've turned into such a beautiful girl. Sorry, beautiful woman." She reached across the table as if to take my hand. "I'm just so happy we are together again. You have no idea how much I have longed for this day."

I jerked away, sudden anger piercing through the shock, sadness, and despair. "If that's true, where have you been my entire life? You abandoned me with a pack that hated me! Where no one wanted me, not even my own father! Do you know what I've had to endure all these years?"

Celeste drew back, and a flash of remorse went through her eyes. "I'm so sorry, Ayla. For everything."

"How?" Tears began to stream down my face. It was all too much. Kaden. My mother. This weird place. I covered my eyes as my whole body trembled with the grief and pain. "How could you leave me?"

I felt Celeste's hand on my back, light and tentative, as if she was unsure if she was allowed to touch me. "It was the hardest decision I had to make," she said, her voice cracking. "I'll explain everything to you, I promise, but right now you need to rest. You've been through so much in the last twenty-four hours, and I don't want to burden you with anything more until you've had a chance to recover."

"No, I don't want rest." I shook my head vehemently. "I need answers!"

"Soon." Her hand moved up to pat my head as her eyes gazed into mine. They began to glow with faint silvery light. "For now, let your mind clear, and your body relax. Rest, my darling girl."

Her cool, calm magic seeped into me, and though I tried to fight it, it was impossible. I was already on the verge of passing out from pure exhaustion and heartache. My eyes drooped, my limbs grew heavy, and all I could think about was how good a nice, warm bed sounded.

"Fine," I muttered, as I rested my head on the table. "But then I want those answers."

"Of course."

Celeste took my arm and helped me up, and in a half-asleep trance, I followed her, abandoning my half-finished hot cocoa on the table. She led me up a spiral staircase and into a bedroom, though everything about the journey there was a haze.

"This is your room," she said, as I struggled to keep my eyes open. "There is an attached bathroom, and though we don't have electricity here, we've made do with magic. Your shower will be warm whenever you're ready to use it."

I mumbled something in response, though I wasn't sure what exactly, and then I blinked and I was in the bed and alone. A semblance of clarity returned to me as I struggled to remove my shoes, along with an odd, horrible feeling in my gut, one that was all too familiar. Though I'd felt it many times before, I never got used to it. *I just want to go home.*

But where was home without Kaden? It crashed over me again that he was *gone,* and I was trapped in this random place with no one I could trust. My mate, my *true* mate, was dead, and there was no way my heart or soul would ever recover from that. *Dead.* The word rolled around in my head, and though I didn't want to believe it, I'd held Kaden's body in my arms and known he was gone.

The emotions became too much to handle and I buried my face in a pillow, covering the tears already escaping from my eyes. I'd dealt with loss before, more times than I could count, but it never got easier to handle. Even Wesley's death hadn't hit me this hard. This was so much worse because Kaden's death had taken part of my soul too.

I can't do this without him.

My body physically hurt as sobs wracked through it. I shoved a fist into my mouth to stifle any sounds. I'd wanted to find my mother and the Moon Witches for so long, but not like this. Kaden was supposed to be by my side, going through this with me. I wished desperately that Kaden was here with me, reassuring me with his cocky attitude and his inner strength. He would know what to do, what to say. But he was gone, and I was here alone with half my heart missing. And unless I could find a way to save him, he'd be gone forever.

The thought caused another set of sobs to wrack my body, and I pressed my face into the pillow, trying to make the feeling go away. It was a relief when the magic finally swept me into a dark, dreamless sleep.

CHAPTER TWO

I WOKE UP SLOWLY, feeling so groggy I wondered if I'd truly slept at all. I had no recollection of getting to this room, and when I blinked my eyes open, they were crusty. I must have fallen asleep crying. *How did I get here?*

I sat up and rubbed at my eyes, trying to clear them so I could better look around the place. The bed I was in had a dark wooden headboard and footboard carved with tiny stars and moons. Silvery light streamed in through an open window that brought with it the smell of the ocean.

Everything came back to me as I drew in a deep breath of sea air. Celeste—my *mother*—had cast some kind of sleep spell on me last night, even though I'd desperately wanted more answers. A surge of anger propelled me out of bed. I was going to stomp down there right this instant and demand she answer my questions immediately—no more excuses. She sure as hell wasn't casting any more spells on me either.

But when I stood, I stopped at the sight of the blood and dirt on my clothes. My head began to spin as some of the despair from last night returned. The sudden grief was so heavy it felt as if I had weights pressing down on my limbs, and I knew how easy it would be to simply wallow in it. Maybe it was better she'd knocked me out. At least I'd had a brief respite from this misery.

Then I remembered Celeste's words from last night. She'd said there was a chance for me to save Kaden, and even if it was the smallest bit of hope, I would cling onto it. I'd put all of my energy into training to become the best damn Moon Witch the Zodiac Wolves had ever seen.

I looked outside instead of dwelling on the pain of losing Kaden. It was dark out and still raining softly, droplets of water hitting the window in a soothing cadence. How long had I slept?

I went into the attached bathroom, surprised to see a set of towels and toiletries set out already next to the claw-foot tub. Celeste probably wanted to make a good impression on me, but she'd need to do a lot more than that to wipe away twenty-two years of abandonment. Not even a fancy little soap shaped like a seashell could put a dent on that pain.

The claw-foot tub had a shower attachment and I gave it a skeptical look as I turned it on, but the water instantly turned warm. Not as hot as I would have liked, but it was hard to complain when it was fueled by magic. I wondered if they'd teach me that sort of thing too.

I took my time in the shower, washing the blood from my skin and scrubbing dirt out from under my fingernails.

When I finally emerged, ready to face whatever the Moon Witches threw at me, I spotted a set of clothes resting on the counter. I toweled off and unfolded the clothes, finding plain white cotton underwear plus a long, gray dress made of thicker fabric. I traced the crescent moons embroidered along the hem with one finger and wondered if it was hand-made. I put it on, surprised to find it fit like a glove, as if it had been made for me.

After dragging a brush through my tangled hair—still red, thank you very much—I headed down to the kitchen and steeled myself to face my mother. I found her in the kitchen, frowning down at the stove as if it was giving her a hard time.

She turned and gave me a warm smile. "Good morning. I hope you slept well."

My eyes narrowed. "Don't ever do that again."

"Do what?"

Her innocent question only brought the anger rushing back. "That sleep spell. You had no right to do that to me."

"I'm sorry. I only wanted you to rest. You had such a traumatic day..." She wiped her hands on her apron, her smile falling. "You're right, I was out of line. It's been a long time since I dealt with anyone outside of our little commu-nity here, and I guess I forgot my manners. I promise I won't use magic again on you without your permission."

I pressed my lips together to hold back a smart-ass response but decided to let it go. Instead, I stared out the big windows at the waves crashing under the moonlight. "It's still dark out. How long did I sleep?"

"You slept about nine hours. It's morning here now, or at least what we consider to be morning since it's always dark in Lunatera. During the day you'll notice the sky gets a bit brighter, almost like the sun is getting ready to crest the horizon, though it never does."

"Do you ever miss the sun?"

"Not especially. I suppose I'm used to it after all this time." Her smile returned, though it was more tentative now. "Would you like something to eat? I can make whatever you want for breakfast. Do you like eggs and bacon, or pancakes maybe?"

"I like all of them, and if you hadn't abandoned me as a baby you would know that," I muttered. I couldn't help myself.

Celeste's face fell and she turned away, toward the stove. After a moment I saw her shoulders lower in a sigh. "Yes, of course. Breakfast will be ready soon."

I watched her light the stove with magic again and felt a little bad for being rude to her. She was going out of her way to be nice to me, to do as much as she could to make up for the time she'd been away, but twenty-two years of utter hell were not easily forgotten. Not to mention dragging me here against my will and casting a sleep spell on me.

I'd spent my entire life wanting my mother and wondering who she was and why she'd left me with my asshole father. And all that time she'd been here, alive and well in this hidden realm. She could have come back for me at any point in my life, but she hadn't.

So, yeah, I felt bad, but not bad enough to take it back.

Celeste owed me a big, fat apology as far as I was concerned —along with the answers I needed to save Kaden.

Celeste moved around the kitchen, gathering ingredients and putting them into various bowls and pans. Once the eggs sizzled in a pan next to some bacon, and the pancake batter had been mixed up, Celeste poured me a cup of coffee from a French press.

As she handed me the coffee, I searched her face for any trace of hurt or anger, but it remained smooth and calm. Did anything ever rile her up? I was beginning to think I'd gotten my smart-ass attitude from my dad's side.

"The Moon Witches came to this dimension many decades ago when we were being hunted to extinction by the Sun Witches," Celeste said, as she flipped pancakes. Maybe she sensed I was ready for those answers now. "I was the High Priestess then as well, and I decided it would be safer for us to disappear and make the Sun Witches think we were all dead."

"Wait. You've been High Priestess for decades?" I asked, blinking at her. No wonder I couldn't pinpoint her age.

"Yes. One of the benefits of living in a realm with no time is that we don't age. But you must understand there is a downside to such immortality—we cannot have children here. We have to return to your world for that, but when we do, we are often found and killed by the Sun Witches, who can sense our magic. As soon as they detect it, they hunt us down tirelessly."

Celeste paused to serve up the eggs and bacon and slid two pancakes onto each plate as well. She took a seat across the table from me and the warm smell of the food made me suddenly ravenous.

"Is that what you did?" I asked, as I took a bite, which tasted as good as it smelled. "Went to Earth to have a baby?"

"Not exactly." She poked at her food, and her voice sounded distant as she continued. "I went with the intention of finding a place for us to live there. We can't stay isolated forever in this realm. Many of my people want to return to Earth, but it isn't safe as long as the Sun Witches are in control." She took a long sip of coffee. "I knew my best chance was to convince the Zodiac Wolves to help us, but they were all under the thrall of the Sun Witches—all but one."

"The Ophiuchus pack," I guessed.

"Yes. I met with the alphas of the Ophiuchus pack, and though they were sympathetic, they were unable to help us. They had a young son and a baby girl, and they wanted to protect them more than anything else."

"Kaden and Stella," I realized.

Celeste nodded. "Indeed. They offered to let us live on their lands, but I was hesitant to put their people in danger. Besides, with their outcast status among the Zodiac Wolves, they wouldn't be able to provide the kind of aid we would need against the might of the Sun Witches anyway. So I went to the Cancer pack next."

"Why them?" I found myself leaning forward, eager to hear more, especially now that we'd come to the part with my former pack.

"Other than the Leos, they were the most powerful pack

at the time. They also have a strong connection to the moon, so I thought they would be more sympathetic."

I couldn't help but snort. "And then you met my father and realized he was anything but."

She chuckled softly at that. "Actually, he agreed to meet with me, though only in private. To the Sun Witches and the Zodiac Wolves, we were still considered enemies, and I understood his need for safety. We met alone at a cabin he owned in Oregon."

My mind flashed back to the cabin where we'd held the solar eclipse meeting. "The same place you found me."

"Yes. We spent several days there, and he seemed very sympathetic to our cause." She looked far away as if she was reliving her past before her eyes. "And he was just so...charming. And handsome, of course."

I tried not to gag, though it must have been true, considering how many women he'd managed to knock up. I could admit he must have some kind of charisma to maintain control of one of the largest packs for so many years, but he'd definitely never showed me that side of him.

"I hadn't had feelings for a man in decades, and I knew I was a fool to fall for him. Even so, when our time came to an end and Harrison said he couldn't help us, I was shocked."

No surprise there, I thought. *Dad wouldn't do anything that would have risked his own neck.*

"I thought we had something together, but he told me that our time together meant nothing and that he was mated to someone else." She glanced down, and I saw genuine hurt in her eyes.

No matter how much I resented her for abandoning me, I couldn't help but sympathize. Before I'd known that Jordan was my half-brother, I'd felt his scorn and rage at having me as a mate. His rejection had been humiliating and painful, and we'd hated each other from the start. I couldn't imagine what it would be like to think someone truly cared for you and then tell you it meant nothing.

Celeste drew in a deep breath. "I was hurt, but I thought at least he would be willing to help my people."

"Let me guess. He said no." That sounded more like the father I knew.

She let out a long sigh. "Correct. He wasn't willing to stand against the Sun Witches. They're simply too powerful. But I didn't want to give up. I left the Cancer pack and traveled across all of North America to make inquiries with some of the other packs. I thought that some of the water sign packs would be sympathetic, but they were all too scared." She paused. "Eventually I realized I was pregnant."

I swallowed hard, my food forgotten, desperately hanging onto every word she said. This was it—I would finally learn the reason she'd abandoned me.

"I went back to Harrison and told him, but he didn't want his mate to know what had happened between us. He gave me some money and told me to go to the cabin in Oregon, where I might be safe. I stayed in hiding and stopped using magic so the Sun Witches wouldn't find me, and then after nine months I had you." Celeste paused and smiled at me again.

I looked away, my heart clenching. I'd always known I

was born from an affair between Harrison and another woman, but to hear how little he'd done for Celeste only brought all the pain back.

"I wanted to take you to Lunatera, Ayla. You would have been safe here, but then you would have never aged. You would have been an infant forever, and that wasn't fair to you. So I stayed on Earth, and I was prepared to raise you there."

"So what happened?" I kept my voice steady, but I wanted to scream at her, as some of the anger from last night returned in full force. "Why did you leave me?"

Celeste drew in a shuddering breath. "When you were four months old, the Sun Witches found us. There were so many of them and only one of me. It didn't matter that I was High Priestess and the most powerful of the Moon Witches, I was outnumbered and overpowered. I barely escaped, and you were injured in the struggle. I returned to Harrison as a last, desperate resort and begged him to take you and raise you as his own. He was upset, and his mate was even angrier. I thought she'd rip my throat out, but I kept begging until they agreed."

"You gave me up," I said, my voice bitter.

"I had to, Ayla. It was the only way to keep you alive. I almost lost you during the attack, and I couldn't let that happen again." A single tear rolled down her cheek. "Harrison agreed to say you were half-human. I made your hair red and locked away your Moon Witch magic. You would blend in with the other shifters, and no one would be any the wiser. It was the only way to stop the Sun Witches from finding you."

I shook my head, almost wishing I'd never heard this story. "There must have been another way."

"I wish there was." She raised her chin and met my eyes. There was deep pain in them, but it was overshadowed by an iron will. The face of someone who had lost everything and overcome it somehow. "I returned to Lunatera, heartbroken. I cried for months, and I almost returned a hundred times, until I reminded myself that I would be putting you in danger. If the Sun Witches caught even the faintest whiff of Moon Witch magic around you, it would draw unwanted attention. I wish more than anything that I could have been there with you growing up, but I knew we would be reunited someday. It was the only way to keep you safe and let you grow into a young woman. And I swore when you turned twenty-two and had your wolf unlocked, I would find you again."

"But you never came." I practically spat the words.

"I did," she said softly. "My Moon Witches and I went to the Convergence, but we were too late and you were gone. We couldn't find you, not until the other night when I sensed your magic starting to break free. I rushed to you as quickly as I could, and now you're here."

I pushed my plate away with trembling hands. My stomach turned, and I knew if I took another bite, I'd throw it all up. "Do you have any idea what it was like for me growing up? I was the outcast of the pack, the lowest of the low, treated like trash for being half-human. Dad was never a real father to me, and he hardly treated me like a shifter either. And Jackie? She was even worse. All my life I was abused, bullied, and beaten, and not just by other shifters, but by my own parents. I never knew love from anyone except my brother. If you really cared for me, how could you abandon me to that?"

"Ayla, you don't understand," Celeste said. "It was the only option—"

"You should have found another way!" I stood up quickly and the chair hit the wall behind me in punctuation. Celeste rose to her feet, but I couldn't hear another word from her mouth excusing what she'd done. I stalked away from the table, and she didn't follow me. The thought of staying in this house made me want to scream. I turned toward the front door and flung it open, then rushed outside toward the beach.

I found myself running, trying to escape Celeste's words. My whole life had been a lie. Even my fucking *hair* wasn't real. And my dad *knew* the whole time. He'd known I wasn't half-human, that I was part Moon Witch, and yet he'd lied to me my entire life and treated me like shit the entire time.

And Celeste? She'd known my dad was a piece of shit who went back on his word, a coward who refused to actually stand up for what he believed in. She could say what she wanted about *protecting* me, but no one had protected me from my own family. The only time I'd ever known safety and love was with the Ophiuchus pack—and with Kaden. But he was gone, and I was left with nothing.

CHAPTER THREE

AFTER A WHILE, my angry rush to escape turned to a much slower trudge through the sand. I tried my best to reign in my emotions as my body physically calmed down. Even in the daytime, the sky was dark with stars glittering above. The moon illuminated the ground in front of me, and although it was no longer raining, the air was crisp, cooling the tears on my cheeks.

Soon I spotted a cluster of small buildings up ahead and headed toward them, curious to see more of this strange place. All the buildings were painted white and almost sparkled under the moonlight, with rounded corners and flat roofs. The village started at the water and then continued up a hill, reminding me of photos I had seen of Greek islands. There was a dock too, where a few sailboats bobbed on the calm waves.

As I entered the charming seaside village I was drawn toward the sound of people, and soon found myself at an outdoor market where stalls displayed handmade clothing, shoes, candles, soap, pottery, and artwork. I kept walking, and at the other end of the market, I spotted a vast array of fruit, vegetables, fish, and cheese. As I watched, I noticed shells being exchanged for fruit, and at the next stall over, a woman passed over a bolt of beautiful fabric for a collection of candles. Most of the people I saw were women with that ageless quality, though some looked on the older side, and none looked younger than me. Each wore a similar dress to mine in a pale color, while the few men I saw wore loose shirts and trousers. Once again I was struck with the feeling of being caught in a mishmash of time periods.

Everyone turned to look at me as I passed, and the entire market went quiet. It was as if a pocket of silence followed me around, and I felt the prickle of everyone's gazes at the back of my neck. I guessed that since they lived out of the continuance of time, they didn't get many visitors. At least they all smiled at me or nodded politely when I met their eyes, so I didn't sense any hostility at my presence—only curiosity.

A lanky girl with pale blond hair broke away from the crowd and started toward me with a big smile, and I blinked at the sight of the first kid I'd seen in the village. "Ayla!" she called out. "You're finally here! What happened to your hair?"

My mouth fell open as I tried to make sense of her strange comments. "I'm sorry. Do I know you?"

"I'm Larkin," she said, her voice bright. As she smiled, I

noticed a patch of freckles across her nose and cheeks that only made her even cuter. "I'm your cousin."

I stared at her. "My cousin?"

"Yes, my mother was Celeste's sister." She took my arm and led me to the side of the market, under a tree where we could talk quietly without the crowd moving around us.

"Was?" I asked softly, still reeling from the news that I had a *cousin*. I stared at her, trying to see anything of myself in her features.

Larkin's smile fell. "She was killed by Sun Witches when I was ten, along with my father."

"I'm so sorry. That must have been terrible."

"Thanks. It was a long time ago, but you never really get over that sort of thing." She paused before adding, "Aunt Celeste saved me and brought me to Lunatera. After I finished my magical training, I tried to go back to Earth as much as possible to keep aging, but it's dangerous there with the Sun Witches hunting us. Physically, I'm probably about twelve or thirteen, but I don't know for sure."

I raised my eyebrows at her. "Physically?"

"I can't grow older while I'm here. I'm stuck being a child forever." Sadness filled her voice, along with a hint of bitterness.

"How old are you really?" I asked, horrified by the thought.

"Forty-two. I think. Although it's rude to ask someone their age, you know." She grinned at me to show she was kidding. "Last time I saw you was when you were a baby. Celeste brought you here briefly to meet everyone before taking you back to Earth. Now, look at you, all grown up. And with red hair too! I like it."

I shook my head, trying to wrap my brain around what she was telling me. Larkin looked like a gawky kid about to become a teenager, and yet she was old enough to be my mom. *This could have been me,* I thought. *Stuck as a child forever.*

"I'm glad you're back," she continued. "Though I've always been jealous you got to grow up on Earth. You're lucky Celeste could hide you there so you wouldn't share my fate. Trust me, it's miserable being trapped in a kid's body with an adult mind."

"Why couldn't she hide you too?"

"Celeste did offer to try to find me a human home, but I wanted to stay here with her. She was the only family I had left. Besides, the Sun Witches already knew what I looked like and had felt me use magic. If I'd gone back to Earth, they would have found me eventually and I would have put another family in danger."

I was starting to understand why Celeste had made the difficult choice to hide me with my father. I couldn't imagine being in Larkin's shoes, stuck as a gawky twelve-year-old for decades, unable to ever truly become an adult. No thank you. Suddenly my life with the Cancer pack didn't seem so bad anymore. At least it had turned me into the adult I was today, and made me stronger emotionally and physically. But Larkin? She would never get that sort of growth. My heart ached for her and all she had missed in life.

She took my arm again, her touch light on my skin. "Come

on, let me show you around Crescent Cove. It's the main village here in Lunatera." We headed back toward the stalls and she gestured at them. "We make everything ourselves here. We have to be completely self-sustaining, since going to Earth is so difficult and dangerous for us. We have fields beyond the hills with farms, and of course, the ocean also provides for us. We don't have money, so we barter and trade instead, or just share whatever we can. We all try to look out for each other."

I studied the market with a frown. "If there's no time here, how do you grow food? Or catch fish? Wouldn't they need to be born and grow and all that?"

Larkin shrugged. "Selene provides for us. We don't question it."

"You don't need anything from Earth?" I asked.

"We do sometimes. There will always be things we can't get here, so we take turns volunteering to go to Earth for supply runs. I volunteer as often as I can. We have a few stores we've partnered with where we can sell our hand-made goods for money to buy what we need." She gave me a wry smile. "I'm always surprised what humans will pay for a crescent-shaped pendant or a box with the moon and stars painted on it We don't even put any magic in them! I personally make bath bombs that sell like da bomb." She laughed at her own joke. "Hey, do people still say that?"

"Um, no." I couldn't help but smile at her. "What do you use the money for?"

"Me? I buy books. I would go crazy without them. We don't have TV here, so as you can imagine it gets pretty boring at times. I read every genre, but romance novels are my favorite. I need my daily fix of trashy romance, or I'll die." She paused as if realizing she had said too much. "Do you like to read?"

"Sure, but I'm mostly into photography. Most of the books I read are to help me be better at it." I glanced around at the market with a pang, remembering the camera Kaden got me. I sighed and said, "I wish I had my camera now so I could take photos of this town. I bet I would get some really interesting shots in the half-light."

Larkin perked up. "I'd love to see some of your photos from Earth. Do you have any with you?"

"No, I didn't exactly get to pack a suitcase before being dragged here against my will."

"Oh, right."

I sighed as we headed toward an area with knitted sweaters and scarves. "So if time stays still here, do you always go to the same day on Earth? Celeste said she could send me back to the moment I left."

"No, we go to the current day on Earth, even though time is frozen here in this realm. It's sort of like looking through a window at the world outside. You can see storms gather and rain begin to fall, and if you go outside you'll get wet, but while inside you're sheltered from it. The same is true here of time. At least that's how it was explained to me. But sometimes, with strong magic and a lot of prayers to Selene, we can perform miracles. Like sending you back to the moment you arrived here."

"It's hard to believe." I gestured around at the different stalls. "All of this."

"I bet. I'm happy to answer all your questions though, so fire away."

I sucked in a breath, trying to figure out what to ask first because my brain was just screaming *WTF?* over and over. I settled on a pretty basic question. "I don't see many men here. Why is that?"

"Ah, so you've figured out the other reason we need romance novels here," she said with a grin. "We do have some male Moon Witches, but they're rare and usually not as powerful as the women. Many of the men here are simply humans who fell in love with a Moon Witch and decided to come here."

"And no children..." I said slowly, realizing how lonely a life many of these people lived.

"No... We had many people who wanted children and went back to Earth, but they were all killed off. A few of them managed to live long enough to bring their families back here as adults. But it's mostly us single people or couples like Elsa and Kena. They have dozens of cats instead of children, and every time they go to Earth they come back with another one. Since the cats never age, well...let's just say their house does not smell great."

I laughed at her story but felt a pang of sadness too as I began to truly understand how these people lived. They had a great community where everyone cared for each other, that was clear, but they were in hiding too, unable to have children or find partners. They were frozen in time just as much as Larkin was in her child's body. All because of the Sun Witches.

"I've never seen a male Sun Witch either," I said.

"No?" She tilted her head. "That's odd. There used to be many powerful male Sun Witches, since the sun god Helios has a masculine energy. They were even ruled by a High Priest back in the day. I wonder what changed."

I had no answer to that, but I also couldn't envision Evanora, the High Priestess of the Sun Witches, sharing her power with anyone.

A thin woman with brown curls streaked with white came up to us with a big smile and thrust a purple scarf in my hand. "It's so nice to have you here, Ayla. I'm your mother's third cousin, and I thought you could use this since it does get chilly here. Oh, although you're half wolf aren't you? Maybe you don't get chilly!"

"This is Mariel," Larkin explained.

"Thank you," I said, wrapping the knit scarf around myself. "That's kind of you."

Other women seemed emboldened by Mariel's actions and came up to me too, introducing themselves and handing me gifts. I tried to remember everyone's name but it quickly became overwhelming, and my hands got so full of candles, soaps, and other trinkets that Larkin got me a carrying bag.

"Give her some space, she's only just arrived," a man said with a crisp English accent.

I turned and met the cool gray eyes of a man who was so handsome I stopped breathing for a second. He looked too perfect to be real, his face too smooth, his black hair too shiny, his movements too effortlessly graceful. It was...un-natural. But I couldn't look away.

"I'm Killian," he said, extending his hand. When our fingers touched, his skin was ice cold, and I jerked my hand back. He smiled in response, and I saw...*fangs?* "A pleasure to meet you. It's been so long since we've welcomed someone new to our town."

I took a step back, while my wolf woke inside me and wanted to bare her canines too. *Vampire,* she whispered. *Must kill.*

"Killian is our resident vampire," Larkin explained, while I mentally told my wolf to chill the fuck out. "Don't worry, he's harmless."

"So they say." He gave her an amused smirk that only made him better looking, then turned back to me. "I simply wanted to introduce myself and welcome you to Crescent Cove. If you ever need anything, don't hesitate to ask."

He flashed me a charming smile and then turned away, continuing his stroll down the road until he turned a corner and disappeared. Larkin used the opportunity to drag me away from the crowd, and I followed while carrying the many items the townspeople had kindly gifted me.

"I thought vampires were the enemies," I said to Larkin once we were walking down a quieter street. "But you have one living here?"

"Killian married a Moon Witch decades ago and now is an outcast of his kind. Even though his wife is gone, he decided to stay here with us. He's currently mayor of Crescent Cove, actually. Don't worry, he's a good guy."

I nodded, but unease turned my stomach. Shifters and vampires had never been friends, and I didn't know what to think about seeing one here. My wolf had some kind of instinctual urge to fight him like it recognized his kind as an age-old enemy. I didn't need to add to my troubles by getting into fights here, so I had to keep her in check. I just hoped he didn't feel that same instinctual hostility toward me at the scent of my wolf.

"I'm going to head home," Larkin said, breaking me out of my thoughts. "But I'll see you soon, I hope. I asked Celeste if I can help with your training."

"I'd like that. Thanks."

She hesitated, moving toward me like she was going to hug me, but then reached out and patted my shoulder instead. "It's good you're here. Celeste has missed you so much. We all have. But now you're home."

Home.

As she turned away, I bit back my response—that this would never, *could never*, be my home. Home was Kaden and the Ophiuchus pack, not this strange place with a night that never ended. I headed back to the beach, away from the village full of well-meaning strangers who somehow only made me feel worse.

I walked for some time along the sand until my legs gave out on me and the weight of my emotions knocked me down. I curled up into a ball as tears streamed down my face, but instead of fighting the pain or pushing it down, I let it wash through me. I allowed myself to cry and feel every-thing—despair, guilt, anger, resentment, and all the things that didn't have a name but somehow consumed me. I cried until it was hard to breathe, mourning Kaden's death, raging at Celeste, and grieving what might have been. I wanted to scream to the moon that it was too much, to ask Selene why she'd allowed all this to happen to me, but I knew she wouldn't answer.

It all felt so damn unfair, but that's how my life had always been—and somehow I'd carried on. When others might have given up, I'd kept fighting and grown stronger, and I would do it again, and again, and again, for as long as I had to. I would survive. And I would win. I didn't know any other way to live.

I let out a hollow breath and wiped my tears, feeling empty inside but better too for embracing my pain. Running away never solved anything. I knew that better than anyone.

I got up and walked back to the house to face my mother again.

CHAPTER FOUR

WHEN I ENTERED THE HOUSE, Celeste was pacing in the living room, looking distraught. She paused when she saw me and smoothed down her white hair. "You're back," she said with a big exhale. "Ayla, I'm so sorry for everything, you're right to be upset—"

I held up a hand. "I understand why you did what you did. I don't like it, and I don't know if I'll ever be able to get over it or forgive you...but I understand."

"You do?" she asked in a soft voice. "How?"

"I met Larkin."

"Ah." She nodded slowly, her face grim. "I won't ask for your forgiveness. I don't deserve it. I only hope you know that everything I did was to protect you, and when I left you with Harrison I thought my heart would never heal from the pain. I knew it was necessary to keep you alive, but it was the hardest thing I ever had to do. Missing your entire child-hood...the thought still tears me apart." A single tear fell down her cheek. "Especially now that I know how bad it was for you. I truly thought Harrison would raise you with love. I'm so sorry, Ayla."

I saw the pain in her eyes and knew she meant the apology. I realized I had a choice then—I could continue to be angry and upset about the past and the choices she'd made, or I could accept it and try to move on. She was here now, trying to help me, giving me the chance to have a relationship with her, even if it wasn't a normal mother-daughter one. No, my mother wasn't what I'd expected, but she was the only mother I had.

I stepped forward and Celeste's arms tentatively wrapped around me. The hug was stiff and awkward at first, but then I drew in a breath and tried to relax. She squeezed me tight with a relieved sigh, the tension leaving her body, and I found my arms going around her too. As she held me, something changed and shifted inside me, like the petals of a flower slowly unfurling. *This is what a mother's love feels like*, I realized. I'd never felt it before, at least, not in my memory.

Celeste pulled back and wiped at her eyes with a smile. "Can I get you something to eat? I want to make sure you have energy for your training later."

"No thanks, I'm still full from breakfast." My heart raced at the thought of beginning my training. "How soon do we start?"

"Tonight, when the sky is darkest and the moon is just overhead. Feel free to rest until then."

I thought about going up to my room, but this seemed

like an opportunity to get more answers. "Actually, I'd like to just...talk. Maybe over some tea?"

"Oh," she said, clearly surprised, but then her face split into a bright smile. "I'd love that. We have so many years to catch up on."

I followed her into the kitchen and asked, "What will we do for training?"

"I'm going to unlock your magic, and then we'll teach you some basic spells to test your strength," Celeste said as she moved to the stove and used a dash of magic to light it. "How much magic have you been able to use so far?"

I stared at the flame with envy. "Not much. I can teleport through moonlight—that's the only thing that's come easily to me since the Convergence."

Celeste nodded, as if unsurprised. "I can do that as well —it's a special gift from Selene that runs in our family. But we both know you're capable of so much more."

I blew out a breath and leaned against the counter. "I'm not so sure. I've blasted the Sun Witches a couple of times, but it was always by accident. I tried to make wards with Kaden, but nothing happened. My magic only seems to work when I'm in danger."

"That will change once I release it. I'm surprised you were able to do as much as you did." She tilted her head as she considered. "I suppose that when the Sun Witches cast the spell that unlocked your wolf, it freed your magic a little too."

"So it's true then? The Sun Witches put a spell on my wolf that locked it away?"

"Yes, when you were only a few months old. Harrison had to take you to the Convergence to be blessed by the Sun Witches, just like all the other wolf babies." She put the kettle on the stove, then went to get some tea bags from her pantry. "That's why I had to make sure your hair was changed and your magic was tightly locked away before you went. I couldn't risk them recognizing you as my daughter."

I nodded slowly. "They always told us the blessing was to save the Zodiac Wolves from the Moon Curse, to stop us from going feral during full moons."

"I'm not surprised they told you that," Celeste said. "They'll do whatever they can to paint Moon Witches as the villains in order to make themselves the saviors. But the Moon Curse was removed by us centuries ago. It was wrong, and we regretted ever creating such a horrible spell."

"Why would the Sun Witches lock away our wolves until we're twenty-two?"

"They do it to keep the packs weak, and to keep them reliant on the Sun Witches." She shook her head with a scowl. "If the Zodiac Wolves believe they need the Sun Witches to protect them from this curse, they won't rebel. They'll gladly return every six months to the Convergence to allow the Sun Witches to cast spells on their children."

"That's why the Ophiuchus children can turn into wolves, isn't it?" I asked. "The Sun Witches never cast the spell on their babies."

"Exactly. That's the way it should be for all of you wolves. A natural shift with no spells needed for any of it. The same is true of finding a mate."

"Yes, I know all too well how the Sun Witches can control the mate bonds," I muttered. "I wonder how many other mate bonds are fake too."

Celeste gave me a sad look as she poured the tea. "Oh, Ayla... All of them are fake."

"All of them?" I asked as shock ran through me. Celeste dropped a tea bag in a mug and offered it to me, but I was too stunned to do anything but stare at it.

She set it down in front of me instead. "The Sun Witches use the same blessing spell on babies to lock away your mates too so that you won't feel the natural mate bond, and then they pair up shifters to further their own ends. They move wolves between packs like pawns on a chessboard."

"What?" *Every single one is fake?* "But what about mates who truly felt like they'd met their true love? How could they all be fake?"

"It's possible a few here and there would have paired up naturally," Celeste admitted. "But the Sun Witches are very good at manipulating emotions too. The spell they use makes it very hard to resist the mate bond."

I shivered and rubbed my arms. "Yes, I know. They mated me to someone I hated in the Leo pack. Later I learned he was actually my half-brother."

Celeste looked horrified, her face even more pale than usual. "Your half-brother? Did you...?"

"No. He rejected me, and then when he did want me, I was able to resist." I shuddered a little at the thought of that night when we'd almost completed the mate bond.

"It's a testament to your will that you were able to resist for so long. Most people are unable to fight the spell."

"But why would the Sun Witches do this?" I asked. "I understand wanting to control us, but why choose who we mate with?"

"As far as I can tell, the Sun Witches want the shifters to be their slaves again." Celeste sighed and took a small sip of her tea. "Centuries ago, the Sun Witches and Moon Witches were one coven. Light and dark, sun and moon, day and night, masculine and feminine, in perfect harmony. Everything changed when vampires started killing the witches off and drinking their blood to steal their magic. The vampires became incredibly powerful when they did this, and the witches knew they had to stop them before they threatened to destroy the entire world." She paused and grimaced. "Our ancestors enslaved the wolf shifters to help them in this battle and tied their powers to the stars, giving each pack extra abilities to use against the vampires. The Moon Witches also inflicted the Moon Curse upon the wolves then, which made them turn feral at the full moon. It was the only way they could enslave them, by having the packs rely on them for the antidote spell. With the wolf shifters' help, the witches were able to defeat the vampire threat. The Sun Witches cast the Sun Curse on the remaining vampires, making it so they couldn't go out in the daylight, and the war ended."

I'd heard similar things from Kaden, but I'd never been sure how much of it was true. After all, when I was growing up in the Zodiac Wolves the Sun Witches were considered allies and saviors, while the Moon Witches were the villains. Since the Convergence, I'd seen many times who the real villains were, and it was nice to hear about our history from a real Moon Witch now. "I didn't know there was a Sun Curse too, but I guess that explains the lore about vampires not being able to go in the sun. What happened after that?"

"After the war ended, the shifters grew tired of being slaves, rightfully so. The Moon Witches removed the curse on the shifters and were sympathetic to their plight, but the Sun Witches didn't want to give up control. This led to a division between the Sun and Moon Witches, and eventually, they split completely. At first, the Moon Witches were allied with some of the packs, including Cancer and Ophiuchus, but many shifters still didn't trust us because of the Moon Curse. Over the years, the Sun Witches got into their heads and turned each pack against us, one by one. They claimed we were the ones who wanted to keep control over the wolves and that the Moon Curse was still active. Only the Ophiuchus never wavered in their alliance, and eventually, they were cast out of the Zodiac Wolves because of it."

"That's a very different story than the ones the Zodiac Wolves and Sun Witches tell," I said.

"I'm not surprised. The Zodiac Wolves have been manipulated by the Sun Witches for years, while we were painted as the villains and hunted down. Meanwhile, the Sun Witches have bred shifters like dogs to get the traits they wanted."

My spine stiffened. "What do you mean?"

She poured us more tea as she explained. "Each pack

shares some of the same qualities and personality traits as their Zodiac sign, as I'm sure you already know. Over the years the Sun Witches have purposefully arranged mates to create offspring with the traits they want, which are usually the more negative aspects of each sign. They've bred the Zodiac Wolves to be the darkest versions of themselves, focusing on all the negative aspects. As an example, Leos became aggressive and arrogant rather than courageous and generous, while Cancers became vindictive and suspicious instead of caring and loyal." She shook her head. "And it's all to control them."

"Why?" I whispered, feeling shaken to my core. I'd known the Sun Witches were evil, and that they'd been manipulating us, but I'd had no idea just how bad it was. "Why would they want to do that?"

"They want to sow chaos and conflict so that you all fight amongst yourselves instead of rebelling against them. Perhaps they're betting that you'll eventually implode and kill each other off."

"Which is exactly what happened at the Convergence," I said with a sigh.

"So it seems. And now they will swoop in and take control again."

I thought of the way the Leos and the Sun Witches were working together and knew she was right. Kaden had said similar things before, and I'd thought it was just an unhealthy hatred for all the packs and the Sun Witches, but it looked like he had been right—and it had been *worse* than even he had thought. I hadn't realized how bad it really was, or how deep the corruption went. How would we ever stop them?

"Can the packs be saved?" I asked. "If everything good has been bred out of the Zodiac Wolves, and they're all being controlled by the Sun Witches, is there *anything* we can do?"

"I don't know," Celeste said. "I wouldn't even know where to start. I fear it may be too late for them."

I set my tea down and met her eyes. "No, I won't accept that. The people in the packs are not all bad. Even though I had a hard time in the Cancer pack, I know there are some good people there, and in the other packs too. I've seen it. My brother, Wesley, and my best friend, Mira, are good people. Some of the other shifters I met recently seem like they might be decent people too. Not every shifter is bad, and I won't give up on them."

"I hope you will be the one who will be able to save them," she said, tilting her head and smiling at me. "You are certainly capable of it. But first, you need magic. Shall we head outside and get started?"

I blinked, and then quickly downed the rest of my tea, eager to get begin. "Yes, I'm ready."

We stepped outside onto the sand, and the moon was so bright overhead it cast a silver glow across the waves. Celeste stopped once we were close to the water and turned toward me. I had no idea what she was planning, but I was ready for it.

Celeste raised her hands and began chanting. I didn't understand what she was saying, but I felt the power growing all around her. No, around *us*. The moon's light got so bright I lifted my hands to shield my eyes, and that's when I realized I was the one glowing. Brighter and brighter until I felt like I would burst from the amount of power being poured into me. It quickly became uncomfortable, like there wasn't any room for any more of it to go, and I felt like I couldn't breathe from all the pressure inside me. I opened my mouth to tell Celeste to stop, that this wasn't going to work, and then suddenly some barrier broke down inside of me and the magic burst free, turning the whole area white.

I staggered from the release, sucking in a huge, ragged breath. As the burst of light faded, the power came back and settled inside me, right at home in my skin. I stared down at my still-glowing skin, mouth agape. It was true. I was half Moon Witch, and I could use the magic inside me. I looked up at Celeste, who was smiling like a proud parent, eyes shimmering brightly in the moonlight.

"Good, now we can begin," she said.

CHAPTER FIVE

THE MOONLIT GLOW SLOWLY FADED until my skin looked normal, but there was a feeling that stuck around, a power inside me bubbling just under the surface. It reminded me of when I'd gotten my wolf—a feeling that I was more complete, as if I had suddenly found access to a limb I'd never known existed before.

"Now you will be able to access your moon magic completely," Celeste said when I glanced up at her, wondering what would happen next. "Before you were able to use it under duress, but now you should be able to call it at will."

"Really?" If I could shoot out anything similar to the Sun Witches' sunbeams, I'd be able to fight them better in my human form. "But only when the moon is out, right?"

"No. Your magic will be stronger at night and under the moonlight, but the moon is always out there, orbiting the planet, even if you can't see it. Your moon magic will always be inside you too."

That was oddly comforting. I opened and closed my hands, eager to use this newfound power inside me. Then I saw something flying overhead, that at first I assumed was a seagull until it got closer and I realized it was Larkin. She flew on a trail of silvery light like she was Supergirl and my mouth fell open at the sight.

"Will I be able to do that too?" I asked.

"Maybe," Celeste said with a small chuckle as Larkin touched down on the sand beside us. "Larkin will help with your training since she's the youngest witch here and went through training more recently than any of us."

Larkin—who was really in her forties despite her appearance—was the youngest witch here? Damn. They really were in dire need of some new blood.

"You will meet here every night to train," Celeste continued. "Until we feel you are strong enough to go back and protect your pack."

And save Kaden, I mentally added, as the moon's strength flowed inside my blood. The thought of being able to use this power to help Kaden and my pack sent a bolt of pride through me. No longer was I the outcast half-human shifter from the Cancer pack. I was a Moon Witch and the Ophiuchus pack alpha female—and I would use my combined heritage to save the other shifters.

"I'll let Larkin take over now," Celeste said, as she stepped back and clasped her hands.

"We're going to start with some very basic spells." Larkin

looked me over as if assessing me for strengths and weaknesses. Her young face had a very serious expression on it, and it was still hard for me to accept that this freckle-faced girl was really a mature woman. "The kind they teach children when they're first starting to use their power. You're going to have to chant a bit in ancient Greek, but Celeste and I will teach you what to say."

"Ancient Greek?" I asked. "Is that the language you were speaking in before?"

"Yes, our kind began in ancient Greece as a cult that worshiped Helios and Selene, the sun and moon gods," Celeste explained.

My eyes widened at that. I hadn't known that the Sun and Moon Witches had been around for so long. Obviously, they played a long game, like the Sun Witches were doing with the shifter packs now.

Larkin lifted her hands and said a few words in that same language—ancient Greek, I knew now. She enunciated them slowly and clearly and looked at me as she did so. A ball of moonlight appeared between her palms, pulsating softly. I'd seen the Sun Witches do something similar, but it had usually been hurled in my direction while I'd been attempting to flee. Now I could simply watch as Larkin manipulated the silvery ball, letting it expand and get brighter, casting enough light on the surrounding beach so it almost looked illuminated by daylight. Then she let it flicker to almost nothing, before releasing it completely.

"Did you catch those words?" Larkin asked.

"I think so," I said, before repeating them for her out

loud. She said one of the words again, putting emphasis on a different syllable. We went back and forth like this a few times until she was satisfied I could say the entire phrase correctly.

She created another ball in her hands as a demonstration. "Good, now try to summon a small amount of light. You should be able to feel the energy within you—let it pull toward the moon and bring some of the energy down."

I opened my mouth to ask her exactly how I was supposed to do *that*, but she shook her head at me.

"Close your eyes, and you'll feel it," she said.

I sighed and did as she requested, closing my eyes and feeling for that power inside of me. I thought about the times I'd used my magic to jump between patches of moonlight, and when I reached for that same magic now it wasn't a struggle like it had been before.

A huge amount of energy went through me like a lightning bolt. I said the words out loud, trying to imagine a small ball of light appearing in front of me as I stretched my hands out to face each other, just like Larkin had done. My eyes popped open to an almost blinding amount of silvery light pouring out from between my fingers. *Oops.* That wasn't exactly small. I wondered if I'd done it wrong, or if this was just what happened at first?

I looked up to find Larkin holding her hand in front of her eyes, grimacing at the blinding light. Celeste was as well, but she was peering through her fingers at me and smiling. I let the magic go, and the light faded to nothing. "How was that?"

Larkin lowered her hand with an amused smirk. "Well, that was bigger than I thought it would be. Usually, young witches can't get much more than a little bit of light."

"It was perfect," Celeste said, clapping her hands together, her eyes beaming. "Your magic is strong, Ayla. The goddess favors you."

Her praise sent a pleasant little shiver down my spine, and I found myself standing a little taller.

Larkin lined up a bunch of smooth sea stones between us, then said another set of words. I repeated them in my head, trying to copy the intonation exactly. For a few moments nothing happened, and I flicked my gaze up to Celeste. Unlike when she had called the moonlight, Larkin's brow was drawn down in a slight frown, as if she was struggling with this. Finally, the rocks began to glow, and when I leaned closer, I could feel the heat coming off of them. Then the glow began to fade and when I reached out to touch one, it was lukewarm.

"We can create heat," Larkin said. "Although it isn't one of our strongest talents. The Sun Witches rule the heat and the sun, but we can use the moon to capture some of that energy. I want you to try it, and see if it feels different for you than calling down the moonlight. Some Moon Witches have an easier time of it than others. I am not one of them, sadly."

"You have many other areas where you are strong," Celeste said to Larkin with a warm smile, and I realized the two of them had a close bond. Almost like mother and daughter themselves.

I repeated the words back to Larkin like last time, and she coached me a bit on the pronunciation until she was satisfied I was saying it correctly. I pointed at the rocks and imagined them heating up. This was more like how I had struggled before. The magic inside of me stirred slowly, as if waking up after a long nap, and it wasn't quite sure what I wanted it to do.

"Imagine that you're holding a laser that will direct the moonlight in a very concentrated way, and think about fire and warmth while you do it," Larkin said.

I tried to visualize what she said and the magic slowly poured out from my fingertips, while the rocks began heating up. They didn't get as hot as they had for Larkin before the magic slipped out from my grasp. I gasped, struggling to hold onto it, but the stones went cool once more.

"That is a lot harder, you're right," I said with a sigh. "Does it get easier? I noticed the magic slipped out from under me, like it didn't want to do that. Is that normal?"

"The short answer is yes," Larkin said. "Our strength lies in making things cool instead of warm, and your magic is out of control because you're so new. It'll 'slip out from under you' a lot in the beginning. You'll need a lot of discipline to be able to control it well, and especially under dangerous circumstances like a battle with a Sun Witch."

"But the shower, and the stove..." I glanced at Celeste. How had she made a flame or kept the water warm enough for me to take a long shower? Making heat had been almost draining, like I'd just run for a long time, even though I hadn't moved from my spot on the beach.

Larkin followed my gaze. "Celeste is strong in all magic."

"*All* magic?" I asked, raising an eyebrow. "Even sun magic?"

"Let's just say I'm old enough to have picked up a few tricks from the Sun Witches," Celeste added with a mysterious smile.

Did that make her centuries old? Or more? It was hard to fathom being in the presence of someone with so much power and wisdom. Or believe that she was my *mother*.

"Let me show you how to make these rocks into icicles," Larkin said. "I think you'll have more fun with this."

As she cast the spell, ice quickly grew along the rocks like a head of hair. Thicker and thicker it grew until it coated each rock entirely in a hard shell of ice. When I picked one up, it was icy and cool under my touch and I dropped it quickly. "Impressive. Can you freeze water as well?" I asked, glancing out at the ocean.

"Yes, although it's harder when it's moving water," Larkin said with a wry smile as the ice melted away. "How about you start with these rocks before you try to freeze the entire sea?"

I huffed out a breath of laughter. She was right, I was getting carried away, feeling giddy and powerful with the magic pulsing inside me. I didn't even know if I could encase the rocks in ice like she had.

I followed Larkin's instructions for imagining the stones becoming so cold that they iced over, and the magic rushed out of me. The stones easily froze, but so did the sand, and when I glanced at Larkin she was hastily stepping back as ice sped along the ground toward her and then ran up her leg. I let go of the magic immediately.

"Oh no," I said, "I'm so sorry!"

Larkin shook her head as she brushed ice off herself. "It's okay. I should have expected this. You have a lot of power, but you need to learn how to control it, especially since you're starting so late in life. Normally we learn these things when we're young."

I nodded, feeling a mix of emotions ranging from worry, guilt, and sadness all at once. I desperately wished I'd been raised among the Moon Witches and had been trained in magic from the beginning, even though I knew there were good reasons that I wasn't.

"Did I hurt you?" I asked.

Larkin scoffed. "What, a little ice? It would take a lot more than that to hurt me."

"You'll learn control with more practice," Celeste said, resting a hand on my shoulder. "That's why you're here now, to learn, and we'll be here to guide you every step of the way."

Her words sank in and calmed me immediately. I wasn't alone anymore, and they would help me with all of this. Over time, I would get better. I had to—for Kaden.

I took a deep breath and said, "Let me try again."

CHAPTER SIX

THE NEXT FEW DAYS—OR rather, *nights*—passed in a blur. I spent most of my time learning magic, and only dragged my aching, tired body to bed when I couldn't cast spells anymore. It reminded me of the early days of training with Kaden, when I had no idea what I was doing and felt like I would never get better. But slowly, I did—both then and now.

Larkin taught me a few more spells, and I practiced alone on the beach even when she wasn't around. I was so determined to learn quickly that I pushed myself hard, and though Celeste said I was progressing at a rapid, almost unheard-of pace, it didn't feel fast enough. I was driven by desperation, knowing that the sooner I mastered the magic, the sooner I would get back to Kaden and my pack. I missed them so much, but I kept reminding myself that I had to stay strong and focused or I'd never be able to save them.

The rest of the time I stayed in the house with Celeste,

and although there was some awkwardness at first, everything soon fell into a strange sort of rhythm. She helped me learn a little more ancient Greek, and over meals, we talked about all sorts of things, like two strangers trying to get to know each other better. Although I wanted to learn about Celeste's history, she insisted on asking me questions about my life instead, saying we'd have plenty of time to talk about her later. She wanted to know everything about my childhood, my friends, my hobbies and interests, and of course, about Kaden. I told her all about what had happened to me at the Convergence and afterward, about joining the Ophiuchus pack, discovering my mate was my half-brother, and how the Sun Witches had arranged it all. Yet every time I asked her about herself, she gave vague answers or turned the question back around to me. I knew she was old, much older than I'd imagined, but little else.

I spent a lot of time with Larkin too, of course. She also wanted to know all about my life, but she was much more open than Celeste about her own. I learned she grew up in Boston and that both her parents were Moon Witches, though it pained her to speak of them much.

"Supposedly one of my great-grandmothers was burned in the Salem Witch Trials," she told me one night while she was teaching me how to shoot moonbeams, similar to how the Sun Witches hurled sunlight as a weapon.

"Really?" I asked as I tried to get a moonbeam to fly across the beach. I couldn't even make it float from my hand slowly, let alone lob it through the air like a softball. The moment I tried, it fizzled out and died.

Larkin gathered moonlight into a projectile again and launched it toward the waves. "So I'm told. Witch trials around the world were originally started by the Sun Witches to root out Moon Witches. They like fire, as you know. But then humans got involved and took it too far."

When it was my turn, I focused the energy into my hand. *Okay, Ayla. Pretend a big, scary Sun Witch is over there and you need to kill her before she kills you.*

I lobbed the bolt of moonlight toward the waves, but it flew a few feet before fizzling into nothing again. Damn. That was a bit better, but not good enough. And I didn't have time to make mistakes.

"Let's take a little break," Larkin said.

I opened my mouth on a firm denial—I needed to keep working until I got this—but one look at her face told me that wasn't an option. We were taking a break whether I wanted to or not. She sat down on a large piece of driftwood and motioned for me to join her, as well.

I sat beside her with a sigh. "Why am I not getting this?"

"Because it's hard and takes a lot of practice," Larkin said wryly. She rooted around in her backpack, then pulled out a travel mug with water in it, along with a bag of potato chips. "Here."

I took a long sip of water, then eyed the chips. "How did you get these?"

"I grabbed a ton of them on my last trip to Earth." She popped open the bag with a satisfied smile. "They might be a bit out of date by now, but they still taste good."

I ate a couple chips, but all it did was make me nostalgic for home. "You make the magic look so easy."

She took the bag back from me. "I've been doing magic since I could walk, and I have a lot more years on you too."

"I don't have years to learn." I took another sip of water and then started getting up. "I need to get back to work."

Larkin muttered a few words and a chain of moonlight wrapped around me and dragged me back down. "Sit. Your break's not over yet."

I huffed in frustration. "Am I in trouble?"

Larkin laughed. "Not at all. I just hoped that relaxing a bit might make the spell come easier to you. You're so focused on doing it right that you're getting in your own way. But we're not going to think about magic for a while, all right?"

"Fine." I leaned back and tried to relax. I wasn't sure what we could talk about that would take my mind off of my growing frustration with my progress, but I was open to anything right now, no matter how counter-intuitive it seemed.

"You do realize there's no real rush," Larkin said. "You can spend years here learning everything you can and then go back to the exact minute we took you. They won't even know you were gone."

"They won't, but I will." A lump formed in my throat as I thought of that moment when I'd held Kaden for the last time. "Every day without Kaden is torture. I need to get back to him."

Larkin sat up straighter. "Your voice gets softer when

you talk about him. Do you love him? Even though he's not your mate?"

"Yes," I said without hesitation. I never got a chance to tell him, and I prayed I'd be able to change that soon. I'd been scared to say it out loud, but now the thought of losing him forever made my chest ache. I couldn't imagine a future without Kaden in it at this point. "As far as I'm concerned, he's my true mate, and I know he feels the same. He named me the alpha female of the Ophiuchus pack."

"Wow," Larkin said, practically going starry-eyed. "That's so romantic. I wish I had someone like that."

"You will," I said.

"Not as long as I'm stuck here," she muttered, before turning to me, her cheeks rosy. "I bet Kaden's good in bed too. All the guys in romance novels are."

"Um..." I looked over at her, raising my eyebrows. "You do realize romance novels aren't real, right?"

"Yes, of course." Her face fell. "But they're all I have to go off of. I've never even been in a relationship. Or had sex."

"Never?" I opened my mouth to ask her why, but closed it just as quickly. One look at her and it was obvious why. "I'm sorry."

She kicked at the sand in front of her. "Any decent man would feel weird about sleeping with me since I still look like a kid, and it's not like there are a ton of available men around here anyway. Luckily I have a whole house full of books to keep me company." She laughed it off, but I could see how much it hurt her.

My heart broke for her, and I grew angry at the Sun

Witches all over again. This was their fault—if they hadn't killed Larkin's parents she wouldn't have been forced to hide here as a child, cursed to never age.

She crumpled up the empty bag of chips. "Come on, break time's over."

She started to get up, but I grabbed her arm. "When I go back to Earth, you should come too."

Her eyes widened, making her look the age of her body, but then she shook her head. "You know I can't. It's too dangerous out there for me. For all of us. Until the Sun Witches are defeated, nowhere on Earth is safe for us."

"That's why you're training me, isn't it?" I grinned at her, trying to get that sad, defeated look out of her eyes. "I'll protect you."

Larkin still didn't look convinced, but she gave me a half-hearted smile as she stood. "Better get back to it then. You're not going to be protecting anyone if you can't make a proper moonbeam bolt."

I jumped up and shook my limbs out, feeling a little better after all. Maybe Larkin had been right about taking a break. Besides, now I had even more motivation—I had to save my cousin too.

THAT NIGHT, Celeste invited some of the other witches over for dinner. They spilled into the house with laughter and warmth, bringing various dishes ranging from green bean casseroles to stuffed grape leaves to fruit pies. Each one of them gave me a hug like I was a member of their family, and I diligently tried to remember names—Mariel, who had given me the scarf in town and had the warmest smile; Elsa and Kena, both covered in cat hair, their arms linked together the entire night; Erik, one of the few male witches I'd seen, along with his wife, Patricia, who brought me tea they'd made themselves; and Rowena, known as the oldest witch in Lunatera, with paper-thin skin and eyes that shone with wisdom. To my surprise, Killian came too, and though my wolf kept wanting to growl at him, he only offered me a polite smile that showed only the tips of his fangs.

"You know, you're the first visitor we've had in a long time," he said as we all sat down to eat. "A decade, at least."

"How long have you all been here?" I asked, raising my eyebrows.

"Some of us have been here for centuries," Mariel said, with a nod to Rowena.

"Aye, I've been here long enough to forget what Earth is like," the elderly woman said with a slow chuckle.

"Most of us came here in 1861," Patricia explained. "That's when Celeste decided it would be safer for Moon Witches to live here than on Earth."

I glanced between all of them, trying to imagine how they'd survived here for over one hundred fifty years without losing their minds. "What happened?"

"The Sun Witches attacked us during one of our coven meetings," Elsa said. "They slaughtered so many of our people..." Her voice faded and she shook her head, while Kena wrapped an arm around her.

"That's when most of the men were killed," Patricia said, clasping onto Erik's hand. "Including Celeste's husband."

My eyes jerked back to Celeste's face. She'd had a husband?

Celeste looked down at her food, and when she spoke her words were laced with pain. "The Sun Witches had been hunting us for some time, and though we tried to fight back, I knew the only way we'd survive was if we went into hiding."

"She saved us," Mariel said, raising her glass of wine in a salute. "And we've been safe here ever since."

I swallowed my bite of food and asked, "How do you stay sane?"

Larkin laughed. "Hobbies. Lots and lots of hobbies."

Then they each told me all about their hobbies—baking, painting, making candles, embroidery, learning new languages, and so many others. They all seemed happy on the surface, but I sensed deep pain and longing inside all of them.

"And you?" I asked, turning to Killian, who had been quiet all this time. "How did a vampire end up here?"

"I fell in love," he said with a charming smile as he swirled his wine. "How else?"

Rowena patted his arm. "Killian joined us a century ago when he married one of our kind."

"Yes, I was lucky they accepted me here." He bowed his head. "Alas, my dear Lucy was murdered by the Sun Witches during a visit to Earth a few decades ago."

"I'm sorry to hear that." I knew what it was like to lose

someone I loved to the Sun Witches. I still woke up most mornings with the image of Kaden being blasted by the Sun Witches' magic.

He nodded in response. "I debated going back to Earth, but at that point, I'd lived here so long, it felt like home. Besides, I'm protected from the Sun Curse here, since there's no daylight."

"How do you get blood?" I asked, but then wanted to bite my tongue. "Sorry if that's a rude question. I've never met a vampire before."

Luckily Killian didn't seem to mind. "I don't need much of it, since time moves oddly here. But when I do, people in town donate for me."

"Killian is a great help to our people," Mariel said with a big smile. "We're happy to make sure his special needs are met."

I bet they'd like to help with some of his other needs too, I thought as I watched the way the ladies all made heart-eyes at him. I couldn't blame them. Killian was freaking gorgeous, and there was something about him that drew you in and made you want to get closer, like some kind of allure. It didn't work on me though—partly because I was taken, and partly because my wolf kept wanting to bite him.

"I do love it here," Killian said, flashing the ladies some more of his charm. "Even if I were to go back, I'm not sure if I would be welcome among my own kind anymore, or how I would adapt to not going out during the day. It's been so long."

I shrugged. "Well, we have the internet now, and you

can order pretty much anything you want from the comfort of your home. You wouldn't have to leave at all during the day."

"Tempting," he said with a wicked smile that sent a shiver through me. "Perhaps one day I will return. I've heard Larkin and some of the others talking about all the wonderful modern conveniences, but I didn't consider how they could help someone like me."

"You should come back with me," I said, then turned to face all the witches there. "All of you. We could use your help standing against the Sun Witches."

Their faces flashed with fear and many of them shook their heads and shrank back. I got the sense I'd said something wrong.

"We're not fighters, dear," Kena finally said. "We're like the moon—calm and serene, flowing like water through time."

"We've already lost too many family and friends to the Sun Witches," Erik said.

"Our place is here," Rowena added, and many others nodded with her.

"I'm sorry, Ayla," Celeste said, resting her hand on my shoulder. "I wish we could help you, but it's not safe for us to return to Earth."

"But you can't just sit around and wait for things to get better," I said, as frustration welled up inside me. "Change won't happen unless you *make* it happen."

"That's why you're here," Mariel said, her eyes bright with hope.

I shoved my food back and stood up. "So you just expect me to save you all? To stand up to the Sun Witches on my own? *That's* why you brought me here?"

"Not alone," Rowena said. "With your shifter allies."

"Right. The shifters you abandoned all those years ago." I shook my head, feeling sick to my stomach. "You want us to fight your enemies for you, but you won't lift a hand to help us."

"Ayla—" Larkin started.

I held up a hand. "No, I get it now. I understand why you brought me here and why you're training me. Don't worry, I'll do my best to fight the Sun Witches because I have no choice. But if I fail, know that it's because you sent me to do it alone."

I stormed out of the room, leaving behind the shocked expressions of the witches there. As I stepped outside, I heard footsteps behind me and spun around, ready to tell my mother to leave me alone, but it was Larkin. With a sigh, I waited for her to catch up to me.

"I'm sorry about all that," she said. "Everyone here wants to help, they really do, but change is hard for them. They're all afraid."

"I am too." I rubbed my arms as I stared up at the endless night. "Some days I'm so terrified it's hard to breathe. But I can't stand back and do nothing, or I'll lose everything."

"Most people here have already lost everything," she said softly. "They're just surviving each day as best they can while praying for a miracle. I hope you can forgive them for thinking it might be you."

I blew out a long breath and looked out at the waves, letting my anger wash away with the tide. I understood what it was like to live each day in survival mode, and the more I saw of the people here, the more my heart ached for them. They were alive but not truly living, stuck in this strange place where nothing changed, too terrified to do anything to save themselves. The unknown was frightening for them, and it felt safer to do nothing than to risk getting hurt again. I got it, I truly did, but I didn't have the luxury of waiting around for someone else to save me.

I didn't want to be anyone's miracle, but it seemed I didn't have a choice. This was my fate, my destiny, my calling. I only prayed Selene had chosen the right person for this burden.

CHAPTER SEVEN

AT SOME POINT, I stopped counting the days, weeks...months? One night simply flowed into the next, and it was hard to know how much time had passed when things never really changed. Sure, they had clocks in Lunatera, but there was little else to mark the passage of time. It was soothing to constantly see the moon above and to feel the touch of power from it, but I also missed daylight too. And Kaden...always Kaden. He was my reason for pushing myself so hard, for all the long hours spent training and studying with Larkin and Celeste, even when it felt painstakingly slow or frustrating. Even when I wanted to give up because it was too hard. But I didn't, and I never would.

Eventually, when I'd learned how to throw moonbeams, got good at freezing things, and mastered all the other spells Larkin taught me, Celeste decided it was time to teach me some of the more advanced spells.

"Tonight I want you to learn to shield yourself from the Sun Witches' attacks," she said, as we stood on the beach alone with the wind whipping at our hair. At least it wasn't raining. The weather here was one of the only things that did change, and it was completely unpredictable. The Moon Witches said it was just Selene being moody. What a goddess had to be moody about, I wasn't sure.

"Larkin taught me that already," I said, before chanting a phrase in ancient Greek and throwing up a moonbeam shield around myself. It should protect me from any of their sunbeams, assuming I got it up in time to block them.

"Very good," Celeste said with a nod. "But there are other attacks you need to be able to defend against, and shielding them is much harder."

I let the shield dissipate. "What kind of attacks?"

"Mental ones. Some witches have a gift for mind magic, and I need you to be prepared in case they try to enter your thoughts."

I shivered a little at the idea of the Sun Witches inside my head. "I didn't know that was possible."

"It's a rare and very difficult spell that few can master. I pray you'll never come up against it, but I want you to be prepared in case you do." She paused and studied my face. "I'm going to have to do it to you so you know what it feels like, and then I'll teach you how to stop it. I apologize in advance."

I drew in a breath and stood a little straighter. There was still a part of me that wanted to impress my mom. "I'm ready."

She didn't even say a word out loud or move her hands, but then I felt it. A voice inside my head telling me to *kneel*, while Celeste's eyes bored into mine. I wanted to resist but it was impossible, and before I knew it, my knees hit the sand and my head bowed. I was hers to command, and terror raced through my veins, knowing how easy it had been for her to control me.

Then she released me and stepped back, turning her head away. "I'm sorry," she said, her voice cracking. "I never wanted to do such a thing to my own daughter."

"It's okay," I said, though my voice was a little shaky too as I got off my knees. "How did you do that?"

"It's not something we teach among Moon Witches, but I learned it from my father long ago." She pursed her lips before adding, "He was a Sun Witch."

I recoiled, taking a step back. "I have Sun Witch blood too?"

"Yes, though I don't think it's very strong in you. The Moon Witch and Cancer blood leave little room for the sun."

Thank the goddess for that.

"You never speak about your past," I said softly.

She let out a long sigh. "No, I try to think of it as little as possible, but I suppose you should know your family history. My father was the High Priest of the Sun Witches and a truly evil man. He raped my mother, a Moon Witch, and then took me from her as a child to train me as a Sun Witch. Eventually, the Moon Witches rescued me from his clutches, but my mother lost her life defending me. I trained with the Moon Witches after that." She swallowed hard, though her face remained stoic. "Perhaps you can see why I was desperate to avoid a similar fate for you."

"I understand." I took a step closer to her. "The Sun Witches have taken so much from you. Your mother, your husband..."

She lightly cupped my cheek with her hand. "Yes, but none of those compared to the thought of losing you." She sniffed a little and then composed herself. "Now, we need to make sure you're protected before you return and face them."

"Show me." I lifted my chin and steeled myself for another of her mental attacks.

She waited for the moon to come uncovered from a few clouds, before murmuring a few words. As I watched, moonlight infused her whole body, pouring out of her as if she'd swallowed it and it was coming out of her very pores.

"Did you catch what I said?" she asked, as the glow faded away.

I repeated the words back to her slowly, paying special attention to the enunciation. I'd learned a lot of Greek these past few weeks, and I was fairly certain that if I heard new magic being spoken by the Sun Witches or Moon Witches, I could piece together what it meant.

"Good, that was correct. As you say the words, let the moonlight flow through you. Give yourself over to it, and let it take control. Allow Selene to protect you with her grace."

I shook out my hands and stepped back, eager to try it. We'd practiced this many times, just letting the moonlight soak into me to give me more power or recharge my energy. It felt like welcoming in an old friend, pulling her in for a hug, and immediately feeling like I was home. I could bask in that kind of energy forever if I had the time.

"Speak the words," Celeste said. "And imagine that the moon is holding you, protecting you, building a shield around your mind and soul."

I said the words of the spell, feeling the power flow through me even faster. It filled me up and strengthened me, and I imagined the magic forming a barrier around my thoughts. When Celeste mentally ordered me to kneel again, I was able to grit my teeth and fight back, though it made sweat break out on my brow. My knees shook with the desire to bend, but I resisted, gathering more moon magic around my mind until I felt her back off.

She beamed at me. "You are so strong, my daughter. Only a few are able to get it on the first try."

My heart hammered in my throat as I dropped the mental shield. "Can the Sun Witches really do that?"

"A small number of them can. Unfortunately, Evanora is one of them." Celeste hesitated, and then added, "You should know that she is my half-sister. We grew up together."

Shock and horror ran through me. "Somehow I doubt you were one big happy family."

"No, with the father we had, there was no happiness in our home."

We practiced a few more times until Celeste was satisfied that I could quickly pull up a shield to block a mental attack. "You're ready," she said. "There's nothing more I can teach you that you need to learn before you go back to Earth."

"Ready?" I asked, as my heart lurched. "I can go back now?"

"Yes, you can return tomorrow after we initiate you as a full Moon Witch." She came forward to squeeze my arm. "I'm so proud of you."

I threw my arms around her, tears welling up in my eyes. I'd worked so hard to reach this point, and sometimes I'd thought it would never happen, but it was really here. *Kaden, I'm coming.* "Thank you."

"No, thank you." She hugged me back tightly. "These have been the best few weeks of my life."

I closed my eyes and pressed my forehead against her shoulder, wanting to commit this moment to memory. "I'm so happy I got to spend time with you."

Celeste pulled back and wiped at her eyes too. "I don't know what I will do when you're gone."

"You could come with me." I glanced in the direction of the village. "You and the other Moon Witches could help us fight, instead of hiding. If we face the Sun Witches together, they won't stand a chance." *And I don't want to lose you again,* I thought but didn't say out loud.

Celeste looked pained, as if she'd heard my words in her head. "I cannot, I'm sorry. None of us can. I have to protect my people, and the Moon Witches are not fighters any longer, but you can always return to Lunatera for safety." She paused, as if she wanted to say more, and I let her have the few moments to decide. "Or just to see your mom, perhaps."

"Of course I will come back for that reason," I said, hiding my disappointment. I'd known what her answer would be, but I'd had to try anyway.

"I truly hope that you can save Kaden," she said with a kind smile. "I'd love for you to bring him the next time you visit."

The thought of introducing Kaden to Celeste made something hurt in my chest. "I'd like that too."

Something in the sky caught my eye, and I looked up just as Larkin swooped down at us.

"When do I learn *that* spell?" I asked.

Larkin grinned at me, her freckles shining under the moonlight. "Hey, you have your gifts, and I have mine." She turned to Celeste. "Did she pass the test?"

"Yes, she did," Celeste said with a warm smile for both of us. "Tomorrow she will become a true Moon Witch."

"Congrats," Larkin said, giving me a hug. "I knew you could do it."

"Mostly thanks to you," I said, squeezing her back. "You're a great teacher."

She bit her lip and tugged on her nearly white hair, which made her look young again. "Is the invitation to return to Earth with you still open?"

My heart raced faster. Was she really considering it? "Of course it is."

"Then I'm coming with you," she said, her eyes shining with resolve. "You've convinced me I can't stay here any longer, wishing things would change without doing anything to actually change them. If I want to have a real life, I have to fight for it." She nudged me in the side. "Besides, you'll need my help. I think I might be able to break your mate bond with Jordan too."

I pressed a hand to my chest as it filled with hope. "Really?"

"I can try at least," she said with a shrug. "Celeste and I have been discussing it and we think we've worked out a spell that could break it. We'll need Jordan to do it though."

"We'll get him, somehow." A huge wave of relief settled over me, along with a dash of newfound hope. "Thank you. I'm so happy you're coming with me, and I'll try to keep you safe. I can't promise anything, but I will do everything in my power to make sure we get out of this alive."

"I had a feeling you would go," Celeste said to Larkin with a sad smile, before turning it back on me. "Take care of each other. You both mean the world to me, and I'll miss you so much, but I've kept Larkin here too long as it is."

As I glanced at my newfound family, I felt a rush of unexpected sadness knowing I would be leaving this place already. As much as I wanted to get back to Kaden and my pack, I would miss Celeste too, and all the other people I'd met in Lunatera. But at least Larkin would be by my side when I returned.

CHAPTER EIGHT

ANTICIPATION MADE my blood race as I walked onto the beach the next night. I could hardly believe this moment had finally arrived. After all my training, grieving, praying, hoping, and fearing, it was time for me to return to Earth. To my pack. To Kaden.

Many of the Moon Witches I'd come to know were gathered on the beach in a circle, talking in hushed tones as they waited. Tonight they wore the dark purple robes they'd had on when they'd brought me here. As I approached, they turned and looked at me, falling silent.

The moon was full and bright, shining down on the beach and illuminating the serene faces of the Moon Witches. I gazed at Larkin, Mariel, Elsa, Kena, Patricia, Erik, and even Rowena, before finally settling on my mother. Celeste's robe was black and silver, distinguishing her as the High Priestess, and her moon crown glowed atop her long white hair, making her look like a goddess. She stood in the center of the circle and opened her arms, embracing me quickly before directing me to the spot where I should stand.

As I stepped into the center I drew in a deep breath and let the moonlight fill me, stealing some of its power to give me strength. Larkin gave me a quick thumbs-up, which made me smile, and then I faced my mother.

"Under the watchful eye of Selene, tonight you will become one of us," Celeste said. "A true Moon Witch. Do you accept this as your destiny, Ayla Beros?"

"I do."

She gave me a smile so full of pride it took my breath away. "Then with the blessing of the moon goddess, I invite you to join our coven."

Around me, the other Moon Witches began chanting softly in ancient Greek. It wasn't a spell, but more of an intonation—a prayer to Selene to bring me happiness and power, and to let the moon always shine on my face. Celeste raised her arms and began chanting too, and the moon illuminated her like a spotlight. She let it surround her, making the air sparkle almost like snowflakes, and then pushed the magic toward me. As the moonlight hit me, it washed over me like a cool wave, dancing across my skin, before swirling around one of my fingers. When I raised my hand, a new tattoo had appeared along my middle finger of a crescent moon and a tiny star. Marking me as a Moon Witch, like my Ophiuchus symbol marked me as one of their pack.

"This mark will tie you to Lunatera, so you may return

any time you desire," Celeste said. "You are one of us now, and you will always be welcome here."

The other Moon Witches looked on as she unfolded some cloth in the same purple shade as their robes. As the heavy fabric settled around my shoulders, my throat tightened with emotion. I'd been reaching for this goal the whole time I'd been in Lunatera, and this was the final hill to crest.

"Thank you," I said, as she pulled the hood up over my hair.

Celeste patted my cheek, her love shining from her eyes. "I'm so very proud of you, Ayla. I'm going to miss you so much, but I will pray to Selene every night for your safe return."

"I promise I'll be back." We hadn't had nearly enough time together, and I still had so much I wanted to learn about my mother. Only the knowledge that Celeste would always be here in Lunatera waiting for me allowed me to leave this place. Still, a tiny part of me wanted to stay by her side for the rest of my life, to be a child again with a mother who actually cared, but her path had diverged from mine long ago. We led different destinies now, and it was time for me to return to my other family.

Just as my eyes began to fill with tears, she released me. The other Moon Witches each came up to grasp my hands in theirs, to welcome me to their coven, and to say small prayers for my safety and strength. One by one, until only Larkin remained, her eyes wide with the same mix of fear and excitement twisting in my gut now.

"The robes look good on you," she said.

"I wouldn't be wearing them if not for you," I said, my throat tightening with emotion. "You stuck with me, making sure I learned everything I needed in record time."

"Of course I did. You're family." She threw her arms around me and squeezed me tight, and I hugged back her small frame. As I did, I noticed she was trembling a little.

"You ready for this?" I asked her as we pulled apart.

She swallowed hard. "As ready as I'll ever be."

When the other witches stepped back, I realized this was it. I'd been waiting for this moment ever since Celeste had told me I could travel back and save Kaden, and my stomach was a swirling mess of sadness, excitement, and fear. Would I be able to save him? Or would I have to face my grief all over again?

"It's time." Celeste gazed between the two of us with a sad smile. "Take care of each other. You both mean the world to me, and I want to see you again soon. With Kaden, I hope."

I laced Larkin's fingers through mine as I faced my mother. "We'll all come see you soon, I promise."

"I'll hold her to that," Larkin said.

Celeste nodded and blinked back tears, before stepping back, closing the circle of witches around us. She began muttering something different in ancient Greek, something I didn't quite understand, and moonlight filled the circle around me and Larkin. The other witches joined in, voicing a steady, solemn chant, one that was very different from the initiation spell.

"Picture the moment when we took you," Celeste said,

while the others kept chanting around us. "Form it in your mind."

I closed my eyes and conjured the image immediately. Kaden in my arms, his skin burned and blackened. Jordan was only a few steps away, and Zodiac Wolves and Sun Witches fought a deadly battle all around us in the woods outside my father's cabin. The smell of blood and sweat had choked the air, while the sound of snarls, shouts, and cries of despair had filled my ears.

With the moment solidified in my mind, I opened my eyes and nodded to my mother. Larkin squeezed my hand and tilted her head back to let the moon cast its light down on her face, as Celeste's chanting got louder and louder, the words crackling with power. The moon seemed brighter all of a sudden, nearly blinding me, bathing us in Selene's light. Then there was a loud crack, as if time itself was splitting apart

And then I was back on Earth.

I stood over Kaden's body with Larkin at my side and the battle raging on around us. Daylight, bright and hot, shone down on me instead of moonlight, and at first, I was too stunned by it all to move. Even my sharpest memories hadn't captured the sheer pandemonium at the moment I'd left, but worst of all was Kaden, lying there on the forest floor. My mind had dulled the pain of this moment to keep me sane, but now I faced the reality of it again, and doubt and horror crept back in. How could I possibly save him?

I quickly threw up a shield and Larkin did the same,

right as a sunbeam flashed toward us. It hit my shield and fizzled out, just as I dropped to my knees beside Kaden.

"I'll cover you!" Larkin said as she conjured her own moonbeam.

I gave her a quick nod, then gathered Kaden in my arms. His burnt body was so much worse off than I'd remembered, and there was no heartbeat, no breath, no *life* left in him. What if this didn't work and I'd trained for nothing? My hands shook as I cradled his face in my palms, trying to find some sign he was still in there. *Kaden, I'm here. I've returned. Come back for me too.*

I reached out to the moon and drew power from it, though it felt sluggish here compared to in Lunatera, especially with the sun still out. With the magic bursting inside of me, I used my Ophiuchus healing powers and ran my tongue along Kaden's cheek. Celeste had told me that my moon magic could boost my wolf abilities, and that's what I was hoping for now.

The magic poured into Kaden until we were both glowing softly, and slowly his skin began to heal, his burns fading away until his tanned skin remained. My breath caught as hope fluttered inside me at the sight, but when it was done, he still didn't move. His body was healed...but he was still gone.

No, I thought, *I'm not leaving here until you come back to me, you stubborn alpha. Please, Kaden.* I pushed more power into him, while tears streaked down my face. Some ancient Greek words suddenly spilled out of my lips, though I wasn't sure what exactly I was saying. A prayer to Selene, begging her to lend me her power for one small, impossible miracle. *Selene, if you care for us at all, please help me save him.*

Moonlight lit up the entire forest in a flash and a sudden rush of power that didn't feel like mine washed through me. It blasted into Kaden's body like a freight train and he jerked with the force of it. Then he drew in one, deep breath that was the most beautiful sound I'd ever heard.

I let out a sob and held his face, waiting for him to open his eyes. The glow faded from both of us, just as I heard the soft, steady sound of his heart beating again. I dared not hope it was real, not until I knew for sure.

Then he opened his eyes.

CHAPTER NINE

"KADEN," I exhaled with another sob, almost delirious with relief. I pressed my forehead against his, breathing in his scent, feeling his chest rise and fall with each breath. The battle raged on around us, but I didn't even care. I just needed to prove to myself that he was alive again.

"Ayla?" he asked, his voice rough.

The sound of his voice healed something inside me. I let out a wild laugh and kissed his face all over, while his brows drew down into a confused frown. I pulled back just enough to check his body for any injuries, but he was completely healed. Through some miracle that I wasn't going to look too closely at, Selene had helped me save him. She'd brought him back from death, like some kind of magical CPR, and now I was never letting him go again.

I pressed my lips into Kaden's skin, warm once again. I moved to his neck, dragging my lips against his pulse point repeatedly. It quickened under my touch before Kaden drew back and pressed his lips to mine. I closed my eyes and let myself melt into him. I'd missed him so much, and I hadn't been sure if I'd ever see him again, but now that he was here, whole and hale, I found myself shivering. I was crying, so overwhelmed with joy and gratitude that it filled me to the brim. I tried to convey how happy I was to see Kaden in my kiss, and from the way his hands tightened around my body, I'd managed it just fine.

A sunbeam fizzling against my shield brought me back to my senses. As much as I wanted to simply sit here and bask in the feel of my mate, we were still in the middle of a battlefield.

Kaden's hands came up to cup my face. "Ayla?" he asked again. His eyes skimmed over me, taking in my new hooded purple robe. "What happened?"

"I'll explain everything," I said. "But let's get out of here first. We're not safe, and the Sun Witches are really going to want my head now."

As if to punctuate my words, a beam of Sun Witch magic hit the tree next to us, sending splinters everywhere. The branches instantly caught fire, and I shot a blast of frozen moonlight to put it out, muttering the spell in ancient Greek. Kaden's jaw dropped when he saw me use the magic, but I didn't have time to worry about what he thought, because Larkin was fighting three Sun Witches under the tree and needed help.

I jumped up and shot a few beams of moonlight into the fray. One caught a Sun Witch in the shoulder and she stumbled back. I let loose more magic, dividing the Sun Witches' attention between Larkin and myself. Despite all her talk about how she wasn't a fighter, Larkin brought down the two witches she was battling, and then together we took out the last one.

"What the fuck?" Kaden asked, slowly standing beside me. He looked at me like he didn't recognize me anymore. "When did you learn to shoot magic out of your hands? And who is that girl?"

"Later," I said. "I have a lot to catch you up on, but we need to find Jordan first. We might be able to break the mate bond if we can take him back with us."

At the thought of Jordan, the mate bond rose up in me like bile in my throat, that heady mix of desire and disgust with a tug on my gut that told me exactly where he was. While I'd been in Lunatera the bond had been completely cut off, further proof it was all Sun Witch magic fueling it. Now that I was back on Earth the heavy weight of the mate bond came back like boulders crashing down on my shoulders. I couldn't wait to be rid of it.

"Just take me to him, and I'll handle it," Kaden said, eyes narrowing as he searched for my half-brother in the crowd.

Cocky alpha, I thought with a smile. Kaden shifted into his giant black wolf in an instant, and then raised his nose in the air and inhaled sharply, no doubt trying to find Jordan's scent trail. Jordan had been only a few feet away when Kaden had fallen, but he must have escaped while I was healing him—but I sensed him easily with the mate bond.

North. I gazed at the clearing in front of the cabin and saw that the battle had started to wind down, with many shifters either defeated or already fleeing from the chaos and death. The woods around us were smoking, and some trees were on fire from the Sun Witches' magic. I searched for any familiar faces, but saw no one I recognized, and prayed everyone else I loved had managed to escape.

"This way," I told Kaden as I started walking away from the battle.

Kaden let out a low growl in return and loped alongside me like my own guardian wolf. I debated letting my wolf free too, but I wanted to stay in human form in case I needed to do more magic. I kept my shield around both of us as we moved deeper into the woods. At the sound of movement behind me, I spotted Larkin flying after us, though she struggled to weave through the forest as easily as we did.

Jordan wasn't far away, standing under a large tree with some of the other Sun Witches, along with three of his Leo shifters in wolf form. Jordan seemed to be arguing with the Sun Witch Roxandra, his hands waving frantically, but I couldn't make out the words, not in human form, anyway. When they spotted us coming, Roxandra promptly vanished in a flash like a firework going off, leaving only a trail of smoke behind. Jordan's shifters charged us, but before the Leos even got to us, I threw up a wall of moonlight. They slammed into it and fell back, dazed, and then Larkin quickly tied them up with some magical chains. They snapped and fought, but remained trapped.

Kaden charged toward Jordan with a fierce growl that sent a shiver down my spine. Jordan let out a Leo roar that made Kaden pause, but my shield protected me from the effects, and Larkin seemed to be okay too. Jordan shifted then, becoming a big golden wolf, and the sunset colors made his fur look even more glorious. He was as big as Kaden and fast too, and when they collided in a flash of teeth and claws I cringed a little.

"Don't kill him!" I yelled, as Kaden bit down on Jordan's flank. "We need him alive!"

At first, I didn't think he would listen, but then he let go and looked up at me, lips curled back in a growl. Jordan's blood stained his massive fangs, and my half-brother stumbled a little from the Ophiuchus poison now running through his veins. Hopefully only enough to knock him out. Kaden shook his head, and I could almost hear the way he wanted to protest, but he backed away.

I blasted Jordan with some of my moon magic, and together Larkin and I tied him up like the other wolves. Jordan then hit the ground hard, his eyes closing, even as his limbs still struggled and tried to escape. But eventually, he succumbed to the poison and went limp.

"Stop!" a familiar voice called out, and I turned around in time to see Evanora striding toward us. My aunt, according to Celeste. Evanora was the High Priestess of the Sun Witches, and I wasn't sure if even Larkin and I could take her together. It didn't seem to stop Larkin from trying though. She shot a beam of moonlight toward Evanora. The High Priestess swatted it aside as if it were an annoying pest and raised her hand to shoot back.

"Kaden!" I yelled and motioned for him to bring Jordan over while Larkin raised her hands and projected another wall of moonlight. Evanora's first sunbeam hit the wall and fizzled, although Larkin grunted.

"Damn, she's strong," she said, her brow furrowing as she reinforced the magic.

"Shit, we have to get out of here," I said. "Come close!"

Kaden, back in human form and completely naked, now had Jordan slung over one shoulder like a sack of potatoes. I gave myself one split second to enjoy the view I'd missed so badly, then grabbed hold of Kaden and Larkin and let the magic pour through me once more. I had yet to try teleporting in the daylight, but Celeste had assured me I would be able to do it now that I had full access to my magic.

When we'd invited all the other packs here for our solar eclipse meeting, Wesley had made up a map of the cabin location for everyone, and about two miles away he'd marked a rendezvous spot where we'd said we would meet if we ran into any trouble. Kaden and I had briefly checked it out when we'd arrived, and I felt confident I could get us there now, and hopefully find our friends waiting there. I pictured the spot and reached out with my magic, and in a flash, we were all there.

I let go of Larkin and Kaden and glanced around. No one else was here yet. Dammit. Where were they? Had anyone made it out alive?

Kaden dropped Jordan on the ground unceremoniously and then turned to us with demands already on his tongue. "Someone better tell me who the hell the kid is, and why you're wearing a hooded cloak, and how you can shoot magic all of a sudden."

"I'm not a kid, thank you very much," Larkin said, rolling her eyes as if this was something she was used to saying. "I'm probably older than both of you put together."

Kaden frowned at her. "What?"

"This is my cousin, Larkin," I said. "A lot happened while you were...passed out. I'll tell you everything later."

Movement in the bushes put us all on high alert, but then Harper and Dane burst out of the trees, both naked and a little bloody, with the Pisces alpha, Amos, right at their heels. I breathed a sigh of relief at the sight of them, hoping others were coming too. But when no one else came through the trees, my heart sank.

"Glad you made it." Kaden nodded to them both. "Have you seen any other survivors?"

Dane shook his head, and Harper replied, "No, not yet. The forest is on fire and it's spreading fast. It's a nightmare back there. I'm not sure if anyone else is coming."

"No," I whispered. So many of the people I cared about were still out there. Wesley, Mira, Jack... Plus all the alphas and betas we'd invited to the meeting. Surely some of them must have survived the attack. I drew in a deep breath. If there was even the slightest chance that some of our allies were still alive and needed my help, I couldn't abandon them. "I'm going back to find them."

Kaden shook his head immediately. "No fucking way."

"Someone has to go search for survivors," I said, propping my hands on my hips. I'd missed Kaden's possessive alpha attitude, but now was really not the time for it. "I can teleport in and out, and I can defend myself against the shifters and witches." Most of the witches anyway. Evanora was another story, but I hoped I could avoid her altogether.

Kaden let out a low growl. "No. It's too dangerous."

"Trust me," I said softly. "I swear I'll return to you. I didn't bring you back from the dead just to let something happen to me now."

Kaden blinked at that. "Back from the dead?"

"Like I said, we have a lot to talk about." I desperately wanted to stay with Kaden now that I had him back, but there were other people out there who needed me more right now. As alpha female, it was my duty, and in Kaden's eyes, I saw the grudging understanding of an alpha who knew we had to do this to protect our pack.

I stepped back and vanished.

CHAPTER TEN

THICK SMOKE BILLOWED into the air, turning the sky black. The fire had spread quickly through the woods, making it almost recognizable from even a few minutes before. I coughed and stumbled through the burning forest, looking for anyone friendly, knowing I would have to hurry. I debated shifting, but my nose was useless now, so clogged by the smoke that I doubted I'd be able to smell anything but fire for the next few days.

I checked the cabin first, covering my mouth and nose with my hood as best I could to shield myself, but the place was already engulfed. I tried to peer inside anyway, calling out for any survivors, when a beam fell from the ceiling, sending cinders everywhere. I narrowly teleported just in time to avoid getting crushed. So much for my father's cabin. If anyone was in there, it was too late for them. I had to move on.

I heard a familiar voice cry out behind me. *Mira.* I ran

through the forest as fast as I could toward it, sidestepping the burning areas, while fear bubbled up inside of me. I'd wanted her here, and if she died, I would never forgive myself.

I stumbled into a clearing a short distance away from the smoke, where the fire hadn't reached yet. Mira was in her human form, while her mate was beside her in wolf form and covered in blood, defending her against another wolf. At the sight of me running toward them with a moonbeam in my palm, the enemy wolf darted off into the woods, and Mira let out a small cry of relief. She stumbled toward me, and I noticed she was limping.

"Oh, I'm so glad you're all right," she said and embraced me.

I hugged her tight with a lump in my throat, before drawing back to look her over. For her, it had been only minutes, but for me, it had been an eternity since I'd seen her. Dirt and blood smudged her olive skin and her long black hair was tangled with a few leaves in it. "Are you okay?" I asked.

Mira grimaced as she moved her leg. I noticed a long slash in her jeans, still sluggishly oozing blood, even though it had begun to heal already. "I'm in better shape than Aiden," she said, motioning toward her mate, who struggled to remain standing on all four paws.

"You're safe now. I can get you to the others and they'll heal you up." I grabbed Mira with one hand and then rested my other on Aiden's back. As soon as I transported them both back to the clearing, I yelled out, "We need healing!"

Harper and Dane immediately came forward to help them. Kaden started toward me, but I teleported back before he could stop me. Wesley was still out there, and I'd be damned if I was leaving him again.

The fire was already worse when I returned. I said a quick prayer to Selene, since it seemed like she might actually be listening, and set off looking for any other survivors. A quick magical shield blocked me from the smoke and fire as I searched, but all I found were the dead, some torn apart by claws, others burnt and blackened by Sun Witch magic.

Then I caught the briefest trail of a familiar wolf scent. *Wesley.*

I found him surrounded by fire, fighting with another wolf—a Leo. They were both injured, neither able to get the upper hand, and the flames were getting closer with every second that passed, caging them in. I blasted cold at the area around them, hoping to keep it at bay, and that distracted the Leo wolf enough for Wesley to knock it down, sinking his teeth into its neck. The Leo let out a last, shuddering breath before stilling.

I ran toward my brother, holding back a cry of relief at the sight of him still alive. I dropped down and wrapped my arms around his furry neck, hugging him tightly. He panted heavily and I saw blood all over his fur, but he nuzzled his head against me, showing he was relieved to see me too.

For a few seconds I considered searching for others, but there was no point. The fire burned almost too hot to handle around us, and there were dead shifters and a few red-cloaked Sun Witches lying on the ground everywhere.

There was no sign of Evanora or her daughter though—they must have fled before it got bad.

"Let's get out of here," I said. But just before I could teleport, Wesley's ears perked up.

He jerked his head toward the south, and I heard it then too—the sound of someone sobbing. Shit. Who else was out here? I shared a glance with Wesley, and we started moving toward the sound as one.

A naked female crouched above a fallen shifter, crying and rocking back and forth. It took me a moment to realize it was Eileen, the female beta of the Sagittarius pack—and Kaden's former lover. She was hardly recognizable under the blood and dirt covering her. Then I caught sight of the dead shifter she was hugging. *Her mate.*

"We have to go," I said, leaning down and shaking Eileen's shoulder. She glanced up at me, her eyes filled with tears. She shook her head violently, her fingers curled into the fur of her dead mate's body a bit tighter.

"I'd rather die here," she sobbed, the words hardly coherent. "At least I'll be with him."

I tried to pull her to her feet, but she was strong and wouldn't let go of his body. "Eileen, it's not safe here. He would want you to keep living. Please come with us."

Eileen shook her head even more violently. "No, I just want to be with him. You don't understand. I've lost half my soul..."

Wesley shifted back to his human form and frowned at her, clearly unable to understand her desire to simply *die.* But then again, he didn't know what it was like to have a mate. If I hadn't carried the hope of saving Kaden in my chest, I wouldn't have survived my time in Lunatera either.

"We need to go," he said.

The fire was starting to close in around us, and I didn't want to be here when it started consuming the bodies. As much as Eileen didn't want to leave her mate, I doubted she actually wanted to die here. As a Sagittarius, she wouldn't actually be hurt by the fire—but then again, neither would the Aries or Leo shifters, and there was no telling who else might find her here. Besides, I owed it to the Sagittarius pack and to Kaden to get her out of there safely. She would have to deal with her grief later, but there was nothing I could do about that.

I tore off my clothes and tossed them to Wesley, then shifted into wolf form. Before Eileen had a chance to understand what was going on, I sank my teeth into her shoulder and bit down, releasing my Ophiuchus poison. She let out a scream and struggled, trying to free herself, and I let her go. She scrambled away, looking wildly between Wesley and me like we were the enemy.

Wesley held his hands out in supplication. "We're just trying to help you."

She snarled but then keeled over to the side, passed out cold. I sniffed at her to make sure she was still alive, and then shifted back.

Wesley handed me back my clothes but stared at Eileen the entire time. "Do you think she'll hate us when she wakes up?"

"Probably. But I'd never be able to live with myself if we

left her." I didn't have time to get dressed—the flames roared closer, unbearably hot. We had to leave *now*.

My brother stepped forward and picked her up easily in his arms, even though he was still hurt. Like a true alpha. "Me either."

I grabbed onto Wesley and teleported us away. Once we were in the safe zone, Wesley laid Eileen gently on the ground and I donned my clothes again. Kaden's head snapped to face us, and though he glanced at Eileen's prone form, it was me he came toward.

"Are you hurt?" His eyes were worried, and my heart softened as he ran his hands over my shoulders.

"I'm fine. The blood isn't mine."

Kaden called for Harper and Dane to check on Wesley and Eileen before he took my elbow and led me farther into the woods. Mira and Aiden were resting on a log while speaking with the Pisces alpha, and I spotted Jack standing with the Libra alpha, Ethan. I was relieved to see a few other shifters with them too. Not enough though.

"Did anyone else make it?" I asked.

"No," Kaden said, his voice low.

Jack looked up with tired, dead eyes. "The Capricorn beta is dead. I tried to save him, but..." He shook his head.

I swallowed hard. We'd lost so many today, and there was no way I could go back and search for any more survivors. The fire had grown too intense, and now that I'd stopped moving, a bone-deep ache settled in my body. I'd overextended my powers, even with all of the rigorous training I'd done.

Larkin stood in the shadows, away from everyone else, watching and listening. I felt a flash of regret go through me. Had I made the right decision to have her come with me? I needed her help, but look at the world I'd brought her into. A world where she didn't belong.

Everyone in the clearing was quiet, and most were wounded, tired from the battle, and covered in ash. Some looked like they couldn't quite believe this had happened, and others were obviously heartbroken. The attack had been so unexpected and brutal, leaving us all shell-shocked. My mate bond tugged me toward Jordan, who was still unconscious a few feet away. *This is his fault.*

"We lost so many," I whispered to Kaden. He met my gaze, and his eyes were haunted. I couldn't imagine what he was feeling after being brought back from death only to be thrown into another desperate fight for his life.

He clenched his jaw. "There's nothing we can do for the dead right now. What matters is getting everyone who survived back to safety. The fire is going to consume this area soon, and we need to get everyone up and moving quickly. We don't know where the enemy packs went, or if any Sun Witches are waiting in the shadows to pick us off."

I looked around the group of remaining shifters. Getting them to move quickly would be impossible in their current state, and we'd left our cars back by the cabin. Kaden was right—this would be the optimal time for the Sun Witches and the Leos to make their big move to take us out. We had to get out of here somehow—and there was only one safe way to do that.

"I have an idea, but I don't know if it will work," I said, though the thought of it exhausted me even more.

Kaden gave me a skeptical look. "Why do I not like the sound of that?"

"Just gather everyone over here," I said, before walking over to Larkin. "I need your help."

She hesitated, her eyes wide. "With what?"

"I'm feeling a bit drained and I need a lot of power for this next bit—can you help somehow?" I asked.

She nodded. "I can do that."

"Good." I let out a long breath. "This might be the only way we're getting out of here alive."

She gulped at that and immediately called forth the moonlight into her hands, then shot it at me. Power filled me up like water pouring into a cup, and I drew upon my own connection with the moon too. There were soft gasps as I started glowing and people gathered closer around us, especially once Kaden called everyone over.

Once I felt like I held as much power as my body could hold, I let it out like a breath. The entire clearing became covered in moonlight, shimmering in the twilight gloom. Many of the shifters reached out to touch it, and I closed my eyes and focused on transporting us *away*. I visualized the Ophiuchus pack's hideout in Canada, trying to spin up the image from memory and hold it in my mind's eye as clearly as possible. I'd never transported myself this far, let alone with a group of people, but I'd also had my full magic unlocked and spent months training to use it and grow stronger. I just had to *believe* it would work.

With a rush, I felt the power take hold of my intention, and there was a huge pull to my gut. I almost lost grip of the magic as a wave of exhaustion washed over me, but at the last second I was able to hold onto it, and then we were gone.

CHAPTER ELEVEN

I OPENED my eyes to a glimpse of the Ophiuchus hideout as we all arrived, but then my vision swam. The moment the spell was complete, my knees went weak, and I stumbled forward a few steps. Every single lesson Kaden had taught me about falling rushed through my mind as I tried to land gracefully, but I never hit the ground. A pair of big, strong arms encircled my waist, halting my swift descent, and then I was held against a muscular chest. I gasped, everything still spinning, and sagged gratefully into Kaden's arms.

He pulled me tighter against him with a low, protective growl. "That was reckless."

"No, that was necessary to save our people," I said with a small smile. It must have worked, or he wouldn't be so annoyed with me. I basked in the feeling of his body against mine, so solid and real. I laced my hands together behind his neck and snuggled closer to him. "I thought I'd lost you."

He tightened his hands around my waist. "It's time you finally told me what's going on."

We had so much to talk about, and we needed to get the injured shifters cared for, and we all needed a good night's sleep. But before any of that happened, we needed to talk about our next steps, and what we planned to do.

"I'll tell you, but it's a long story, and the other alphas and betas should be here for the discussion. What I have to tell you will affect everyone."

"Fine, but I expect another report later...once we're alone." He set me down, making sure I could stand before letting me go.

The door of the alpha's cabin burst open, and Stella came running out. A few other Ophiuchus shifters gathered around us, trickling out from their own cabins at the sound of the new people outside.

Stella skidded to a halt in front of us, eyes bright. As she looked at the state of everyone, she frowned and then turned to us. "What happened?"

I stepped forward and hugged her, unable to stop myself. I hadn't realized just how much I'd missed her until she was here in front of me. "I missed you so much."

Stella drew back and gave me a questioning look. "I missed you too," she said. "But it's only been a few days."

I shook my head. It was an odd feeling, knowing I'd been gone for so long, while for them almost no time had passed. "We need healing, food, and shelter for everyone here. And I need to talk to the alphas and betas about what happened."

"Understood," she said and moved away to speak to some of the other pack members.

Kaden turned to Dane, who was carrying Jordan now. "Get him tied up and put somewhere where he won't escape."

Jack joined Harper and Dane as they took Jordan away. I watched them go, but it didn't feel real. After all of this time seeing Jordan as the ultimate enemy to defeat, we had him in captivity, and Larkin would help me take the mate bond off. This would all be over soon.

"Everyone else, please join me in the cabin," Kaden said, addressing the others who had come back with us from the meeting.

Some of the others began moving inside, but before we could join them, Clayton rushed over to us. He looked harried, almost frantic, as he moved to speak with Kaden in a low voice. "We have a problem."

"What is it?" Kaden asked.

Everyone in the area could hear the conversation, but at least they all pretended to give Kaden and Clayton a moment of privacy, though I noticed the Pisces and Libra alphas lingering outside. Probably waiting to see if this new problem affected them too.

"Tanner left around the same time you did for the solar eclipse meeting." Clayton's brows furrowed. "They haven't returned yet, and they took a small group of Ophiuchus with them. Another shifter who stayed behind said they were going to the Sun Witches."

"Tanner betrayed us to the Sun Witches?" Kaden

growled low in his throat, and I felt the tension pouring from him. He was *pissed* and rightfully so. If Tanner had done this, he had condemned so many shifters to die, including his own pack members.

"I can't believe he would do that," I said, though it would explain how the Sun Witches had found us so easily at my father's cabin. I'd worried it was because of me and my connection with Jordan.

"Tanner must have felt that their only option was to ally with the Sun Witches for protection," Stella said softly, looking between Kaden and me. "Especially if he worried they were going to wipe out the Ophiuchus pack."

"That's what I think too," Clayton said grimly. "Which leads to another problem."

What, another one? I thought as the bone-deep tiredness dragged at me. I didn't think I could stand another crisis tonight.

"Go on," Kaden said through gritted teeth. I could see how much he wanted to let his anger show, but he was doing his best to contain it and keep calm.

"Tanner knows where we're hiding," Clayton said. "After the Sun Witches regroup, I have no doubt their next stop will be here."

Kaden swore under his breath. "We'll have to leave tomorrow. The entire pack."

"Where will we go?" I asked. We'd only just returned here, and I'd been dreaming of it for the entirety of my stay in Lunatera.

Wait. *Lunatera.* Could I bring the Ophiuchus pack

there? No, that would mean telling our allies about the secret hiding place of the Moon Witches. I wanted to believe they would stay on our side, but if our own pack members were betraying us, I couldn't do that to the Moon Witches and the other residents of the village. If the Sun Witches ever found the place, they would kill every last person there.

Ethan stepped forward and addressed Kaden. "The Libra pack will shelter you." He extended his words to the rest of the crowd. "All of you."

Kaden took in the other alpha with a long look. They were about the same height and both had dark hair and muscles for days, but Ethan was a contradiction of tattoos and sophistication, while Kaden was all rugged mountain man. Ethan's business suit had been abandoned in the fight, and now he had a piece of ripped cloth wrapped around his waist, but it barely covered anything. If I hadn't been mated already, I would have let my eyes linger on the dark hair descending into that cloth. Stella and Larkin definitely noticed it and were having a hard time looking away.

"You would take in the Ophiuchus pack?" Kaden asked with surprise, or perhaps suspicion, in his voice. I couldn't blame him—only months ago the Ophiuchus pack had been the outcasts of the Zodiac Wolves, and Kaden had been shunned at the Convergence by every alpha there, including the Libra one.

"Yes, the Libras will protect your pack in Toronto," Ethan said. "I wanted to attempt diplomacy with the Leos and the Sun Witches, but I see now that there is no way to reason with them. The only way is to stop them. Together, as allies." He offered his hand to Kaden, who took it after a split second of hesitation.

"Thank you," Kaden said. "That's a very generous offer."

The Libra Alpha inclined his head. He looked ready to say more, maybe an actual apology—*Kaden deserves one,* I thought wryly—but after a moment he simply stepped back.

"We'll leave tomorrow at sunset." Kaden turned back to Clayton. "Start getting everyone ready to move out. Pack up only the essentials and leave the rest behind."

Clayton nodded, though his brow was pinched. "We'll be ready, although the pack won't like it."

"Better they're pissed off than dead," Stella said with a shrug.

"I'll address everyone when I can," Kaden said. "We'll do what we must to keep our pack safe. We always have."

Clayton bowed his head and headed off, while Kaden stared off into space with a frown on his lips. I could see the weight of being an alpha on his shoulders, and I knew the news of Tanner and other shifters leaving us and possibly betraying us was a crushing blow. They'd once been friends before Tanner had disagreed with the way Kaden had been running the pack and challenged him as alpha. I'd had to fight in that battle too to claim my position as alpha female, defeating Tanner's mate, Lindsey.

Kaden shook off his worries and led me inside his cabin, and I heard the others slowly following us as we entered the house. For a second I stopped at the door and breathed it in, savoring the familiar sights and sounds. Then we all settled in around the living room, and Stella began passing out drinks and some food, along with some blankets and clothes since pretty much everyone else was naked. To my disappointment, Kaden threw a shirt and some jeans on, while I accepted some crackers and cheese gratefully. I'd been too nervous to eat breakfast this morning before leaving Lunatera, and I hadn't noticed how ravenous I was until the food was in front of me.

I leaned against Kaden as we ate and sipped some water, while I surveyed the others. No one was so badly hurt that they needed immediate care, and with food and drink in their systems, the shifter healing process could work its magic. Amos, the Pisces alpha, was clustered at the island counter with Mira and Aiden, while Ethan took the chair across from where Kaden and I were seated on the couch. Wesley had set Eileen down in another chair, and she was waking up and crying softly. Together that made four packs joining the Ophiuchus here: Pisces, Libra, Sagittarius, and Cancer. No one from the Capricorn pack had survived, I noted with a grimace.

Larkin leaned against the wall, her small arms crossed, observing everyone while looking out of place and uncomfortable. Even though she appeared to be a kid, she was one of the oldest people in the room, but she was also the only one who had no shifter blood. I'd have to find a way to make her feel more welcome among these people.

Kaden waited until everyone had taken a few bites of food before standing and addressing everyone. "I hope you see the severity of the matter now. The Leos and the Sun

Witches plan to slaughter anyone who stands in their way. They won't spare anyone, and diplomacy is out of the question."

He didn't even know the full extent of it. Something twisted in my gut as I realized I'd have to reveal to them that they'd been pawns of the Sun Witches all along and that everything they knew was a lie. How would they react to such unbelievable news?

"It's worse than you know," I said, as I rose to my feet. "I have a lot to tell you."

"Is it about the bright light we all saw you make in the forest?" Amos asked, crossing his arms.

I nodded. "During the battle, the Moon Witches took me away to a place called Lunatera. It's a realm outside of time, where they can hide from the Sun Witches. A place where they can be safe. I was there for what felt like months, though they were able to bring me back to the exact moment I'd left."

Wesley held up a hand with a worried expression. "Wait. The Moon Witches kidnapped you?"

"Not exactly. They trained me to use their magic so I could use it to fight the Sun Witches. It turns out my mother is their High Priestess." I gestured at Larkin. "Larkin is a Moon Witch too, and my cousin. She's come back with me to help us."

"Wow," Stella said, her eyes wide. "So you know all sorts of Moon Witch spells now?"

"Yes, and Larkin and I can teach them to any of the pack

members who have Moon Witch blood. We'll need every advantage we can get against the Sun Witches."

"How can we trust the Moon Witches?" Ethan asked, eyeing Larkin skeptically. "And how would this one teach us? She looks barely old enough to drive."

"I'm older than you are," Larkin said with a scowl.

"Larkin's body has been trapped in time. It's complicated." I sighed, realizing this would be a lot harder than I'd expected. "The Moon Witches are not the evil people the Sun Witches led us to believe they are. They just want to live in peace."

"What about the Moon Curse?" Amos asked.

"There is no Moon Curse," Larkin said. "We removed it long ago from all shifters."

"How do we know that?" Ethan asked, arching an eyebrow.

"The Ophiuchus pack doesn't suffer from it," Kaden said. "And we never get the Sun Witch blessing as babies."

I took a deep breath and looked around the room. It was time we began taking back our own power, and it had to start right here, in this room. "That's how they're locking away your wolves and your true mates. The ritual they perform on newborn shifters isn't to bless them and protect them from the Moon Curse, it's to make sure that they can't shift until the spell is lifted. They've convinced the Zodiac Wolves that you all need their spells to keep you safe from the Moon Curse when in reality they're using it to control you—all to keep us weaker and ensure we stay reliant on their magic."

There was a murmur of surprise around the room, and some of the shifters shared disbelieving glances.

"You're all welcome to meet our wolf pups while you're here," Stella said. "They begin shifting when they're toddlers, and learn how to control it by the time they're five or six."

"You said they're locking away our true mates too?" Mira asked, her eyes wide. Beside her, Aiden's jaw clenched, as if he was scared to hear the answer.

I swallowed, knowing this would hit her hard. We'd both talked about wanting to find our fated mates for so long, and she'd been ecstatic when she'd been paired with Aiden. Learning that was all a lie? I didn't want to tell her, but she had the right to know.

"Yes, the Sun Witches also lock away our ability to sense our mates," I said, my voice soft. "All so that the Sun Witches can create fake mate bonds, like the one they made between me and Jordan.

"No, I can't believe that," Aiden said, taking Mira's hand. "What I feel for my mate is real."

I gave Mira and Aiden a sympathetic look. "There might be a few that are real, but from what the Moon Witches have told me, those are rare."

"Why would they want to control the mate bonds?" Ethan asked.

"They've been breeding us like dogs for years, shaping and guiding each pack into what they want," I said. "All so they could make us weaker and easier to control."

"Prove it," Amos said.

I lifted my chin and met his gaze directly. "I can't. Not yet. But we know my bond with Jordan is fake—Wesley already told you that he found proof the Sun Witches created that bond. But what he didn't tell you is that Jordan is my half-brother. We share the same father."

Amos's jaw dropped nearly to the floor. "Harrison had a child with a *Leo?*"

Others around the group also muttered their shock and outrage, but I held up my hand to request silence. "Yes, and we've captured him now to try to break the fake mate bond with Larkin's help. If it's possible, we'll be able to break other ones too and prove that the Sun Witches have orchestrated them all."

"We'll also interrogate him on what he knows about the Sun Witches," Kaden said with a dark tone. I had no doubt his interrogation of Jordan would be...intense.

"I don't think Jordan will tell us anything," Wesley said with a snort.

Ethan leaned forward and met my eye. "If this is true, the other packs need to know. All of the Zodiac Wolves should have the opportunity to learn the truth and make the decision to leave the Sun Witches and join our side."

"I don't know if any of the packs would believe it," Amos said. "Hell, I can hardly believe it."

"We have to try," Wesley said. "We need to unite as many of the packs as we can against the Sun Witches. We know that the Leos won't be swayed, but we have to get the other packs on our side if we want to break free of their control."

"The Capricorns will join with us once they hear what happened to their betas," Amos said. "I will pass along the information. There is no way they can ignore this now."

Eileen sat up straighter. Her eyes were red and wet with tears, but she pulled her shoulders back and looked Kaden square in the face. "I will return to my pack and tell them everything. You will have the Sagittarius's full support."

Though I'd once felt hesitance or jealousy when it came to Eileen, now all I felt was sympathy. She'd lost everything today, and yet here she was, still trying to put on a brave face and help lead her people. Her eyes flicked to me as if she'd heard my thoughts, and they were so full of pain, I shuddered to think I'd have been in the same position if I hadn't been able to help Kaden today.

"I can contact the Virgo pack again," Wesley said. "Now that we have more packs on our side, they might be more receptive to joining us. Especially after the events of today, they really can't ignore what's going on any longer. If we have most of the packs on our side, we might even be able to convince the Aries, Taurus, and Scorpio packs to turn against the Leos as well."

I didn't think that was possible, but I wasn't going to tell Wesley as much in front of so many of the other packs. We needed to present a united force. And it was possible, just not probable.

"I'll contact some of the other pack alphas too," Ethan said. "I've tried to remain neutral in all other pack conflicts, so they'll listen to me when I tell them neutrality won't work any longer."

Kaden nodded. "Then we all know what to do. For now, we must rest and recover, because tomorrow we will leave this place."

"I'll help get everyone settled," Stella said, rising to her feet. "Come with me and we'll find a place for everyone for the night."

She led the other shifters out, leaving Kaden and me seated beside each other. He looked over at me and arched an eyebrow. "You look like you're about to pass out. Time for bed."

"Yes, please," I said with a groan. Before I could stand up, Kaden was already on his feet. He leaned over and lifted me up, bridal style. I pretended to struggle. "Hey, I can walk."

"I doubt that, little wolf," Kaden said dryly, and carried me up the stairs to the door of our bedroom. "You need to rest."

I opened my mouth to protest again but then decided against it. I was in Kaden's arms, the exact place I'd wanted to be for the past few weeks. I leaned my head against his chest and listened to the beat of his heart until he set me down on the bed.

I was home.

CHAPTER TWELVE

MY HEART RATE picked up as Kaden began stripping his shirt off. He stopped and gave me a hard look as I ogled his muscular chest.

"Don't even think about it," he said.

"I can't help it. It's been months since I saw you." Emotion welled up inside me and I took a long breath. "I didn't know if I would ever see you again, but here you are, in front of me. Alive."

He stopped and cocked his head. "Did I really die?"

"You did." I shuddered a little at the memory. "And then the Moon Witches dragged me away and I didn't know if I would be able to save you."

"But you did."

"With Selene's help. I prayed to her when it seemed like my healing wasn't working. She's the one who really saved you."

He cupped my cheek and gazed into my eyes. "Because

of you. When I was...dead...all I saw was darkness. No light coming for me. Nothing. But then I heard you say my name and I found my way back to you."

He bent down and kissed me softly, and I slid my hands across the hard planes of his chest. I was exhausted, but I wanted him too. I'd been craving the touch of his skin for what felt like *years*. I needed to feel him inside me to know this was real.

He pushed me away when my hands slid down to his jeans. "No, you need to rest." When I opened my mouth to protest, he raised a hand. "I will *make* you sleep if I have to."

"Your alpha command won't work on me," I said, giving him a wry smile. "You can try, of course, but you'll just look dumb."

"I'll have to bite you instead," he said, nuzzling my neck. "Knock you out like we did with Jordan."

Jordan's name was the last thing I wanted to hear right now, but the thought of Kaden sinking his teeth into the soft flesh that joined my shoulder to my neck made my breath catch. I remembered all too well how that felt, and one day I wanted to mark him as my own too.

Kaden breathed in my scent with a dark chuckle. "No, I can tell you'd like that too much."

I sighed and fell back on the bed, and caught a whiff of the smoke that still wafted off of me in waves. There was no way I could go to sleep smelling like a forest fire. I looked down at my hands, which still had streaks of blood and ash across the backs of them. Yeah, there was no way I was going to bed like this. "Fine, but I need a shower at least."

"You'll fall over if you shower, but I can give you a bath," Kaden said.

"Yes please." I perked up at the idea of Kaden giving me a bath. I started to stand up, but before I could, Kaden was there. He scooped me up into his arms and carried me into the bathroom, ignoring my protests. He set me down on the counter beside the sink and went to turn the water on.

When he turned around, he eyed me closely. "You're going to have to tell me more about these clothes you're wearing and how you got them."

I look down at my dress and winced. I hoped I could get all the blood out—I'd come to really like the Moon Witch attire. "Lunatera, the Moon Witch's realm, was like being stuck in the past. They all wore handmade clothes like this, though sometimes they supplemented with things bought on quick trips back to Earth."

"I want to hear all about it later," Kaden said, as he tested the water again. Then he came toward me and slowly slid the cloak off my shoulders, making my pulse race. His touch was so gentle as he removed my shoes and socks, and then finally began unlacing the back of my dress. Each touch sent a shiver of desire through me.

"I have so much to tell you," I said, leaning back into his arms.

He pushed the dress down, baring my naked flesh, his soft touch across my skin driving me mad. "I want to hear about your mother. The High Priestess, you said?"

"Yes. I think you'd like her. I was angry with her at first for leaving me with the Cancer pack as a baby, but when she told me the full story, I understood why. She went to such great lengths to protect me from the Sun Witches—she even magically dyed my hair red."

Kaden's eyebrows raised as he finished sliding the dress off my body. "You're saying you're not naturally a red-head?"

"Nope, my hair should be white like hers. She asked if I wanted to change it back to its original color, but I told her no."

Kaden fingered a strand of my fiery hair. "Good. I like it red. It was one of the first things I noticed about you," he murmured, his lips brushing my ear.

I wanted to pull him closer, but then he picked me up and gently put me into the tub. Warm water sloshed around me as I settled into the tub and immediately relaxed. Oh yes, this was exactly what I'd needed.

It got even better when Kaden grabbed the pitcher sitting on the side of the tub. He filled it up and poured water over my head. I closed my eyes as the warmth washed away some of the horrors of the last few hours. Then he got some shampoo and began working it through my hair with infinite patience. I relaxed back into him as his fingers worked at my scalp. It felt amazing, and I let out a small groan. He lingered on my head for a few more minutes, letting me tilt my head to encourage him to reach different parts, and then his fingers lifted.

I opened my eyes to find him reaching for the sponge. He dipped it into the water and then picked up one of my arms. I let myself relax back against the side of the tub as he ran the sponge over my arm and then continued across my chest to my other arm. He washed my entire body with a gentleness that made my heart ache. Even my legs and my thighs.

"You're dirty, too," I murmured as he finished with my left leg. "You should get in. Save water."

Kaden gave me a look, but then stood up and took his pants off as well. I had seen him on the battlefield, but I hadn't given myself permission to *really* look at him. He was whole, alive and well, his body just as beautiful as ever. He climbed into the tub, and I reached up for him as he sank down. Immediately, it became clear that there wasn't enough room for us, and I climbed on top of him, straddling his legs. I leaned in and kissed him, running my hands along his body. I trembled as I did so, so happy to finally be doing this after wishing for it during the entire time I'd been in Lunatera. Kaden was very real under my hands, solid and warm, and sexy as sin.

"I was devastated when you died," I whispered. "My mom wouldn't let me come back here, even though I begged her to let me go. Every moment of the next few months that I spent training, I missed you so much I could hardly breathe." A few tears slipped down my face as I thought about the pain I'd felt, not knowing whether I'd ever see Kaden alive again. This felt almost too good to be true, to finally have him back in front of me in the flesh. "But it helped me learn the magic faster. You were my biggest motivator, and the reason I can do everything I can today."

"You're incredible," Kaden said, pressing another kiss to my neck, right where my pulse point was picking up at the light touches. I could feel his cock stirring, pressed against my thighs, and wondered if maybe he'd changed his mind after all. "I can't believe I have you as my alpha female."

I thought the exact same thing every single time I set eyes on him. I leaned in close again and pressed another kiss to his lips. Kaden shifted me slightly in his lap, hands cupping around my ass to pull me closer to him. I gasped against his lips, letting him slip his tongue into my mouth. He reached between us and stroked my slit. I was already wet, so ready for him, and he let out an appreciative noise as he slid his fingers inside of me. He drew them out just as quickly and guided his now rock-hard cock into me.

I broke the kiss to look down between us and watch his cock disappear inside of me. I shifted my legs a bit so I could help, and together we set a low, lazy rhythm, meeting each other halfway. The water steamed all around us, splashing up against the sides of the tub. I traced a droplet of water with my finger as it cascaded down Kaden's chest. I watched in wonder as his muscles clenched in response, tensing and releasing to follow the line of my finger.

Kaden kept his hand between our bodies, thumbing at my clit, and I reached out to grasp at his shoulder, needing to steady myself as the pleasure built more quickly than I thought possible. I had so much pent-up *need*, but I hadn't been able to do anything about it the entire time I'd been in Lunatera.

"I know, I know," Kaden murmured, running a soothing hand over my waist as I shuddered, all the emotions I'd been too busy to really comprehend came crashing over me. "I'm here now. We're together."

The waves of emotion mixed with the pleasure in a confusing rush, and I began moving faster. Kaden's breathing became harsher as we picked up the pace, his hips lifting to meet mine. My fingers tightened around Kaden's shoulder, digging into his flesh as I let go of all logical thought and started just focusing on the pleasure, the way our bodies met and melded together in the perfect way they always had. The water added a hazy element, a sharp contrast to the growing need building up in the pit of my stomach. The steam rolled against my skin, making everything slippery and that much hotter. Kaden leaned forward and licked my collarbone in a way that sent strong shivers of pleasure sliding through my entire body.

It tipped me over the edge when Kaden latched his teeth onto my collarbone, just putting enough pressure onto it that I could feel it, each tooth pressed into my flesh. I shuddered, stilling on top of him as the pleasure crested. He growled and slid his hands underneath my ass again, helping to move me up and down, making the orgasm even more intense. The splash of water became louder as he picked up the tempo. My other hand slid on the slick porcelain of the tub as I tried to hold myself up for Kaden, but I couldn't quite manage it.

It didn't matter, Kaden's harsh breathing and stuttering rhythm let me know that he was getting close as well. He pounded into me through my orgasm, and all I could do was hold on for dear life as he let go of my collarbone with his teeth and drew me close to him. He shuddered to a halt, buried deep inside of me, and let out a moan that resolved itself into my name. I wrapped my arms around him as he came, and pressed our lips together. I felt like I wouldn't be close enough to him until I'd crawled into his skin, merged us together.

The water settled around us, and I sank back down, letting Kaden slip free from inside of me. He cradled me as I slumped over him, cheek pressed into his shoulder, and for a while, we simply sat, tracing lazy droplets down each other's skin.

"I love you," I said, once I had the energy to speak again. "Every day in Lunatera I regretted not saying it before. So I'll tell you now, and every day after, as long as I can."

"I love you too, Ayla. Even in death, my only thought was of coming back to you." He touched my cheek, his eyes staring into mine with awe. "But not even death can keep us apart."

I'd never felt so content as in this moment, wrapped in Kaden's arms, still feeling the afterglow of the orgasm we'd shared. Everything I'd been desperately working toward had finally happened. I had Kaden here in my arms, alive and breathing, pressing soft kisses to my neck. But eventually my eyelids began to droop.

"Come on," Kaden said, as he rose to his feet in one fluid motion, lifting me up at the same time with his hands on my ass. Water sloshed everywhere, but I was past caring at this point.

I'm pretty sure Kaden toweled us off, but I barely

noticed, and then he carried me back to bed and drew the covers back. I gratefully let go of him to snuggle into the pillows. This had to be the softest bed I'd ever slept in. Before I knew it, I was drifting off to sleep, and only felt the bed dip under his weight when he joined me. Then his arms wrapped around me, and I was gone.

CHAPTER THIRTEEN

I WOKE up to the sun slanting into the room, casting its warm rays over my feet, but the heavy weight of Kaden's arm around my waist was more comforting than anything else. His arm was curled protectively around my body, hand splayed flat across my stomach, and I smiled before I even shifted around to look at him.

He was still asleep, and I watched his face for a few moments in silence. He looked younger and less serious in sleep. I let my gaze skim over his face, down to his chest. The blankets had slipped down during our sleep, baring his torso, and desire stirred up within me again, along with that aching feeling in my chest I now recognized as love. I could hardly believe that I had him back.

He looked so peaceful I didn't want to wake him, and after nearly dying yesterday, he had to be exhausted. But I couldn't stay in bed either. There was too much to do before we left for the Libra pack's territory at sunset.

I slipped on some clothes as silently as I could manage and grabbed my camera. It felt strange to be wearing modern clothes again after spending so much time in the hand-sewn dresses of the Moon Witches, but I had missed stretch fabric. The weight of my camera felt familiar in my palm, even though I hadn't seen it in such a long time. I looped the strap around my neck as I reached the kitchen, where I found Larkin and Stella already there.

I smiled as I heard Larkin's animated chatting before I caught sight of her. They were both cooking something that looked more like lunch than breakfast, and I frowned as I glanced at the clock. It was close to noon already, though I could have sworn I'd only gotten a couple hours of sleep.

I caught the tail end of Larkin's enthused words. "And you just watch the people on this little flat screen, I couldn't imagine anything like it."

Stella grinned over at her. "Just wait until you get a smartphone. You'll be amazed at how many things you can do with a little screen that fits in the palm of your hand."

"Like a television?" Larkin's eyes looked as round as the moon, and she glanced over at me as I approached. "Good morning, Ayla. Or should I say afternoon?"

"Hey," Stella said, grinning at me. "Do you want a sandwich?"

"Oh, yes please," I said, and my stomach growled so loudly that Larkin laughed.

"Coming right up," Stella said, as she grabbed another piece of bread. "But yeah, it's like a TV, Larkin, but even better. You can even read books on it. You can have as many books as you can imagine. Hundreds of them all on the little device that you can stick in your pocket."

"No way," Larkin said.

I sat down in the living room and listened to Stella and Larkin chatter more about the marvels of modern technology. I was struck once again by how odd it was to know that Larkin had spent most of her life without any of these. It was sad, but at least she had a chance to experience it now.

Stella brought a plate over to me, and I took it gratefully. It was a BLT, and my mouth started watering before I even bit into it. I closed my eyes and made an appreciative noise.

"I've missed your cooking so much," I said.

Stella sat down opposite me, and Larkin wandered over to join us. "Everyone is getting ready to move again," Stella said after I'd taken a few bites of my sandwich. "Eileen left early this morning to rejoin the Sagittarius pack."

A bolt of panic went through me. "What about Wesley?"

Stella shrugged. "I think he's outside somewhere. I saw him walking down to the lake earlier."

I polished off my sandwich and took my plate over to the sink. "Thank you," I said again and waved as I headed outside.

I took a deep breath and tilted my head back to let the rays of sun shine onto my face. That was another thing I'd missed in Lunatera. I never thought I could miss the sun quite so much, but standing under it, I realized that I'd taken it for granted. I certainly wouldn't be doing that anymore.

Wesley was seated by the lake, and to my surprise, Mira

was with him. I opened my mouth to call out to them, but stopped. There was something about their posture, something intimate in the way they were curved toward each other, sitting a bit closer than was probably proper. Wesley reached out and touched her shoulder.

I walked a bit closer and caught sight of the looks on their faces. I knew Mira had always had a crush on my brother, but this went beyond that. This was fondness, or longing even—and he wore the expression too. I raised my camera and snapped a picture before I could stop myself. It was too pure of a moment to pass up. When I looked at the picture on the small screen, I smiled. It captured their emotions perfectly.

I looked back up at them, a pang of sadness nearly catching me off guard. If the Sun Witches hadn't interfered, they probably would have been mates. *Once we remove the bonds, they can find out,* I told myself before I could let the sadness completely overtake me. There was still hope for them, and I'd rather focus on that than wallow.

Mira started to say something, but glanced up and noticed me. She paused mid-sentence and waved toward me, and I noticed the bit of space they put between themselves. I wanted to tell them that I didn't care, but bringing it up might be an issue in and of itself. She was still mated to someone else, after all.

I walked the rest of the way out to join them, and Wesley scooted over so I could sit between them. He slung a hand over my shoulder, and I leaned into him. I'd missed all of them, and I couldn't help but smile as I settled between them. No matter how much I'd enjoyed living in Lunatera, this was where I really belonged.

"Did I miss anything while I was asleep?" I asked.

"Amos had to go back to the Pisces pack, but he asked Aiden and me to stay with you and the rest of the Ophiuchus pack," Mira said. "He wants us to keep him updated on everything."

I grinned at her. "I'm so happy to hear that. Now we just need to get Wesley to stay too, and it'll be like old times again."

Before Wesley could answer, a voice called out Mira's name. I twisted around to see Aiden, her mate, standing where I had been just a few minutes ago. I wondered what he would have thought if he'd seen her and Wesley together, and I was glad that I'd been the one to find them instead.

Mira jumped up. "We'll chat more later."

I watched her go for a few moments before turning back to Wesley, whose eyes were glued on Mira.

He finally looked back at me. "What are you grinning about?" he asked, shoving me slightly.

I shoved him back. "Oh, you've got it bad, brother."

"I have no idea what you're talking about."

I shook my head. There was no use trying to push him about it since there wasn't anything that could be done about it until we could remove the bonds. "Never mind. Are you staying too?"

Wesley gave me a look that said he thought I was being crazy again, and then he frowned. "I wish I could, but I have to get back to the Cancer pack. Although I don't have a way back there, since my car was back at the cabin in Oregon."

"Right. At Dad's sex cabin."

"Um, what?" Wesley asked, and the look of disgust on his face was almost comical.

"When I was with the Moon Witches, my mom told me I was conceived in that cabin. Likely, Jordan was too."

Wesley made a noise of protest. "Why would you tell me that?"

"Hey, if I had to be cursed with that knowledge, so do you."

"It's a good thing it burned down then," Wesley said. "After you told me about the fake mate bonds it got me thinking. Do you think that my mom was really Dad's real mate?"

"Probably not." *Although they were a perfect match for each other. Both good at making everyone miserable.* But I wouldn't say that out loud to Wesley. Even though they had been awful to me, Jackie and our dad had still loved Wesley. "The Sun Witches probably put them together, although I don't know why."

"My mom was originally part of the Capricorn pack— the daughter of the previous alpha, in fact—and their bond was the beginning of an alliance between the Cancer and Capricorn packs. That's probably why the Sun Witches wanted them to be together."

"That would make sense," I said.

"I never understood how they were supposed to be

mates anyway," Wesley continued. "They fought more than they got along."

That was true. I hadn't minded the fighting because it meant that they spent less time concentrating their efforts to make my life miserable, but it must have been hell for Wesley. "I don't ever want that to happen again. I'm going to figure out how to remove the spell that the Sun Witches cast on all of us, so we can be free to choose our own mates. It's only right." I let out a sigh. "And it's going to start with Jordan."

Wesley nodded. "Keep me updated on that."

"I will. But first, let's get you back to the Cancer pack." I stood up and held my hand out for Wesley to take.

He looked at it and raised his eyebrows. "What? You're going to take me there? It's a long way."

"Just trust me," I said.

Wesley still looked skeptical, but he stood up and took my hand. I concentrated on the little island I'd spent my summers at, where the Cancer pack was now hiding. I could recall it in almost perfect detail and then reached inside of myself to access the magic I knew was there. It was like stretching a muscle. Still sore after yesterday, but I had no doubts I could get Wesley back to where he needed to go.

Something tugged at the back of my gut, and then the calls of the seagulls up ahead were real. I blinked at the bright light coming off the waves as Wesley staggered, looking around.

"Holy shit," he said, looking around and then turning

back to me. "I'm all for your new powers, but could you warn me next time?"

I grinned at him. "What fun would that be?"

"That's pretty impressive." He sighed. "No one should have ever underestimated you, Ayla. Not our dad, and not the other wolves in our pack. And certainly not the Sun Witches."

There was a sudden lump in my throat that I had issues swallowing past. I nodded, hoping that it would convey everything I felt to Wesley. "Thank you," I managed to say.

Wesley squeezed my shoulder and then stepped back. "I'm going to prepare the Cancer pack to fight and reach out to some of the other packs for alliances. We'll keep in touch, especially now that you can just teleport yourself halfway across the world like it's no big deal." He grinned at me and then opened his arms for a hug.

It was nice to know I could visit him whenever I wanted. This goodbye wasn't as hard as the last one we'd shared, but I still found myself tearing up as I wrapped my arms around his waist and inhaled his familiar scent. "Yeah, we will."

I stepped back, and Wesley raised his hand to me in goodbye as I closed my eyes and focused on getting back to the lake and Kaden. *Home.*

CHAPTER FOURTEEN

THE PREPARATIONS TO leave were in full swing as I got back, with Ophiuchus shifters running around between cabins and calling out instructions and questions to one another. I went back to our cabin and began packing up my own things as well. I heard Kaden's voice from the other room and stopped what I was doing to look out into the living room.

He had Clayton and Harper and a few of his other friends in the living room, and they were pouring over a map, discussing what the best way to travel would be. I watched him for a few moments before turning back to my work and finishing my packing. I moved onto Kaden's clothes and toiletries next, gathering them and putting them in a separate bag.

Eventually, I ran out of things to do, and I realized I couldn't put it off any longer. Jordan was being held somewhere, and I needed to see if we could get the mate bond dissolved. I was terrified of what would happen if it didn't work and I'd be stuck with him forever, but I had to face him and try before we left tonight.

We didn't have a proper prison here like there had been in Coronis, but there was a shed that had once been used as storage for water equipment. It was far enough away from the main cabins that Jordan couldn't disturb us, but close enough that we'd know if he got away. I made the trek toward the shed while Kaden finished in the living room. Larkin was outside, standing by herself and looking at the lake, and when she caught my eye, I waved her over.

"I'm going to talk to Jordan," I said. "In a few minutes can you come in and try to do the ritual for removing the mate bond?"

Larkin nodded. "I'll get Kaden as well," she said and headed back toward the cabin.

I almost called after her to tell her not to bother, that he was busy. But it would make sense for him to be there. He was my true mate, and he deserved to know right away whether it worked or not.

I turned away and walked toward the shed. When I approached it, two Ophiuchus pack warriors nodded to me. "Is he awake?" I asked.

"I can't promise that he'll be lucid," one of the shifters said.

"That's fine." I paused and took a deep breath in. I could do this. I'd dealt with much worse. I opened the door and stepped inside.

It took a moment for my eyes to adjust. There weren't

any windows, and no one had bothered turning on a light. Jordan was tied up with cords, his hands behind his back, and more around his ankles. When he glanced up at me, he looked dazed. *Ophiuchus pack poison,* I thought. It was an ingenious way of keeping him sedated and unable to escape. The second our eyes met, the rush of desire and disgust filled me, but I tamped it back down.

"Are you happy now that the tables have turned and I'm your captive?" Jordan asked, his words slurred slightly. It did nothing to mask the bitterness in his voice.

I didn't want to give him an answer to that, because part of me *was* glad to see him like this, and that part felt a little too much like him for me to comfortably say it out loud. "I'm going to remove the mate bond between us, if I can."

"Good," Jordan said. "I can't wait to be rid of it."

I let out a humorless laugh. "Right, you never wanted to be mated to the half-breed. You made that very clear from the beginning, even before you knew I was your sister."

Jordan stared at me but didn't say anything else. I let the silence fester between us like an open wound for a few moments, waiting to see if he'd say *anything* at all. He didn't. I let out a breath and shook my head. Before I could be the first one to break the silence, the door opened again. Larkin entered, followed closely by Kaden.

"I've never done this before," Larkin said, her young face drawn down into a frown as she looked between Jordan and me. "Celeste thought it might work, but it might take me a couple attempts."

"Glad to be your guinea pig," I said dryly.

"We should just kill him instead and save ourselves the trouble," Kaden muttered. He'd leaned against the door frame, arms crossed. If looks could kill, Jordan would have been dead ten times over by the way Kaden was glaring at him.

"No," I said, shooting him an exasperated look. "We need to know if the mate bond can be removed. We need to free everyone to find their true mates."

Kaden shrugged. "Just as long as he suffers, I don't care."

I rolled my eyes and looked at Larkin. "I'm ready whenever you are."

Larkin nodded, her brows pinched in concentration. She lifted both of her hands up and began chanting, softly at first but growing louder with each iteration. She was saying a phrase in ancient Greek over and over again, and I could feel the pull of power as the spell took effect.

The cord running between Jordan and I drew taut. It was almost uncomfortable in a way it hadn't been since it had been put in place. It was too much too fast, all the emotions I felt when I was close to Jordan suddenly ramping up to a thousand, and I took a staggering step back. Pulsing need flashed through me, and I nearly threw myself at Jordan to rip his clothes off. I opened my mouth to tell Larkin that it wasn't working, but before I could utter a syllable, something else happened.

The effect of the mate bond—the constant need to get closer to Jordan, to give in, to stop fighting—lessened. I took in a deep breath, but before I could tell Larkin that it had worked, the spell ground to a halt. I pulled at the mate bond that still existed between Jordan and me, and let out a frustrated breath.

"It's weaker," I said. "But still there."

"Fuck," Larkin said, and Jordan looked a bit surprised to hear the harsh word on a child's lips. He didn't know that she was older than all of us, but I wasn't about to be the one to tell him. I was enjoying the shocked way he was looking at her too much. "We were both worried this might happen."

"What's the problem?" Kaden asked.

Larkin grimaced. "We need a Sun Witch for this ritual since it's sun magic."

"Oh, great," I said, exasperation rising up in me suddenly. "Can Celeste do it?"

"No, we need someone who knows how the spell was done. Someone who was there at the time it was cast, probably."

I swore under my breath. "Sure, let me go out and ask one of our friendly Sun Witch allies to come in and help us."

Larkin's face fell, and I pinched the bridge of my nose between my thumb and forefinger. There wasn't any reason to lash out at her, but it was so frustrating. Everything had been within arm's reach, and now it might as well be on the moon.

Jordan let out another bitter laugh. "Looks like we're stuck with each other."

I opened my eyes and shot him my own scathing look. "Shut up or I'll gag you."

Jordan fell silent, but I could still see he wanted to taunt me more. I wanted to get out of here before I did something stupid.

"Now can we kill him?" Kaden asked. "That would get rid of it for sure."

"No. We need him alive, and we need a Sun Witch to help break the bond." I sighed and forced myself to calm down. "I don't know how we're going to swing this, but we'll get it done. We always do."

Kaden looked at me, and I saw the acceptance there. He was willing to go along with this plan for now. I wondered how far his patience would run, and when it ran out, how catastrophic the ramifications would be. Jordan was the epitome of everything Kaden hated about the Leos. It wasn't completely about the mate bond, not entirely. There were older, deeper wounds that Kaden still had to heal. I just hoped we could find a viable alternative before Kaden got to the end of that particular rope. I didn't want to be there to see the fallout otherwise.

Breaking the mate bond seemed impossible, but I had to keep trying. We'd find a way—somehow.

BY SUNSET, everyone was packed up and ready to go. It was amazing how quickly the Ophiuchus pack could get everything together and ready to leave. But they'd all had a lot of practice moving around in the last few months. They practically had it down to a science by now.

"It'll take about a full day of nonstop driving," Stella told me as we helped load the bags into our car. Stella, Kaden, Larkin, and I were all in one van, along with Harper, Mira, and Aiden in the back with a couple more bags taking up the eighth seat. I shoved my bag into the tight space and looked at her.

"We have enough people to take short shifts," I said.

Stella hummed in agreement and then narrowed her eyes at the arrangement. "Do you think we need to leave a space for seeing out of the back?"

"I don't think we can," I said and sighed. "I guess we'll have to hope for the best."

Kaden and Clayton dragged an unconscious Jordan between them toward one of the vans that had been converted into a makeshift prison cell. After the failed spell, I'd watched Kaden sink his teeth into Jordan's shoulder once more. He seemed to be enjoying the whole process a bit too much, but I understood it completely. Even now, Jordan's limbs were bound and two guards were accompanying him. Kaden wasn't taking any chances. Jordan was going to be our prisoner until we were done with him. Escape wasn't an option.

I rubbed at my stomach, where the mate bond still sat. It had faded, like someone had put layers of wool blankets between Jordan and me, which made it easier to ignore now. If I was focused on something else, it was almost as if it wasn't there at all.

We got on the road, and I stopped thinking about Jordan at all as I talked with Stella and Larkin while Kaden took the first shift at the wheel. We only stopped for gas and food, and we were in Toronto by sunset the next day.

Stella nudged me awake as we entered the city limits, and I stared out of the window, mouth open wide at the sight of the huge city. There were so many buildings of all different shapes and sizes, with millions of people all going about their daily business. The thought of coexisting among so many different humans was amazing to me. I'd never spent much time in big cities, and now we'd be here for the foreseeable future. It was also hard for me to imagine shifters living so close to humans too. I'd never heard of it being done, but if anyone was capable of it, it was the peace-keeping Libra pack.

When we arrived at the hotel that the Libra pack alpha owned, we all piled out of the van, and I looked up at the huge, shining building. "This is where we're staying?"

From the looks on everyone else's faces, they'd been expecting something rustic, like what we were used to. This looked like a five-star hotel, and I doubted I'd ever stay somewhere as nice again in my life.

Another car pulled up and Ethan got out and adjusted his suit, looking impeccable once more. He was smiling as he approached us. "Welcome," he said, and Kaden dipped his head.

"Is this where we'll be staying?" Kaden asked, his voice skeptical.

"Yes, this is it. I own a lot of hotels in Toronto and other parts of Ontario. This one is finishing up renovations, so it hasn't officially reopened yet. There's tons of space available for your use, so feel free to spread out."

"What do you do when you need to be a wolf?" Kaden asked. The dry tone in his voice seemed to be completely lost on Ethan.

"High Park is nearby for short nightly runs, although we always need to be cautious of humans spotting us, of course. For full moons, we have a large portion of the Algonquin Provincial Park reserved for our use. It's just a three-hour drive away." He paused and grinned. "Sometimes humans go on wolf howling expeditions there to listen to us."

I frowned. That sounded... odd, to say the least. "You let humans join you?"

"Not exactly. They get a presentation about wolves, and then they go a little into the forest to howl at us. They think real wolves are howling back at them, but it's actually just us. They're never any the wiser, and we get to entertain the tourists and teach them a bit about wolves along the way. They're quite popular too—last time we had over a thousand people attend."

"That many?" I asked, surprised. I supposed it was a good way to teach humans about wolves, and the Libra pack was all about keeping the peace—even between different species, it seemed.

"We've worked hard to try to change humans' perception of wolves," Ethan said with a slow grin. "Now let's get inside, I'm sure you're all exhausted after the journey. I know I am."

We followed Ethan into the hotel, while the Ophiuchus pack members from the other vans trickled in after us through the sliding double doors. The lobby was just as nice as I imagined it to be, with white marble floors and huge chandeliers, along with a small fountain in the entry. Ethan stopped at the front desk and spoke to a woman there, who nodded and then directed everyone to line up so she could pass out room assignments.

Ethan brought us an envelope personally with our keys inside. "I saved the penthouse for you two, I hope it's to your liking."

Kaden accepted it with a nod. "Thank you, I'm sure it will be more than comfortable."

"The conference rooms are also available to you for meetings of any kind, and you can even order room service. Basically, you have the whole run of the hotel for now. My staff will help with anything you require."

"That's most generous of you," I said.

"What about a place for the Leo alpha?" Kaden asked.

"I have just the place," Ethan said. "He'll never be able to escape."

"Perfect," Kaden said.

I smiled at Ethan. "Thank you again for taking us in. We all really appreciate it."

"Of course," Ethan said as if the Libra pack hadn't been on the fence about allying with us only days ago.

I just hoped this alliance could last—and that coming here had been a good idea.

CHAPTER FIFTEEN

KADEN and I grabbed our bags and then rode the elevator up to the top floor, which turned out to be entirely the penthouse. It was just as lavish as the lobby, and the furniture was modern, minimalist, and clearly expensive. The couch alone probably cost more than I'd ever made in my years of working put together.

I walked to the huge window and peered out. The city of Toronto stretched out in the distance, glimmering lights switching on as the sun fell behind the horizon. The park was as close as Ethan had said, a spot of darkness between the city lights. But when Kaden stepped up beside me, he didn't look pleased.

"What is it?" I asked.

He bared his teeth a little as he looked outside. "I'd rather be in the forest. I don't think we can trust these city wolves. It's not natural for us to be among humans like this."

"Well, I'm excited to explore the city," I said and made

my way over to the huge couch. I knew there would be an adjustment period, but I hoped Kaden could settle in here, along with the rest of the pack. The Libras had been the only pack who'd offered to let us stay with them, so we couldn't exactly afford to be picky about it.

Kaden joined me, sitting close enough that our legs brushed. I leaned my head against his shoulder and he wrapped his arm around me. "I know this is different," I said, "but it's important. This is the first time one of the Zodiac packs has offered to help us in such a big way. It could be the beginning of cooperation on a larger scale."

"I just hope they can be trusted," Kaden grumbled. "I'm taking a huge gamble letting the pack live here among them. Maybe we should just go back to my original plan of taking over all the packs and killing anyone who stands in our way." He only sounded like he was half joking, and I pulled away from him slightly.

"Absolutely not. I won't let you. The Ophiuchus pack is better than that. *You're* better than that." I poked him in the chest, and Kaden let out a huff. "Besides, the other Zodiac Wolves aren't our true enemies, the Sun Witches are. The sooner the other packs see that, the better."

"True," Kaden said grudgingly, rubbing a hand up and down my arm in a soothing motion. "But when it's all said and done, will the other packs let the Ophiuchus pack back into the Zodiac Wolves? Will we ever be accepted as one of them?"

I opened and closed my mouth as I tried to come up with a response. I didn't have a clear answer, and Kaden knew that. "I don't know," I finally said. "But we have to try. Our future as a pack depends on it."

"You're speaking like the true alpha female of the pack now, little wolf," Kaden said, pulling me closer to him. I closed my eyes as he nuzzled into my neck. I tilted my head to the side to let him get better access, and let out a moan of pleasure as his hand slid to my breast, playing with my nipple through the fabric of my shirt.

Kaden hummed, pressing kisses to the side of my neck and following it up with a few light bites, scraping his teeth against the tendon of my neck. I shivered, little bolts of pleasure running through me.

I shifted closer to him, feeling the press of his cock through his pants against my lower back. I wanted to move against him, to get rid of the layers between us and take advantage of this brief period of peace, but duty still pulled at me.

"We should probably go make sure everyone is settling in okay," I murmured.

"Clayton can deal with it," Kaden said, his other hand gripping tighter around my waist. "An important part of being alpha is learning when to delegate to your beta."

He shifted slightly, pulling me against him once more. I tilted my head back, letting Kaden bite at the other side of my neck. His hand slid down, into the waistband of my pants. He slid his fingers against my slit. "God, you're already dripping wet," he murmured. I made a noise of assent and shifted to allow him better access. Kaden slid his finger along my clit, stroking it in the way he knew I liked. I closed my eyes and made another noise.

I pressed back against him, trying to create some friction between us to give him the same pleasure he was giving me. We found a rhythm that worked fairly quickly, gyrating our bodies together as Kaden continued swirling his talented fingers around my clit. The pleasure throbbed, low and hot in the pit of my stomach, and spread out quickly. I gasped as it reached a crest—and then Kaden pulled back.

I bit my lip on a whine and tilted my head back, looking at him. "Are you purposefully trying to piss me off?"

Kaden grinned down at me and slid himself out from under my body. "No, I just had a great idea." He crouched beside the couch and slid his hands under my legs. He cupped my ass and slid me so that I was sitting right on the edge of the couch and grinned up at me. My heart rate picked up at that look, heated and filled to the brim with desire and the promise of what was to come. "Lift your hips," he said, and I complied without questioning it. He might not be able to use the alpha command on me, but I'd still listen to him if he said something like *that,* all deep and sultry.

Kaden slid my pants and underwear down my legs, tossed the clothing over his shoulder, and I gasped as he immediately slid two fingers into my pussy. He worked me like that for a few moments, pumping his fingers in and out, and pausing to look up at me every time I made a little noise or shuddered around his fingers.

I was about to open my mouth to ask him what the hell

he was planning to do if he wasn't going to let me come, but before I could even draw in another breath, Kaden leaned forward and licked my thigh. I gasped, jerking away from the motion, and Kaden slid his eyes up to me, raising his eyebrows.

Do you want this? That look asked, and I settled back onto the couch. I nodded, and Kaden flicked his tongue out again, tracing the same path back down my thigh. He continued crooking his fingers in that perfect way that sent shivers of pleasure zipping up and down my spine, and just as slowly leaned forward and licked the other thigh, right up to the crease, and then paused.

I shuddered and tried to relax my muscles, but Kaden had me wound up so tight after teasing me that I couldn't relax at all. Kaden finally leaned in again and licked right across my slit, tongue catching the sensitive bud of my clit. I grabbed onto the couch and focused very hard on not bucking up into his mouth.

Kaden's eyes were hot on mine as he repeated the motion, two more times. My muscles were tense, trembling, and Kaden took it all in with obvious delight as he continued toying with me. He had me right where he wanted me, and he was doing an excellent job of keeping me just pleased enough that I wasn't frustrated, but not to the point where I would come yet.

Just as I thought I was getting used to the cycle, Kaden sealed his lips around my clit and began sucking. My hips jerked forward again, and this time I couldn't do much to stop them. Kaden slid his free hand to my front and pushed down on my hips, holding me in place while he continued. I threw my head back, panting as the pleasure went from manageable to almost overwhelming. Kaden expertly took me apart with his tongue and hand, drawing me closer and closer to orgasm.

Right before the pleasure crested, sending me tumbling over the edge, I forced myself to look back down at him. His eyes gleamed, seemingly captivated by my reactions. "Fuck, Kaden," I gasped out. He hummed, tongue stroking over my clit again and again, and I saw a glimmer of humor join the captivation just as he pushed me right over the edge, spiraling right into pleasure.

I rode it out with a barely-muffled scream, Kaden's hand pressing me against the couch and not letting me budge an inch as he worked me through my orgasm. Wave after wave of pleasure crashed over me until I thought that it would go on forever.

Finally, it ebbed, and Kaden let me up as my hips started twitching away from him. He drew back and licked his lips as if he'd just eaten a delicious meal. It sent another after-shock of pleasure to see the satisfaction on his face. "You taste incredible."

I let out a laugh, sagging back against the couch as I tried to catch my breath. "Please tell me there will be more."

Kaden pushed himself up onto his knees and ran his hands down my thighs, which were still shaking. "There will be as much as you want."

He kissed me and I tasted myself on his tongue as he slipped it into my mouth. He drew back a moment later, and

I reached for him, sliding my hand down his front. I slipped my hand under his shirt and splayed it across his side.

"What do you want?" I asked.

"I want to fuck you while you're bent over this couch," Kaden growled.

The words sent another wave of desire through me. *Will I ever get enough of him?*

He took off the rest of my clothes, his eyes hungry on me, taking in every inch of me as if he'd never seen me naked before. Then he spun me around and guided me over to the arm of the couch, bending me over it just like he'd said.

Kaden slid his hands over my sides, and then smacked my ass, hard enough that it stung. I let out a moan and pressed back further. Kaden pushed me so that my front was pressed snug against the arm of the couch, and didn't let me up. I relaxed against his hold, letting him do what he pleased with me. He rewarded me with another light slap, on the other cheek this time, and then before I could even register that, he pushed into me, sliding up to the hilt in one, smooth movement.

He filled me perfectly, and I closed my eyes as he paused, running his hands along my back before pulling out and thrusting back in. I gasped at the angle. It was different than anything we'd done yet, and it hit that spot inside of me that had a deep throb of pleasure building up almost instantly. I wasn't able to move as Kaden rammed into me hard, so hard I was surprised we didn't move the couch.

He drew back out and did it again, fingers gripping on tight to my waist. He tilted my hips up a bit more, and I went pliant, allowing him to move me however he wanted. He slid one hand up my back and wrapped my hair around his fist. He pulled me into a tighter arch, and the pressure on my skull would have hurt under any other circumstance, but I was incredibly turned on by it. Kaden had me baring my throat for him while he pounded into me from behind, each thrust getting impossibly faster and harder.

I turned to look at Kaden as he fucked me, his frame painted in the fading light of the sunset. It highlighted his perfect body, each muscle standing out in stark relief. I reached back and wrapped one of my hands around his arm, holding on for dear life as Kaden continued pounding into me.

He growled and let go of my hips and hair. He picked me up by the thighs, shifting me so that I was tilted even further forward, and slammed back into me harder. I put both of my hands back down onto the couch to steady myself. It drove the head of his cock against that place inside of me with every stroke, and I felt the pressure of a second orgasm begin to build quickly. Kaden was relentless, pounding into me without letting me pause for breath. His rhythm was perfect, and I squeezed my eyes shut, trying to hold out for him, to keep the rising orgasm at bay.

It was no use. Kaden knew exactly what he was doing, and my elbows gave way as another orgasm crashed into me like a ton of bricks. I managed to catch myself on my forearms, and Kaden wasted no time yanking me back into the position he wanted. I was boneless against his relentless, pounding rhythm, clenching around him in an attempt to slow him down throughout my own orgasm. It didn't work, and I gave up the battle, simply letting him do what he wanted.

Kaden growled something that sounded like, "Good girl," which sent another shock wave of pleasure through me. I gasped, and Kaden gripped onto me tighter. His own rhythm was getting more erratic, losing its perfect timing, and I held my breath, anticipation rolling through me with the aftershocks of my own orgasm.

"You feel so fucking good," he growled. "I would have you like this every day if we had the chance."

"You can have me as many times as you want. I'm yours. Only yours."

That seemed to be the thing that set Kaden over the edge. He grunted and slammed into me one last time, burying himself as deep as he could go, and spilled himself inside. I closed my eyes, shuddering with pleasure as his cock pulsed again and again and his teeth scraped against my neck.

Finally Kaden let go of my legs, setting me down and slipping out. I collapsed onto the couch, and he climbed over me, pinning me down with his naked body in a way that made me want him all over again. I played with his hair and looked up at him, and then pulled him closer. I let my mouth trail down his neck, finding the same spot where he'd marked me, and then sank my teeth into it. Marking him too.

Mine.

He groaned as I claimed him and his cock immediately sprang back to life. He yanked my legs open and shoved back inside my pussy in a rush. We rocked together, our movements half-feral, our bodies somewhere between human and beast. Then we came again, letting out howls that I knew could probably be heard by many other shifters in the hotel, though neither of us cared.

It didn't matter that the mate bond with Jordan wasn't broken, because Kaden was my true mate, and we both knew it. Nothing could keep us apart—not magic, not time, not even death.

CHAPTER SIXTEEN

THE NEXT DAY passed quickly in a flurry of activity. There were so many things to do that I could hardly keep it all straight in my head. Last night, Kaden had told me that I was speaking like the alpha female of the pack, but being faced with the responsibilities made me have new respect for his coordinating abilities.

To my surprise, most of the Ophiuchus pack shared Kaden's point of view. They didn't want to stay in the city, and grumbled about city wolves and how they couldn't be trusted. Many of them disagreed with Kaden's decision to send the pack here, and I worried there might be another challenge against him, though no one dared to go that far yet.

"Can't we go to the park?" I heard more than once while making my rounds to check on everyone.

After I'd heard it the third time, I went back to Kaden and asked if we could possibly swing that. He'd shaken his head, lips pulled down in a frown. "I'm not a fan of staying here either, but the Libra pack seems to think we're safer here, and after some careful consideration, I agree."

I heard it from Ethan himself later. "The Sun Witches wouldn't dare attack you here. And neither will the other packs."

It made sense. Too many humans around, and the added safety of the big building, though that didn't stop Kaden from heading out with Larkin to put down some magical wards around the perimeter.

While he was out doing that, I decided to go check on Jordan. I wanted to make sure he was being securely held, or that's what I told myself, anyway. But maybe he'd talk to me if we were alone. We'd gotten to a point in the past where he had seemed to be open with me, when I'd gained his trust and let him 'court' me. I wasn't sure if he would ever get to that point again, but if I could even get halfway there, I'd take it.

They were keeping Jordan in one of the basement rooms, right in the middle of where the laundry service would be. I stopped outside of the door, and Jordan's guards melted from the shadows. One of them was Jack. He gave me an appraising look, and asked, "Are you sure you want to see him?"

"Yes," I said, frowning at him.

He hesitated. "And Kaden is okay with this?"

A wave of frustration rose up in me, quick and vicious, and I bared my teeth at Jack. "I'm the alpha female. I don't need his permission."

"Technically, you aren't mated, so..." Jack said, shifting on his feet as he met my gaze.

A growl resonated through my chest, surprising even me. Jack held his hands up, dipping his head in subordination, and stepped aside.

I opened the door, glaring at Jack the whole time. Jordan was standing, and pacing back and forth like a caged lion. I'd thought that he was completely unbound for a few heartbeats, but as he moved, a chain clinked at his feet. I followed the coil of thick chain to where it was sunk into the floor. Not even someone with shifter strength would be able to get that loose.

His eyes snapped to me immediately, and I was startled by the clarity in his gaze. I'd thought that we'd keep him drugged with Ophiuchus poison as long as we had him, but he seemed lucid.

"What the hell are you doing here?" he snarled at me. He turned around on his heel and paced back again. I watched him pull the chain taut, and then turn around and repeat the motion in the opposite direction. "Are you here to kill me finally, put me out of my misery? I'd take it, rather than being stuck in this shitty basement in Libra pack territory. It reeks of humans."

"I'm not here to kill you."

Jordan let out a bitter laugh. "What, then you're going to try and remove the mate bond again? Didn't you get your fill of failure the first time around? We both know that it won't work a second time, either. As far as I can tell, you don't have a Sun Witch yet, and you aren't likely to get one. So I'd get used to the mate bond if I were you."

I knew what he was doing—he wanted me to lash out, to match this violent energy that was pouring off of him. I was tempted to snap back, to let my sharp tongue get the better of me, but I took a deep breath. "Honestly? I don't know why I came. I just..." I paused and shrugged. "I just wanted to talk to you."

Jordan let out another bitter laugh. "We have nothing to talk about," he said. "Unless you plan to free me."

"You know I can't do that."

Jordan watched me, eyes still wary. I had to find some way to prove to him that I had no intentions of hurting him, but there wasn't any easy way to do that. He'd never believe me if I said it. I sat down on the floor, just out of reach of the end of his chain. Jordan watched me as if waiting for an adder to strike.

After a moment, when I didn't pull a knife, or make any moves to hurt him, Jordan sat as well, a few feet away from me. I watched him for a few moments longer. "Did you know?" I asked suddenly, the question leaping out from me without my permission. It was too late to take it back, so I plowed on. "That you were my brother all along?"

Jordan recoiled as if I'd struck him, and the disgust on his face couldn't be feigned. "No. I was just as horrified as you were when I learned that. I definitely wouldn't have kissed you or tried to mate with you if I'd known."

Something that had been squeezed tight for a long time was released in my stomach. "Good," I said.

"If you had come back with me at the solar eclipse meeting, I would have made them remove the bond," Jordan said. "That's why I tried to grab you. I want it gone as much as you do."

"You really think they would remove it?" I tilted my head, finding it hard to believe. "Or that they didn't know all along that we were siblings?"

"I demanded they remove it, and they said they would. They listen to me."

I shook my head. "How can you be working with the Sun Witches?" I asked. "Especially knowing what they did to us."

Jordan clenched his jaw, muscles working as he watched me, eyes still wary. "You don't understand. The Sun Witches want to unite the packs, just like I do. I don't know why they mated us together, but it must have been an error."

I scoffed. I would have believed that before my time in Lunatera, but now I knew that the Sun Witches did everything for a purpose. We were just pawns to them, and they wouldn't care about two shifters' feelings if it meant that they could further their own game. "No, they did it to spark a war. Don't you see that the Sun Witches are manipulating the packs? They have us tearing each other apart in an attempt to enslave us once more."

Now it was Jordan's turn to scoff. "That's ridiculous. The Sun Witches aren't strong enough to enslave all of us." He so blindly followed them. It was almost sad. Jordan's eyes sharpened on mine again. "If you would have just gone with me at the meeting, I would have protected you. I would have—"

"There's no way you can protect me when you're part of the threat," I snapped at him, anger rising once more and washing over me in a sudden wave. "I stupidly thought you weren't as bad as I believed. I tried to put aside my pack's prejudice and hoped there was some good in that black heart of yours, but I was wrong."

I pushed myself up and stormed out of the room, and Jordan didn't say a word as I slammed the door behind me. As I turned away from the door, I ran right into a solid body, and I stumbled back. I looked up to find Kaden standing with Jack and the other guard, watching me with suspicion.

"What are you doing with Jordan?" Kaden asked. The suspicion didn't leave his gaze, and I gave him a wild look. Surely, he couldn't think that I was doing anything bad? Did he not trust me? There was a line of tension running through him, half jealous and possessive, and half resigned.

The anger toward Jordan found a new target: Kaden. "I'm trying to get information out of him."

"You're wasting your time."

"I am not," I said, drawing myself up. "I learned a bit." I shot a poisonous look over at Jack. He'd probably said something to Kaden, and I wasn't in the mood to be questioned like this right now.

"Anything useful?" Kaden asked, folding his arms over his chest.

I stopped and considered. What Jordan had told me wasn't new information. He trusted the Sun Witches, almost to a fault. That was already common knowledge, and Kaden would just be annoyed if I parroted information at him that he already knew. "Not yet, but I will."

Kaden stepped forward, every inch the alpha male I'd met in the forest a lifetime ago, convinced that he was going to kill me on the spot. "The mate bond is clouding your mind. You need to stay away from Jordan until it's broken."

I glared at Kaden rather than backing down. "It's not the fucking mate bond. I don't feel that way at all for him, and I haven't for ages. Or do I need to remind you that he's my *brother?*"

"That doesn't mean that it'll affect you any less," Kaden said. "A mate bond is still a mate bond."

"Dammit, Kaden, I just want to stop the Sun Witches, like you and everyone else here. You should know that by now—" I broke off and shook my head. "Forget it. Just get out of my way."

When Kaden didn't move, I shoved past him, slamming my shoulder into his as he moved to block me. I loved Kaden, but during my time in Lunatera, I'd forgotten how infuriating he could be. After everything we'd been through, I couldn't believe that he wouldn't take me at my word. How many times did I have to prove to him that the mate bond between Jordan and I meant less than nothing?

"Ayla, wait," Kaden called, as he came barreling after me down the hallway and around the corner.

I spun to face him. "How can you still not trust me after everything I've done for you?"

"I do trust you. I don't trust *him*. He's a snake in wolf's clothing."

"That's funny coming from an Ophiuchus," I muttered. "I don't trust Jordan either, but I'm the only one who might be able to get any info out of him."

"Leave me alone with him for thirty minutes and I'll get something out of him," Kaden said with a low growl.

Selene save me from the arrogance of alphas. "No, you won't. Torture won't work on him."

Kaden huffed. "Fine. Just be careful. And I want to know everything he says to you."

I rolled my eyes. "Anything else, alpha?"

"Yeah." He pinned me back against the wall, taking my chin in his hand. His lips crashed down on me roughly, demanding I accept his hard kiss, the swipe of his tongue in my mouth, and his body pressed against mine. "Don't ever forget you're my mate. Not his."

As if I could forget.

CHAPTER SEVENTEEN

DAYS PASSED, and slowly the pack settled into their new home. I avoided both Kaden and Jordan, feeling far too sick of alpha male energy to deal with either of them. I did manage to convince some of the shifters to meet with Larkin for training one evening though. The more people we had using magic against the Sun Witches, the better.

The night air was brisk as I walked to the park with Stella, the streetlights creating pools of warm light in between the cooler puddles of moonlight filtering through the trees. A few of the other Ophiuchus pack shifters trailed after us to where Larkin told us to meet her. I was excited to see how the other shifters fared, and Stella was practically vibrating with excitement next to me as we walked.

We cut through the park to where Larkin was waiting, the moonlight spilling over her. Harper caught my eye as she formed a circle with her twin brother Dane. A few other

Ophiuchus pack members joined us, and to my surprise, a familiar face joined the crowd.

"Mira?" I asked as she jogged over to me. "What are you doing here?"

"The Cancer pack used to be close allies with the Moon Witches," Larkin said. "There's still some Moon Witch blood running in a few of the Cancer wolves' veins. Including Mira's."

"I had no idea," Mira said. She clapped her hands like a small child, and then joined Stella and me in the circle.

We all turned to face Larkin, quieting down as she cleared her throat. I hadn't known how the other pack members would react to her, but they respected her just like they would any other adult. Even though she was trapped in a child's body, she still commanded the attention of an adult, and they realized that.

"The first part of training is about learning how to channel the moonlight," Larkin said. "It's the most basic form of Moon Witch magic, and is something that is taught to us at a very young age."

I was reminded of the very first lessons with Larkin and Celeste and had a brief moment of bittersweet nostalgia. *Soon,* I told myself. *Soon I can go back and see my mother again.*

Larkin met my gaze with a small smile and I nodded at her. I knew she wanted my help for this lesson. We had a lot of shifters to teach, and she couldn't handle all of them, but I was eager to help however I could.

"Repeat after me," Larkin continued, drawing me back

into the present. She spoke a few words in ancient Greek slowly. The shifters all repeated after her, and then she went around the circle, correcting pronunciation where it was needed, and beaming at everyone when they got it right.

I stepped forward to help her after that. We each took half of the students, and I was happy to get Stella and Mira in my group. I demonstrated the magic, and all of the shifters stared at me with awe. Most of them had never seen me use moon magic before.

"Who wants to give it a try?" I asked, trying to give an encouraging smile.

Stella raised her hand, practically bouncing on the balls of her feet. I nodded for her to step forward. It would be easier for her because she already had a Moon Touched gift and came from a strong lineage of Ophiuchus pack shifters. I walked her through the same steps Larkin and I had reviewed earlier that evening. Stella tried, but nothing happened.

"It's all right," I said, trying to encourage her. "If you got it on the first try, I'd be really impressed. It took me forever to learn everything." Which wasn't exactly true, but it had felt like forever. I remembered my frustration, and how that had seemed to impact how I was able to work. "Try not to get upset if it doesn't work, since the frustration only makes it harder."

Stella nodded and tried again. We went through the cycle a few more times before she finally got the barest flicker of light. "I'm glowing!" she yelled and lost it immediately. I stifled a laugh and had her try it again once she had calmed down. After that, it was relatively easy for her to get more and more light every time she called the moonlight down. It wasn't quite as bright as any of the Moon Witches I'd seen, but it was still impressive.

I moved on to the next student, and the process repeated. Everyone had a bit of a different process, I learned after working with a few of the other shifters, and we got varying results. One thing might work for someone, but that might not work for someone else. The amount of moonlight each shifter was able to call down also varied as well. Mira had the least success, but it didn't seem to sway her.

She laughed with joy at the tiny moonbeam she managed to call down into her hand, and I embraced her. "I can't believe I have actual magic," she said, clinging to me. When she pulled back, I was surprised to see tears in her eyes. "Remember how cool we thought the Sun Witches were when we were younger?"

I smiled at her but felt a pang of sadness go through me. I almost wished I could have that level of ignorance once more, to believe that the Sun Witches were these amazing, mystical beings who only wanted to help us. But it was better to know the truth. We would never trust the Sun Witches again, and I hoped that we could convince the other packs to join us in our rebellion too.

After I made it through my half of the students, we rejoined into one big circle again and continued practicing. There was a lull in questions directed toward me, and I walked over to Larkin.

"I'm surprised," I said, nodding my head toward Mira. "I

never would have suspected that a Cancer pack member would have Moon Witch blood."

"The Sun Witches want to wipe us out of the blood-lines," Larkin said. "But we persist."

"Yes, we do." I gestured at the students working, where Harper and Dane seemed to be having a contest for whose moonlight could shine the brightest. "This is a really good start."

Larkin hummed in agreement. "The Ophiuchus pack is especially determined. They dig in and don't let go until they have achieved their goal."

"What do you think you'll be able to teach them?" I asked.

Larkin shrugged. "I doubt any of them will be able to learn true battle magic like you and I can do, but they can help with shielding maybe. Most of them will only be able to shield themselves, but there are a few stronger ones who will be able to shield others as well, and Stella might be able to do some basic spell work that could be beneficial to us during fights." She nodded and looked around, her young face serious. "Overall, this will be a huge asset in the fight against the Sun Witches."

A knot in my stomach unclenched. We'd had the odds stacked astronomically high against us from the beginning, and getting any sort of edge would be incredible. *Maybe, just maybe we can win.* I didn't dare say the thought out loud.

"I wish that we could convince the other Moon Witches to fight with us," I said. It wasn't the first time I'd brought it up, and I watched Larkin's shoulders fall as she also thought about it. I hadn't meant to dampen the mood, but the words had just slipped out.

"They gave up fighting a long time ago," Larkin said.

I sighed and opened my mouth to say something else. Before I could, another figure joined us from the direction of the hotel—Kaden. I stood back as Larkin went up to greet him, but was secretly pleased he'd seen fit to join us tonight. He gave me a long, heated glance as Larkin talked to him in hushed tones, catching him up on what we'd been doing so far.

I watched as Kaden focused, speaking ancient Greek as if he'd been a fluent speaker his whole life. To my surprise, he drew down a huge beam of moonlight, almost as bright as a full-blooded Moon Witch could create. I shielded my eyes as I looked at him, taken aback. I'd seen him use magic before, but I'd had no idea he was this strong in it. Of course, being the cocky alpha he was, he'd best everyone. Why was he so damn good at everything?

A few scattered claps went throughout the group as Kaden let the moonlight go, and the clearing faded back to darkness. Kaden joined Stella, Mira, and me as we continued practicing, but he hung back and watched for the most part. I tried not to feel his gaze prickling at the back of my neck, but every time I glanced over, he was looking at someone else.

Larkin ended the class a bit later, stepping back into the middle of the group and beaming around at all of us. "That was an excellent first class, you are all amazing students," she said. "I can't wait to continue working with you. I'd like to meet up again next week, and every week following if you're interested. And if you could spread the word and try to get anyone else here who thinks they might have Moon Witch blood, I'd appreciate it."

There was a murmur of assent around the group, and a few of the shifters shared meaningful glances. I knew they'd bring more of the pack here, and a jolt of pride went through me at Larkin and the assembled shifters. We were all working together, and I found myself grinning, my annoyance at Kaden forgotten once more as I soaked in the uplifting atmosphere of the assembled group.

As Larkin formally ended the class, I listened in on the exchanges of the other shifters. Mira was almost vibrating with her success right next to me. "I never imagined that I could do anything like that," she said.

"I'm surprised I could too," Stella said, grinning at Mira's enthusiasm. "I knew about my Moon Touched gift, but I never thought I'd have access to actual Moon Witch magic."

"This is so cool, I can't wait to tell—" Mira broke off and glanced over at me. I raised my eyebrows at her. If she had been about to say *Aiden,* why had she cut herself off? I had a sneaking suspicion that she'd meant *Wesley,* and that she knew I was catching onto her continued crush on him. I turned my attention elsewhere, letting it slide for now. There would be plenty of time to rib her about it later.

I overheard Harper speaking to Larkin as everyone headed back home. Dane had a Moon Touched gift, but Harper had never had one. I had the feeling that she made up for it by being one of Kaden's best warriors, but someone like Harper who was clearly competitive was probably happy to be on even footing with her twin. "Maybe I'll be able to do some magic in combat," she said, grinning. Harper was one of the stronger of the bunch, and I grinned as I thought about her lobbing attacks at the Sun Witches.

"I'm going to try to get you to that point," Larkin said. "You would be good at that."

Everyone eventually trickled away, but I walked back to the hotel slowly with Mira, Stella, Kaden, and Larkin. "I'm so glad you came here with me," I said to Larkin. "I never would have been able to teach everyone by myself. Thank you for your knowledge, and your willingness to teach us."

"I'm happy to be here," she said, and then sighed, looking down at herself. "I just hope that I'll finally age up while I'm here too."

"We need to get you some new clothes," Mira said, looking at Larkin's homespun dress. "That'll definitely help."

Stella clapped her hands. "Oh, I've been dying for a chance to go shopping in a big city for a while. All we've had access to are the clothes in Coronis, and they're..." She trailed off and wrinkled her nose in Kaden's direction. "Not the most stylish."

"Yes, please," Mira said. "I need some new clothes as well."

A pang of guilt went through me at the reminder of her leaving everything behind when we escaped the Leo pack. "We can make a trip out of it," I said. I'd never been to a larger city to shop, and I was excited to see what options were available. I still remembered going to the store in Coronis and being overwhelmed, and if Stella thought that their options were limited, I couldn't imagine what it would be like here.

"Kaden?" Stella asked, looking at him.

"Fine, as long as you stick together and are safe." He gave Stella a hard look. "And don't spend too much of my money."

Stella rolled her eyes. "We'll spend whatever we need to spend, won't we, Ayla?"

I was about to answer, but we'd reached the hotel lobby, and Clayton was rushing toward us. Kaden's face went tight with tension as Clayton drew near.

"We have a problem," the beta said.

Shit, I thought. *What now?*

CHAPTER EIGHTEEN

KADEN and I followed Clayton through the hotel to a conference room, and the tension was almost suffocating. He refused to say anything, despite Kaden asking him what this was about. "We need privacy for this conversation," Clayton said. The others—Larkin, Stella, and Mira—all hung back, sensing this was alpha business only.

When we arrived at the conference room, Ethan was already there, his handsome face grim and devoid of any color. "A package arrived for you," he said, before any of us could so much as greet him. "It smells like death."

On the table was a package that looked like it could be anything. When I stepped closer, I saw the label and had to cover my nose from the horrible stench.

"Postmarked Arizona," I said.

Kaden frowned and peered down at the box. "It must be from the Sun Witches or the Leos. There isn't anyone else in Arizona who would bother sending something to us."

I bit my lip. "Should we even open it? It could be a trap."

"Would they have put their location on it if it were a trap?" Kaden asked dryly, and I tilted my head to the side. He had a fair point.

Kaden's hands shifted to claws, and he cut through the packaging with precision. The instant he pulled back the flaps of the box, the smell got even worse, becoming a suffocating aroma of death and decay. I nearly gagged as he pulled the wrapping apart and extracted something from the box.

A head. A *human* head.

And not just any head, but one I recognized.

Tanner.

I drew in a sharp breath and suppressed the urge to scream. I turned away quickly, but it was too late, and the image was branded on the backs of my eyelids. There was no way I could forget it.

Once I swallowed down a few waves of nausea, I slowly turned back and looked again. Kaden stared at the head with an unreadable expression, but I knew he must be upset too. Tanner had been a friend once, and though they'd had a falling out, it hurt Kaden to see any member of his pack killed. Especially in such a horrible way.

Kaden reached into the box again and I held my breath, fearing what else might be removed, but it was only a small card. "'Return Jordan or more Ophiuchus pack members will be sent back to you in pieces,'" he read aloud.

I swallowed hard, thinking of the others who had gone

with Tanner, including his mate, Lindsey. I wondered if she was still alive, or if she'd been killed as part of this point the Sun Witches and Leos were making. The thought of my mate being killed while I suffered alone and in enemy territory made something clench tight in my stomach. She didn't deserve this. No one in this pack did. "Is it signed?"

Kaden shook his head and tossed the note down as if it burned his hand. "I don't know if it's from the Leos or the Sun Witches, but it doesn't really matter at this point. Either way, it proves they know we're here with the Libras."

Shit. I knew we wouldn't be able to keep our location a secret, but we had just gotten here a few days ago. I'd hoped we would have a few weeks of peace at least.

"What are we going to do?" Clayton asked, breaking into the silence. All pairs of eyes turned to Kaden, who had his arms crossed over his chest and was frowning down at Tanner's head.

"We should send Jordan's head back to them," Kaden said in a low, menacing voice.

"We can't," I said, the thought making me feel sick in a different way. "We need him."

"He is the best bargaining chip we have right now," Ethan pointed out. "We can't send him back—alive or dead."

"I'll try to get something useful out of Jordan," I said. "He must know something that can help us against the Sun Witches."

Kaden's eyes flashed with dark anger. "Then we should attack the Leo village in Arizona now and get this over with. They must be holding the rest of the Ophiuchus there."

Ethan raised a hand to halt Kaden. "Let's not be hasty. It might be best if we call a meeting first, with all of the other alphas. Immediately."

"How do you propose we do that?" I asked. "There isn't enough time to get everyone gathered into one place, and our last attempt didn't go so well."

"Trust me," Ethan said. "I'll make sure we have a meeting set up by tomorrow."

Kaden snarled, "Fine. We'll keep trying diplomacy. But when it fails, we're doing it my way."

He left the room, and I trailed after him, my thoughts heavy and bleak. This was going to be a restless night for all of us.

THE NEXT AFTERNOON Kaden and I were summoned to a different conference room, and to my surprise, it was only Ethan sitting in the room with a laptop open.

"What's going on?" Kaden asked. "What are we doing?"

Ethan looked up from the laptop and motioned for us to sit beside him. "I'm calling an emergency conference with the rest of the alphas. We're going to do it on Zoom."

"Zoom?" Kaden asked with a scowl.

"Yes, it's a video conference program," Ethan explained.

"I know what it is," Kaden grumbled. "But I prefer face-to-face meetings for things like this."

"This does seem a lot easier—and safer—than getting everyone to meet in a secret location," I admitted.

"Exactly." Ethan typed a few things into his laptop. "A lot of the packs are hesitant to use technology like this, but I'm hoping I can bring the Zodiac Wolves into the modern era. It would solve so many issues if we could talk quickly without having to wait for representatives to travel between the pack lands."

Kaden didn't look convinced, but he didn't say anything. He just sat back and crossed his arms, his black shirt straining across his muscles, making him look every bit the brooding alpha.

A noise pinged from Ethan's laptop. "Here we go," he said.

One by one, his screen split, and faces appeared. Before I could ask Ethan if there was a way we could see it better, he hit a button and his laptop screen projected onto the wall.

I was shocked by how quickly the alphas started piling onto the call, one after another. Ethan was right, this was a lot easier and faster than trying to call our own meeting— and I was impressed that the other alphas had responded to Ethan so quickly when it had been a challenge to get them to meet with us at all originally.

"I can't believe they all agreed to meet so soon," I said quietly, though we were all on mute.

"Being known as the mediators of the Zodiac Wolves has its perks," Ethan said with a grin. "Most of the other alphas will listen to me if I say it's an emergency."

I was beginning to realize how lucky we were that Ethan had agreed to help us—and how it might open up more opportunities with the other packs in the future. If the alphas saw that the Libras and Ophiuchus were working together, they might come to see our pack as equals too.

There were a few hang-ups as all the alphas tried to get their videos and microphones working, and Ethan took everyone off mute to try to help them through it. Voices chimed in with things like, "Why are we doing this?" and "I can't figure out how to turn on the microphone," followed by another person saying, "It *is* on."

It was clear that not all of the alphas had taken the time to familiarize themselves with this technology, but after a few more moments, Ethan got everyone settled in and we could see all the other alphas on the projected screen. I recognized most of them but was surprised and pleased to see Ethan had managed to get the Gemini and Virgo alphas to show up—something we hadn't been able to accomplish before.

I gave Wesley a warm smile and also nodded to Amos, the Pisces alpha, who looked confused by everything going on, despite having an assistant next to him who kept showing him how to unmute himself. I was pleased to see Thom and Mae, the Sagittarius pack leaders, on the screen too, but no sign of Eileen.

I focused my attention next on the alphas I'd never met before. In the top left-hand corner were the Gemini twin alphas, one male and one female, both of them in their early thirties and gorgeous with blue eyes and golden hair. Unlike the other packs, they always had two alphas, and always twins.

At the bottom of the screen was the Virgo alpha, who was an older woman with darker skin and her long, gray hair pulled into two braids. She had no alpha male sitting with her because the Virgo pack was always led by a woman and had a matriarchal hierarchy.

The final alpha in attendance was the Capricorn leader, Wilson. I'd never met him before, but he was the oldest person in the group and had a surly scowl on his face.

"Let's get this over with," Wilson said, looking like he was sucking on a lemon peel.

The Scorpios, Taurus, Aries, and Aquarius were absent. No one mentioned it or asked where they were. We all knew that they had allied themselves with the Leos and the Sun Witches, and I presumed Ethan hadn't even bothered to invite them to this meeting.

"Thank you for joining us," Ethan said. "Especially on such short notice. We have an urgent matter we need to discuss with everyone, and I thought this was the best way. Many of you have met Kaden, alpha of the Ophiuchus pack, and his alpha female, Ayla, originally of the Cancer pack. They are currently under the protection of the Libras and their pack is staying with us for the time being after the attack at the solar eclipse meeting."

Some of the other alphas looked surprised at hearing we were staying with them, but no one said anything against it. Everyone seemed hesitant to speak first until the Sagittarius alpha spoke up.

"We apologize for not making it to the previous meeting ourselves," Thom said in a grim tone, while Mae nodded beside him. "Eileen told us everything. We're grieving our beta, and stand with you in the fight against the Leos and the Sun Witches."

"I lost my betas too," Wilson said. "Now what are we going to do about it?"

At his question, everyone began to speak at once, as all the alphas clambered for attention, asked questions, or protested being here at all.

Ethan let it go for a few seconds, and then with a push of the button, muted them all. Some of the alphas continued talking, unaware that no one could hear them. He waited until they all looked out at him, and then unfolded his hands from where he'd steepled them.

I was impressed by the sheer audacity he displayed with that move. He clearly had everyone's attention, and he wasn't going to squander it.

He cleared his throat and began to speak with the charisma of an alpha in his element. "During the solar eclipse meeting, which you've all been briefed on by now, we managed to escape with the Leo alpha, Jordan. Now we've received a package from the Leos and Sun Witches containing the head of one of the Ophiuchus pack members." Some of the gathered alphas gasped at this and even muted and hundreds of miles apart from each other, the tension was palpable. "They want Jordan back, but we're trying to get information out of him as we plan our next move. We need to discuss the Leo and Sun Witch threat and make a concrete plan once and for all, especially with the winter Convergence coming up. By now you've all been told what's going on. Maybe you believe it, maybe not. This is your time to bring forward your concerns. I'll go around once more and unmute you one by one. Try to be succinct."

He has balls, I thought again, another wave of respect going through me. To talk to all of the alphas like this? Wow.

To my surprise, he unmuted Wilson first. The Capricorn Alpha glared out at us. "I didn't want to take a side, but my beta's death during the meeting has convinced me that we have to fight back." He didn't sound very happy about it. Ethan waited a moment and then muted him again.

He moved onto the Sagittarius pack next. Thom and Mae shared a look and then nodded. "We're convinced now more than ever that we have to act if we stay free," Thom said. "We don't want any more needless violence, but we aren't going to sit back and let the Sun Witches enslave us either."

Amos was nodding as Ethan unmuted him next. "I don't know how much help the Pisces pack will be unless we get into some water, but we will support you."

That made the last of the packs that had shown up at the meeting. A wave of anxiety ran through me as I looked at the remaining packs. They hadn't come to the meeting and hadn't heard everything we'd discussed then nor witnessed the slaughter firsthand.

Ethan unmuted the Gemini pack first. The twins shared a look and then nodded. "I think that we should stay out of the conflict," the female on the right said.

"I think we should fight back," the male said, shrugging. "We haven't decided yet. We need more time to talk it over."

"Typical Geminis," Kaden muttered. "Can't make up their damn minds."

Ethan shot him a look, and then it was the Virgo alpha's turn to speak.

She looked hesitant, her serene expression shattering. "We've long been hesitant to pick sides in this war. We are the smallest pack, and we are healers, not warriors. But we will fight if we have to." She sighed and rubbed her temples. "I do have a few concerns. What will we do about the Convergence? Who will help us unlock our wolves or help us find mates if we turn against the Sun Witches? There are shifters in my pack who want to go to the Convergence for this purpose. We cannot deny them that. They've waited twenty-two years for this."

A few vigorous nods. Mae raised her hand, and Ethan unmuted her. "A few of our pack mates have expressed their concerns about that as well. I'm sure it's similar throughout the rest of the packs."

Another wave of nods.

The female Gemini asked, "What if we work with the Sun Witches to see what they want?"

"They want to control us," Kaden said, his tone harsh. "There's no way to work with them."

That brought on more protests and questions, with too many people talking at once again. I pinched my brow. This technology was convenient, but it did seem to make real conversation a bit trickier too.

"Can we use the Leo alpha as leverage?" Amos asked. "Or at least get some information out of him?"

"We have tried to talk to Jordan, but he is only interested in speaking with Ayla," Ethan said with a sigh. I saw the tightening of Kaden's jaw at that fact, but he didn't say anything.

"I'll keep trying," I said, hating that I didn't have anything else to say yet. I wanted something concrete from Jordan, but I had to keep working at him to get that.

"If we don't stand together against the Leos and Sun Witches, we're going to go back to being slaves for them," Kaden said into the turmoil. Slowly, the packs calmed down and turned to look back at the screen. Their faces ranged from contemplative to downright disturbed, but everyone was considering it at least. "We should go for the attack," Kaden added.

A few of the alphas immediately shook their heads. Ethan did the rounds again, asking each of them to give their opinions. The general consensus was that it was too rash to attack yet, said in varying ways.

"We're not ready to make such a bold move," Wilson said, and I was surprised that the wily Capricorn alpha would be so quick to wait.

"We are," Kaden replied. "There won't be another chance. This is our best time to strike. We can't put off going on the offensive any longer. If we do, more of my pack members will be sent to me in boxes. This isn't about whether or not you're ready to fight, but the lives at stake. The Leos are weak without their alpha. It's the best time to strike—and rescue my people at the same time."

We went around in circles for a few more minutes, and I

could see Kaden's body winding tighter and tighter with each pass around. No one was getting any closer to making a decision, except all the alphas agreed that attacking now was a bad idea.

Finally, Kaden pushed up from the table with a huff of air. "And this is why the Leos and the Sun Witches are winning."

CHAPTER NINETEEN

KADEN STALKED out of the room without another word. I shot Ethan an apologetic glance and then hurried after my mate.

The elevator door was just closing as I rounded the corner. "Hold it!" I called, half expecting Kaden to just let it close. He looked like he was considering it, but then pushed the button that had the doors sliding back open. I jogged the rest of the way to the elevator. The doors closed, and we started going up.

In this tight of quarters, it was hard to ignore the annoyance flooding from Kaden. It filled the air as he clenched and unclenched his fist. "This is why I can't stand the Zodiac Wolves. Aligning with them was a mistake. I should have stuck to my original plan of just wiping them all out. They're all so far gone, it would have been better to just start with a clean slate."

"I know you're angry, but I thought we were past that.

Besides, we can't stand up to all the packs. We're not strong enough. We need allies."

"Nothing is going to get done when the Zodiac Wolves can't come to any decisions and try to rule by committee," he said. "I'm going to form an attack team and hit the Leos. When are they in heat? That would be a good time to strike. They'll be easier targets."

A wave of panic rushed through me, icy in my veins. "You're lowering yourself to their level just by suggesting something like that. Even if everyone thinks the Ophiuchus are monsters, we are not."

Kaden gave me a dark look. "That's where you're wrong. I *am* a monster. Or at least, I'll become one, if I have to."

I poked a finger at his chest. "I won't let that happen."

He blew out a long huff and finally admitted, "All right, that was going too far. I'm just upset about Tanner."

I put a hand on his shoulder. "I know you were close once."

"Even though Tanner challenged me for alpha and threatened you, I've known him since we were both pups. We had different opinions on things, but we were friends. I valued Tanner's insight, even if I didn't always agree with it. Now he's dead, and his mate is next. Everyone who followed Tanner is going to be on the Leos' hit list now and even though they left, they're still part of the pack. I can't turn my back on them."

I reached out to hit the button that would stop the elevator, then wrapped my arm around Kaden's waist and rested my head against his chest. "I understand. You're frustrated because your pack members are in danger and none of the other packs will acknowledge that or make an effort to save them."

He grunted in response, as his own arms came up around me. "I have to find a way to save them."

"I'll grill Jordan harder," I said. "I'll get something out of him, I promise."

Kaden sighed and wrapped his arms tighter around me. "We're going to have to start coming up with a plan of attack, with or without the support of the Zodiac Wolves."

I knew he was right, but I also worried about jeopardizing our new status among the other Zodiac Wolves. We couldn't afford to lose the precious alliances we'd fought so hard to obtain.

"Just don't lose yourself in the process," I said, as I played with his hair.

"I won't, as long as you're around." He nuzzled my neck, and the spark that had been buried beneath the anger flared to life. The heat was instant, all-consuming. I'd missed him for the days we'd spent apart, and I wanted to feel him closer to me, to soothe his worries for the little bit of time that I could.

Kaden slid his hands from my back to my shoulders as he leaned down and kissed me hard. Before I knew it, he'd pressed me back against the wall of the elevator, much as he'd done the other day outside Jordan's cell.

He broke away from the kiss, breath harsh as he rolled his hips against me. He reached down, sliding his hands to cup my ass. He ground himself against me, harder until there was actual friction between us. I shuddered, chasing my pleasure alongside his. We ground against each other, completely clothed for a few moments before Kaden pulled back.

"I can't wait until we get to the room," he growled. "I need you now."

"You have me," I breathed out, and lifted my shirt above my head, leaving me in just my bra. "Just hurry."

Kaden's eyes were hungry, and he pressed his fingers into my skin and dragged them along my bare flesh. Kaden leaned down and skimmed his nose along my neck. He bit into the juncture between my neck and shoulder, just enough to send a shiver through me. I slid my hand along his front, working at the button of his jeans one-handed as I kept my other hand on his chest, feeling his heartbeat.

He drew in a sharp breath as I took his cock in hand, no teasing, just sliding him out of his pants and pumping my hand up and down his length. Kaden ran his hand along my stomach, up to tease my nipples through my thin bra, and I closed my eyes to enjoy the sensation, my head falling back against the side of the elevator. Finally, as I whined out his name, Kaden yanked my leggings down, along with my panties.

I thought he would take me right then, but he parted my lips with two fingers and slid a third to circle my clit. My hips jerked forward into the pressure, trying to get more of it. I was sopping wet and so ready for him. I leaned my forehead against his still-clothed chest and shuddered, trying to push back my orgasm. It came on quickly, though, pleasure crashing over me like a wave and making me go weak at the knees. Kaden was relentless throughout it, not giving any quarter. He eked every last bit of pleasure out of my orgasm, while my hand pulsed around his cock, the other one clawing at his shoulder.

"You're so fucking gorgeous when you come. I can't get enough of you." He slid his hand out of my pants and lifted it to his lips. He popped his fingers into his mouth and sucked his fingers clean. I kept my hand moving on his cock, feeling it throb and become impossibly harder in my hand.

Then he gripped my hips and lifted me up, wrapping my legs around his waist, and thrust into me in one quick, hard movement. My pussy clenched around him, eager to be filled once more by his huge, familiar cock. He pushed me back against the side of the elevator, and I vaguely wondered if there was a camera inside, but decided I didn't care at that moment if someone was getting a show. Knowing anyone could interrupt us or that the elevator might start moving at any second only made this hotter, our need for release given a hint of frantic desperation.

He grabbed my arms and yanked them over my head as he pounded into me, each thrust banging me back against the side of the elevator. As he circled my wrists with his strong hands, he claimed my mouth too, owning every inch of my body. I loved it when he took control, when he pinned me and used me as he wanted because he always made sure I got what I needed too.

With every second our tempo increased, and the slap of flesh against flesh was louder here in the small elevator. I

couldn't help but stare over Kaden's shoulder at the reflec-
tions of our bodies on each mirrored wall, watching his ass
clench as he pushed inside me, then relax as he pulled out,
over and over.

He hefted me up a little more, hitting my clit with each
thrust, and nipped at my neck while his fingers tightened
around my wrists. His breathing grew harsher, his teeth
grazing my neck again, and I knew he was close. I was too,
but I needed him to come with me this time.

I threw my head back as Kaden's cock brushed against
that perfect spot inside of me just hard enough to set me
over the edge. I gripped his hips with my legs, trying to keep
the rhythm for him as another orgasm crashed over me. I
couldn't hold back the sounds I made, the sheer amount of
pleasure running through me, so strong it felt like it was
trying to burst my body apart. That set him over the edge
too, and Kaden thrust up into me once more before his hips
stilled, his cock twitching inside of me as he groaned his
release.

"We should probably go back to the meeting," I said, as
he set me down on trembling legs. I reached down and
grabbed my clothes, hastily throwing them back on. Now
that the rush of desire and pleasure had begun to fade, I realized how we'd rushed out of the meeting, only to have hot,
rushed sex in an elevator.

"Why? They're probably still arguing over what to do."
Kaden hit the button for the penthouse. "We're on our own.
As usual. And I don't see that changing anytime soon."

CHAPTER TWENTY

THE NEXT MORNING, I decided it was time for me to take matters into my own hands.

I found a pack of playing cards in the penthouse, and on impulse, I snatched them up and tucked them into my pocket.

Last night we'd gotten word that Ethan had moved Jordan into a hotel room a few levels below ours, which was guarded at all times and magically warded by Larkin so the Leo alpha couldn't escape. Ethan hoped Jordan would be more amenable if he was treated more like a guest and less like a prisoner, but I remembered all too well when Jordan had done the same thing to me. A prison was still a prison, no matter how comfortable it was.

When I stopped in front of Jordan's door, the guards didn't question me this time. I felt a wave of satisfaction go through me as I walked into his hotel room. It was smaller

than ours, just one room with a king-sized bed and a small
seating area, plus a tiny kitchenette area.

As I shut the door behind me, Jordan looked up from his
spot on the bed, blinking in surprise. He looked better than
he had the last time I'd visited and wasn't chained up any
longer. Clearly, he wasn't being mistreated either.

"What are you doing here?" he asked, scowling.

"I thought you might be bored." I pulled the cards out of
my pocket and motioned for him to sit at the table and chairs
in front of the window overlooking the city. I hoped I could
take his mind off of interrogation and help him let his guard
down enough to open up to me.

Jordan cocked his head. "You're going to play cards
with me?"

"Why not?" I asked as I unboxed them and began shuf-
fling them. "Do you know Go Fish?"

Jordan nodded grudgingly as he came to sit at the table.

"Good. I'm going to come play Go Fish with you every
day," I said. "Or other games, if we get tired of that one."

"I can't imagine Kaden approves of this."

I shrugged. "You're my brother. I can visit you if I want."

Jordan scoffed but took his cards as I settled in and
began dealing them. At least he was open to me being here. I
doubted he got to talk to anyone much, outside of being
asked questions by his jailers. But I knew Jordan didn't
respond to threats—we needed another way to get inside his
head.

We were both silent for a few moments as we checked

our cards, and then Jordan surprised me by speaking up first. "What was our father like?"

I snorted as I set a card down. "It sounds like he wasn't much better than the Leo alpha. He was a hard alpha to live under and a worse father. To me, at least. To Wesley, he was fair, if not a bit controlling."

"Between my two fathers, I never had any hope of ever being anything but a villain," Jordan said with a dark glower and set his own card down.

I frowned. He was winning. "That's not true," I said, checking my cards subtly once again to see if I had anything to counter him.

Jordan set down another card, ending the match before it had even truly begun. I blinked at his card, and then Jordan flicked his wrist up for me to see and slid a card out. I raised an eyebrow. I hadn't seen him palm it.

"Like I said, incorrigible villain." He grinned, but it didn't hold any humor. "Run back to your nice little alpha, Ayla," he said, flicking his fingers toward the door.

I stood up, gathered the cards, and left without another word, trying not to let him get under my skin. That was what he wanted, after all.

The next day, I returned with the deck of cards again. Jordan looked surprised, and though he pretended to be annoyed, I think he was actually pleased to see me.

"You again," he said.

I sat down, and after a moment's hesitation, he joined me at the table. I dealt us out for Go Fish again, and Jordan slid his cards to his side of the table and picked them up. I watched his hands carefully, but I didn't see any sleights of hand.

We played in silence for longer than yesterday, and a sudden pang of sadness went through me. I could have imagined us doing this as children if we'd been raised together the way we should have been. Maybe Wesley could have joined in too.

"How is it possible that we're siblings?" I asked, breaking the silence at last, as Jordan showed no signs of cheating. "Do you have an ace?"

He handed over an ace. "I asked my mother the same thing after you escaped. She didn't want to tell me at first, but I finally got it out of her. My mom was the daughter of the former Leo alpha before Dixon. Her father never had any sons, much to his disappointment." Jordan set down another card, and I snatched it up. Jordan's eyes flared, as if he'd caught me red-handed. I discarded the ace he'd just given me. "When it came time for her mating, her father chose the strongest male Leo in the pack, Dixon, and paid the Sun Witches to mate them together."

I raised my eyebrows. "Their pairing wasn't a natural mating either."

"No, and I don't think my mom ever loved Dixon." His lips took on a wry twist as he set down a complete book of fives. "I doubt Dixon was ever capable of love. But then my mom met our dad when Harrison came over for some negotiations one time. She felt something for him, and it surprised her."

"Lots of women seem to have felt that way," I muttered,

thinking about what my mom had told me about her relationship with him. I couldn't see it, but there was obviously something there, or women wouldn't have kept swooning into his arms.

"Maybe," Jordan said. "I also wonder if my mom, Debra, was actually Harrison's real mate." When I raised my eyebrows at him, Jordan shrugged. "What? I've had a lot of time to think in here since no one else is willing to come in and play card games."

"If that had been true, maybe their natural pairing would have ended the rivalry between the Cancer and Leo packs."

Jordan made a noncommittal noise and drew one of my threes out of the discard pile and set down another book. I shook my head and drew another card. He was still winning, and there weren't any signs of cheating today.

"Which of course, the Sun Witches wouldn't have wanted," I continued. "They would have done everything in their power to keep Debra and our dad apart."

"Maybe. All I know is that no matter how much my mom and Dixon tried, she couldn't get pregnant," he continued as he discarded another card. I finally had a book of twos. I set them down triumphantly, and looked up in time to see a slight smile curving over his lips. He hid it quickly enough, but I was surprised to see it. He cleared his throat and drew another card. "Then there was a full moon right on the Cancer-Leo cusp, and she spent the time with Harrison. You can guess what happened next. I was born right at the cusp myself, only a few hours into Leo."

My eyebrows darted up at that. He seemed to embody everything *Leo*, so it was particularly shocking to hear that he was a cusp. Hardly even a Leo at all.

Jordan let out a bitter laugh at the look on my face. "Yeah, a cusp baby, and my father never let me forget it."

I grimaced as I looked back down at my hand of cards. "I know exactly what that's like," I said after a moment. I hoped that I could get through to Jordan, to find common ground between us. "Did Dixon know that you weren't his birth son?"

"He figured it out when Griffin, my younger brother, was born on the cusp too."

I sat back at this information. Another brother. My family was getting bigger by the day, by the looks of it. *Do you have any other brothers up your sleeve?* I almost asked, but pulled my attention back as Jordan continued with his story.

"When Dixon found out, he became obsessed with taking down the Cancer pack. He went to the Sun Witches, and they offered their assistance in helping him take down not just the Cancers, but to help him with ruling over all the other packs," Jordan said.

I folded another book down to my left, and Jordan looked at it with a smile. We were now even.

"And the night of the Convergence?" I asked. "Did Dixon know that we'd be mated?"

"No, I don't think he knew anything about that. I think my mother suspected something was going to happen though." He paused and tilted his head to the side, his eyes lost in the memory. "She didn't want me to go to the Convergence. Dixon insisted, of course, even though I'd gotten my wolf a year earlier. But Dixon made my mom and Griffin stay home. He didn't want them there during the fight."

My phone buzzed in my pocket, signaling that it was time for me to go. "Well, thank you," I said. "This has been a rousing game of Go Fish. I'll be back tomorrow." I gathered the cards like I had yesterday, and got up.

"Wait," Jordan said, and I looked up at him. He frowned, as if deliberating over something, and then took in a deep breath. "I'm sorry for being a dick to you about being a half-breed." His lips twisted up with the irony of it. "Of course, that came to bite me in the ass."

I stared at him. That was the last thing I would have ever thought I'd hear Jordan say. "Thank you," I said softly as I moved toward the door.

"I'm sorry about a lot of things, Ayla." For once, he sounded sincere...and almost regretful.

"I accept your apology." I left the room, feeling unsettled by how much his apology affected me. I'd needed to hear it, on some level. It would never make up for the horrible things he'd done to me, but it was a start.

CHAPTER TWENTY-ONE

ONE THING that was nice about spending so much time in the hotel was that Kaden and I were able to take breakfast together most mornings, even though we both had a lot of duties that pulled us apart during the day.

I woke one morning to find Kaden making breakfast, the muscles of his bare back working as he shifted a pan over the fire. I smiled as I watched him for a few moments, before joining him in the kitchen.

He was tense, as he was almost every day. He was still frustrated by the lack of action taken by all of the packs, and I couldn't blame him. We'd talked it over more than once, but it felt like going in circles. We weren't getting anywhere, and it was getting more frustrating by the day. His tension bled into mine, and it was hard to catch these few moments of peace.

I wrapped my arms around his middle and he leaned

against me for a moment before going back to his work. "How are you feeling this morning?"

"Frustrated," he said. "No one seems to care that our people are being held captive by the enemy, and they won't let me do anything about it. Maybe we should go back to the Ophiuchus pack lands since our enemies know where we are anyway."

I shook my head. "Not yet, we're still forming alliances with the Libras and the other packs. It's a slow process and I know it's taking forever, but it'll be worth it, I promise. I know you want to get back to the forest, but this will pay off. Besides, we're all working on Moon Witch training, and I'm getting close to getting Jordan to talk. I can feel it."

Whatever ease permeated the air evaporated at his name. We hadn't gone so far as to discuss our differing feelings on Jordan lately, but it was a constant elephant in the room, impossible to ignore.

"I still don't like you going to see him," Kaden said.

"I know you don't, but he's our best hope of learning what the Sun Witches and Leos are up to. Besides, he's my brother and... I know this sounds crazy, but I don't want to give up on him completely."

Kaden let out a huff of air and grumbled something incomprehensible. He didn't say anything else on the matter though, so I decided to change the subject.

"How's training been going?" I asked, hoping to turn the conversation to something we could agree on, at least. Kaden had begun helping to train some of the Libras with members of the Ophiuchus pack. The Libras were generally peacekeepers, preferring diplomacy over violence, but to my surprise, Kaden had managed to sway some of them, and they were eager to learn.

"Good," Kaden said, smiling a bit. "Ethan is a hell of a good fighter."

"I'd love to see you two spar," I said, and then made sure that Kaden could hear the teasing note in my voice as I looked him up and down. "Shirtless, of course."

"You'd distract me too much," Kaden said, pinching my butt. "The smell of your lust is intoxicating."

I flushed at that and swatted his hand away. "Only to you."

We had an easygoing breakfast after that, and then I got ready and met my friends down in the lobby of the hotel for our much-anticipated shopping trip.

The hotel was located in the middle of a commercial area, so all we had to do was walk down a few blocks to find what we were looking for. Our eyes were wide as we headed out, since like most shifters we hadn't spent much time in big cities, and this was all pretty new to us. Stella and Larkin were chattering away about what sort of clothes they might find, while Harper laughed along with them, and Mira and I grinned at every shop we saw. This was my first ever girls' day out, and I was going to enjoy every second of it.

I looked around as we walked toward the entrance of a clothing store Stella and Larkin wanted to visit, and couldn't control my smile. Kaden was always grumbling about being surrounded by buildings and not being able to see the stars at night, but I found myself enjoying Toronto, even if I wouldn't want to live here all the time.

We entered the store, and something warmed in my chest as Larkin immediately sped off, like she'd never been in a place like this before. I looked over at Mira and Stella, who stood with me in the doorway.

"Well?" Stella asked, grinning at me. "What do you want to look for first?"

I'd bought and lost so many clothes over the past few months alone, I wasn't even sure. I remembered when Stella had taken me to the small store back in Ophiuchus pack lands, and I'd been amazed by the selection. Here there was even more choice, and while I was still awed, it wasn't the same sort of thing I'd felt before. My life had changed a lot since leaving the Cancer pack.

As we waded through the displays of clothes, it felt like something had been lifted from my chest. I'd spent so much time lately worrying about what was going to happen. The Zodiac Wolves couldn't come to a decision about what to do about the Sun Witches, and they were all nervous about the upcoming Convergence. I had to admit that I was fed up with their indecision almost as much as Kaden was. But I didn't think Kaden should charge in and kill the Leos while they were in their mating frenzy either.

I shook my head as I held the sleeves out from a pretty green shirt that would make my hair stand out. This was the time to forget all of that. I was here to shop with my friends and not think about an impending pack war.

I bundled some clothes into my basket and met up with

Harper and Larkin, who were perusing through the junior's section. Larkin was practically shining as she showed me some of the outfits she'd picked out.

"Those will look so nice," I said. "And now you won't get weird stares."

Larkin nodded, and we took our clothes up to the register. I had a feeling Kaden was going to roll his eyes when he saw what it all added up to, but that only made me grin wider as I swiped his card, paying for all of our clothes at once.

Once we walked out, Larkin grabbed hold of my wrist and pulled me to another store—a bookstore. I smiled, remembering Larkin's love of books.

"I might as well check out the thriller section," Harper said as she held the door open for Stella and Mira.

It was a small, locally-owned bookstore, and the setting was much more intimate than the huge clothing store had been. I followed Larkin to the romance section, with Mira and Stella trailing behind us.

Larkin ran a nonstop commentary as she showed me some of the books she already owned, and then gasped several times as she spotted new ones. To my surprise, Stella stepped up beside us and started giggling with Larkin.

"I love the manchest ones," she said.

"I know, right?" Larkin said, her eyes glimmering. "They're the best."

I stepped back with Mira as Stella and Larkin started speaking more in depth about the books. I glanced over at her to see Mira smiling slightly.

"What is it?" I asked.

"They don't have their mates yet. Someday they'll see that romance isn't like what's in the books."

It was only when I heard the tone in her voice that I realized her smile was a little sad.

I rested my hand on her arm in sympathy. "Once I find a way to get rid of the mate bond between Jordan and me, we'll find a way to remove yours, as well. That way, you can be with your true mate, and then maybe it'll be a little more like what you've read about in the books."

Mira looked at me sharply, her cheeks flushed. "Why would I want the mate bond removed?"

I hesitated, worried I'd overstepped my bounds. "I just thought maybe there was something between you and Wesley. Something more like what Kaden and I have."

"I had a childhood crush on Wesley. No more, no less." Her voice shook, and she turned away and walked straight out of the store.

Shit. How had I misread that so completely? I thought that I'd seen something—no, I'd definitely seen something between them when they'd sat by the lake. But Mira wasn't ready to talk about it, and I wasn't sure if she even knew how she felt. There was clearly something more that was going on.

I sighed and checked to make sure that Stella and Larkin were still gushing over the romance books before following Mira out. She hadn't wandered far, leaning against the wall outside of the bookstore.

I leaned against the wall next to her. "I'm sorry. I wasn't

trying to stir up trouble. I thought..." I shook my head and trailed off. "But obviously I was wrong."

"I'm also sorry," Mira said, looking down at her feet. "I shouldn't have gotten upset at you for that. I know you just want the best for me, but that's not Wesley. The thing is..." She took a deep breath, and then finally looked up at me. "I'm pregnant with Aiden's child. I don't want to have the mate bond removed only to find out that I'm supposed to be mated to someone else when we already have this tie between us. What would happen to our baby?"

I drew in a breath. That was the last thing I'd expected to hear today. "I understand," I said after a few heartbeats of silence. "But how did you get pregnant? The Pisces heat is before the summer Convergence."

Mira flushed again. "I went into heat at the first full moon after the Convergence, just like you did. Since it was outside of the Pisces time frame, the midwives tell me I'm going to have the baby early." Her eyes were huge in her face, and there was genuine fear in them. "I'm so nervous about that. I know that giving birth early can be bad. I want nothing more than for this baby to be healthy and happy."

I pulled Mira against my chest. I hated seeing her like this. She was supposed to be always smiling, strong, and carefree, like when we were kids. "Everything is going to be all right."

"Promise?" she asked.

"I promise," I said. "You're strong, and so is your baby. You're both going to be fine."

Mira sniffled and pulled back, swiping at her face to

clear it of any tears. Then the door opened, and everyone piled out. Unsurprisingly, Larkin had a bag of books that looked to be as full as she could make it.

"I'm hungry," Stella said as she stopped in front of us. "Anyone else?"

We all nodded, and walked a little bit further down. There was a French takeout restaurant that we'd passed by on the way, wafting incredible smells out of their front door, and we stopped inside to grab some lunch. Once we'd all ordered, I looked outside. I wasn't quite ready to go back to the real world just yet, and it was a beautiful fall day. Cool, crisp, but not raining either.

"Let's go to High Park and have a picnic," I suggested. It was only a couple blocks to the park, and after that, only a shorter distance to the spot where we practiced magic.

Everyone nodded their agreement, and we took our steaming hot food over to the park. The girls chattered the entire time about things they saw, and then we sat down and began digging into our food.

I was just raising my second bite to my mouth when a twig snapped, much too big and much too close for it to be anything small. All of our heads swiveled toward the sound, and the next moment, a huge blur burst out of the brush. A pale-colored wolf.

We were all up and ready to fight in an instant. Stella, Harper, and I all shifted, our clothes shredding and falling to the ground, while Mira stayed human and stepped in front of Larkin. The pale shifter snarled, crouching down into a defensive position as we all reacted to the situation quickly.

This shifter clearly didn't have good intentions and had wanted to catch us off guard.

It wasn't a second too soon. Several other wolves burst into the secluded clearing, snarling and snapping, and one of them let out a loud roar that made me want to run for my life. *Leos,* I thought wildly, as my companions started running away in a panic. The lion roar of the Leos was hard to resist, but Larkin muttered a few words and threw up a shield around my friends. They stopped and shook their heads, regaining control of themselves.

I was the only one who'd managed to fight off the roar, and I dug my claws into the dirt to steady myself. The Leo wolves surrounded me, my companions too far away now to help, but I snarled and faced the enemy down.

Capture them alive if you can, I told Harper and Stella through our pack bond. If we could get these Leos in custody, they might be able to tell us more of what their pack and the Sun Witches were doing—and no doubt they'd be easier to break than Jordan.

The Leos lunged for me, but I teleported away, unhindered by the lack of moonlight even in my wolf body. A few of them looked confused but then chased after me, but others went for my friends. Including Mira.

The largest wolf leaped for her, fangs bared, and I teleported in front of her just before he sank his canines into her flesh. Pain lanced through my side and I howled, then immediately shifted back and hit the wolf with a moonbeam burst, knocking him back.

"Get help!" I said to Mira. I didn't want her in danger

when she was pregnant, and she'd never been much of a fighter anyway.

She hesitated, unwilling to leave me behind, but then ran away toward the hotel. Just as three more wolves piled on me and tore at my skin. I threw up a shield but it was too late, and there were too many of them. Only Harper and Stella's quick movements managed to get the wolves off me, their Ophiuchus poison knocking some of them unconscious. Larkin took down a few more with her magic, and I managed to topple another one, even in my weakened state.

A yelp sounded from our side, and I swung my head around just in time to see Harper dodging in front of Stella, who staggered back in her wolf form. Blood welled up in her shoulder, and Harper made quick work of the shifter who had bitten her.

When it was all done, we had five wolves dead, and five more knocked out. Stella and I were both injured and could barely move, but Larkin and Harper were all right, and I prayed Mira had gotten away too.

Kaden burst into the clearing seconds later with a roar and took in the sight of us. His eyes bulged at Stella's injuries, and then nearly burst out of his head when he saw my own. I tried to stand, to go toward him, but my thigh was too badly injured and I crumpled to the ground.

"We're okay," I said, my voice weak.

"What happened here?" Kaden demanded as he picked me up in his arms.

"An attack by the Leos," Harper said, as she tended to Stella's shoulder.

"We've captured five of them, but the rest we couldn't take alive," Stella said.

Dane and some of the other Ophiuchus rushed into the clearing then too but stopped once they saw the fighting was over. Kaden inspected my injuries, and I whimpered a little at his touch.

"They did this to you?" Kaden asked, and I'd never heard his voice sound so terrifying.

"I'll be okay," I said softly. "The important thing is that we have prisoners we can interrogate now."

Kaden set me down in the grass and ran his tongue over me, making me shiver, healing me just enough so that I wouldn't lose any more blood. The many bite and claw marks on my body began slowly closing up, and I sighed in relief.

Then Kaden stood and stalked over to the unconscious Leos. With a menacing growl, Kaden's hands turned to claws, and he slashed at their throats, killing them instantly and nearly severing their heads at the same time. Blood sprayed from his attack, splashing against my cheeks and my neck. His eyes flashed with darkness as he turned away from their bodies.

"Kaden!" I struggled to sit up, horrified by what he'd done. Killing in combat was one thing. Killing unconscious prisoners, prisoners we could have used for information, was another thing completely.

"No prisoners," Kaden snarled. "Not after what they did to you."

The others were all staring openly at Kaden, and I realized I wasn't the only one who was utterly shocked by Kaden's actions. Stella kept her eyes averted, as if by not seeing what was going on, she could stop believing it. Harper's face was grim, but I didn't think she would disapprove somehow. Larkin just looked terrified.

Kaden picked me up, ignoring all my protests that I was fine, and carried me back to the hotel. I was too horrified by what I saw in his eyes to say anything—too worried he was actually turning into the monster he'd threatened to become.

CHAPTER TWENTY-TWO

KADEN TOOK me up to the penthouse and made quick work of healing and cleaning me, and I felt too numb to do anything but let him do it. I couldn't believe Kaden had killed all of those shifters, no matter how many times my brain offered up the image of his claws tearing through their necks like paper. I still had the blood clinging to my neck and wondered if any shower would be long and hot enough to get rid of the shock of what he'd done.

The look on his face had been almost monstrous, and I kept glancing at him to see if it was still there. Kaden's face had returned to his normal scowl, but I couldn't help but see him as something *different*. He wasn't the Kaden I thought I knew, that much had been made clear. Something had changed in him.

"What is it?" Kaden asked as he stood over me on the couch.

I opened and closed my mouth a few times before finally spitting out, "You just murdered those shifters in cold blood."

Kaden's eyes narrowed. "I did what I had to do."

"Do you really believe that?" I asked.

"You could have died!" he roared, making me flinch back.

"But I didn't!" I drew in a deep breath. "We'd gotten the situation under control, and captured the shifters so we could interrogate them, and then you killed them all."

Kaden stalked back and forth, an angry wolf caged inside a hotel, eager to be unleashed. "They came into Libra territory and attacked my alpha female and my sister. They had to die."

"You're better than this," I said, imploring him to see reason, if only for a moment.

"I'm not," Kaden said, his voice cold. "And I'm done sitting around waiting for the other alphas to help us. This attack proves we're not safe here, and the longer we wait, the more we'll be in danger. We need to strike now against the Leos and anyone who stands with them. Tonight was a message, and I intend to beat the meaning of it into their thick skulls until every single one of them is dead or fleeing with their tails between their legs. They deserve to suffer just as much as we have."

"Kaden, listen to yourself." He sounded like his old self, like the one I'd first met before I'd convinced him not all the Zodiac Wolves were bad. Something had shifted inside of him, and something dark had taken hold. Was it because he'd almost died? Or had Tanner's death hit him that hard? "Let's call another meeting with the alphas. Once we tell them what happened today—"

"No. After what the Leos have done to you and to others in my pack, I'm done with diplomacy. I thought you would be too." He stood straight and squared his shoulders. "If I have to be the villain, so be it."

His hard words made me reel back. It felt like I was trying to hold onto sand, with Kaden himself slipping right through my fingers. There was nothing to gain purchase on with this slippery, cold surface of vengeful armor Kaden had donned. There was absolutely nothing I could do to stop him. He was beyond reasoning with.

"You're not a villain," I said. "Or a monster. You can't become what the other alphas all think you are."

"I'll become whatever I need to be. I'm not going to argue with you about this. What's done is done, and we can only go forward from here." He gave me a hard look. "And you can either join me or get out of the way."

I slowly rose to my feet and faced him without backing down. "As your alpha female, I can't let you do this."

"There's no way you can stop me," he growled.

He was right of course—he was the alpha, and my position among the Ophiuchus was still tenuous at best. But I was just as obstinate as he was. "You're wrong. It's my duty to tell you when you're out of line. If you won't listen to me, fine. But I won't stand by your side for it."

He opened his mouth like he wanted to say more, to try

to convince me not to do this, but then he stubbornly closed it. When he didn't say anything else, I turned around and left the penthouse, slamming the door behind me. Then I closed my eyes hard, trying to pull my emotions under control once more.

It was a struggle, but finally, I opened my eyes, and they were dry. I didn't know where I would go, but all I knew was that I wanted away from Kaden and this whole thing.

I started walking, and I didn't realize where my feet were taking me until I stopped in front of Jordan's door. I hadn't made the conscious choice to come here. If anything, I would have rather stayed away, gone somewhere else completely. Jordan wasn't someone I should be seeing when I was so emotional. He could use it against me.

Jordan looked up when I entered, surprised. "What are you doing here?" he asked as he sat at the table, eating some lunch. "This isn't your normal time." He studied me closely. "What happened? Are you okay?"

"The Leos attacked us," I said, my voice shaking a little. I sank into the chair opposite him. "You wouldn't know anything about that, would you?"

He snorted. "You think I had something to do with it? I've been trapped in here for days. Or are we at weeks now?"

I blew out a long breath, centering myself. "No, I don't think you did."

Jordan relaxed a little at my admission and his eyes ran over me but with concern instead of desire this time. "You're injured."

"I'm fine," I snapped, then rubbed my face. I shouldn't take this out on Jordan. For once, he wasn't to blame.

"Obviously not." He tilted his head as he studied me. "Why are you here?"

"I don't know," I said truthfully. "I just...wanted to talk to you."

He let out a harsh laugh. "Now I know you're not thinking right. You must have hit your head or something during the attack."

"Kaden and I fought," I admitted. Jordan raised his eyebrows, and before he could open his mouth and say something that would make me regret coming in to talk to him, I continued. "He killed several Leos in cold blood after we'd already knocked them out. I wanted to take them as hostages, but he just killed them."

Jordan's face was grim as he digested the news. "Brutal and efficient. Sounds like something I would do. Did any of them survive?"

"No."

"I'm surprised you care so much about the Leos," he said, leaning back and appraising me. "I thought you'd want to see them all dead after everything that happened."

"No one should be killed like that," I said. "Besides, they would have been more helpful as prisoners that we could interrogate. We need to know what the Sun Witches and Leos are planning, and so far, you haven't been much help. Unless you're willing to finally talk..."

"At this point, I have no idea what they're planning any more than you do," Jordan said.

"Why do I not believe that?" I sighed and pinched my brow. "I'm trying to convince everyone that the Sun Witches are the real enemy, not the Leos. If you would only help me, we might be able to stop this useless pack war before it gets worse. We need to take the fight to the Sun Witches already."

Suddenly Jordan's hand clasped around my wrist. "Stay away from the Sun Witches."

I jerked back, but his hold was steady, persistent. "What?" I asked, startled. I'd never seen him look so serious before.

"Ayla, I'm serious. You have no idea what they can do."

I tried to yank my arm out from his grip, but it was impossible with how strong he was. I was only half shifter and couldn't even compete with one of the strongest alphas alive. "Let go of me."

He did, uncurling one finger at a time before leaning back in his chair. His previous nonchalant attitude returned, but there was an undercurrent left in the air, something that spoke of danger and persistence.

"I have some idea of what they can do," I said as I rubbed my wrist.

Jordan shook his head, and let out a puff of air that could have been a laugh under different circumstances. "No, you don't. They get in your head. Twist things around, make you do things..." he trailed off and slammed his mouth shut. It was almost as if he wanted to say more, but *couldn't*.

Celeste had told me the Sun Witches could get in your

head, and had taught me how to protect against it—was that what Jordan was talking about? Had they used such power on him before? My brain raced, going over every incident we'd had, wondering how much of it was him, and how much was the Sun Witches. "Did they make you do things?"

"Of course not," he snapped.

"Jordan, you can tell me, and maybe I can help—"

"I don't need your help. What are you even doing here?" He shoved back from the table so hard it slammed against me and nearly knocked my chair over. "Stay the fuck away from me."

I stood up and stepped toward the door. Maybe it was a mistake that I'd come here. Maybe I should have just gone for a walk instead. But I supposed I'd thought Jordan needed to know what was going on, and hoped I could get something useful out of him in return. I should have known it would be pointless.

No. I had learned something, and Jordan was working hard to push me away from him, which meant that I was getting somewhere. I couldn't give up now. I turned back to him.

"Please," I said. "Help me end this war with your pack and turn the battle onto the real enemy. You obviously know that the Sun Witches are evil. You just admitted as much."

Jordan stared at me, jaw clenched, eyes unreadable, but didn't answer.

"At least help me get a Sun Witch so we can remove the mate bond," I said.

Still no response. He was being so stubborn, and it was at his own expense.

I tried a different tactic. "The November full moon is coming up. What will you do when you go into heat?" I knew how awful it would be for him to still have the mating bond between us while he was in heat. Even in its dampened state, he would struggle, probably until he hurt himself, and I didn't know what would happen to me either. "It's not like you can just ignore it." *Trust me, I know,* I added silently, grimacing at the reminder of the utter *need* that had overtaken me, utterly uncontrollable and insatiable until the moon had gone down.

"I want the bond broken just as much as you do, trust me," Jordan growled. "But the Sun Witches are too powerful. They—" He stopped and grimaced again, and when he looked back at me his eyes hardened once more. "A pack war is inevitable, and you and I? We're not friends. We're not siblings. We're not mates. We're *enemies.* Nothing more, nothing less. No matter how much you try to convince yourself otherwise every time you come here and play cards with me. Now get out."

His words stung, even though I didn't really believe that he meant them. He was trying to push me away as a defensive tactic, to prevent me from learning anything. I couldn't let him get to me, even when I was already feeling bruised to my core.

"Say whatever you want," I said. "But I know there's something you're hiding, something about the Sun Witches. I'll get you to spill it eventually."

I walked out, anger simmering in my chest at both the alphas in my life. They were so damn stubborn, both of them convinced they were always right—but then again, so was I. And I wasn't going to let either of them push me around.

CHAPTER TWENTY-THREE

UNSURPRISINGLY, security was doubled from then on. When I went down to check on Stella, I was shocked at the sheer number of shifters walking around on full alert, as if expecting an attack at any moment. Stella was fine, fully recovered, but a little sore when she moved her shoulder. My own recovery would be a bit longer, but I was determined to not let it slow me down.

"No one is allowed to leave without a sizable escort," Kaden ordered everyone at the pack meeting the next morning when he'd finished explaining what had happened to us, and how he was working on taking the fight to the Leos in retaliation. Tensions ran high among the people in the crowd, and I heard many people whispering that we should just go back home. Some agreed that we should attack the Leos head-on, and others muttered that we should go back into hiding and stay out of the conflict like the Ophiuchus pack had done before. I didn't know what the answer was, I just knew I refused to live in fear.

Kaden tried to talk to me after the meeting, but I had nothing more I wanted to say to him. I'd said it all the other night, and Kaden had completely refused to listen to it. Would he listen now? Doubtful.

Over the next few days, training increased in different areas of the hotel. Shifters learned how to fight one another during the day with Kaden and Ethan, and in the evenings, Larkin and I held classes on magic—both using it and defending against it. Every night the classes grew in size, although most of the shifters didn't have any magic to speak of. They still wanted to know what they could do if they came face to face with a Sun Witch. Unfortunately, we weren't allowed to do the classes in the park anymore, but at least the hotel had a nice outdoor garden that also worked for our purposes. I loved seeing my fellow Ophiuchus pack members along with Mira finding this power within themselves, even if it was the smallest spark. Anything would help us in a battle.

Ethan called another Zoom meeting with the alphas to tell them what happened with the Leos, but no matter how much we tried to get them to make a decision, to put aside their differences to come together and defeat a common foe, it was hard to get them to agree on anything. We were getting closer, but at the rate we were going, it would be a whole year before everyone was satisfied, and we didn't have that kind of time. All the alphas had stubborn streaks, and I was beginning to wonder if it was a prerequisite to becoming one.

I knew Kaden planned to attack the Leos soon, but he remained quiet about his actual plans, both with me and with others. At one point I found him arguing in hushed tones with Ethan, and paused outside the conference room door, careful not to make any noise.

"We need to go to the Leo village and see what we can find," Kaden was saying.

"That's madness," Ethan said. "And besides, what are you going to do, slit all their throats while they sleep?"

"Maybe," Kaden growled. "They deserve it, after attacking my sister and my mate in the park on *your* territory. Does it not bother you?"

"Of course it bothers me." Ethan sounded as if he'd had enough of Kaden's bullshit. "But it's wrong."

"So is the fact that we have all suffered at the hands of the Leos for so long. Or that some of my people continue to suffer. We could get another head in a box at any time."

There was a short, tense silence, as if they were having a staredown, and then Ethan continued. "I can't control what you do, but if you bring the ire of the Sun Witches, I won't be able to help you."

"I already have the ire of the Sun Witches," Kaden snapped. "We're going at the next full moon, and no one can stop us."

Damn. I needed a way to stop him from becoming a villain. I'd hoped I could convince Jordan to give up more information, but the last few times I'd visited he hadn't responded at all, and refused to play card games with me. He either ignored me completely, or snarled at me to leave, and that was it.

A week after I overheard Kaden arguing with Ethan, another package arrived. Kaden, Ethan, Clayton, and I all gathered around it, grim and tense. This time there was no doubt about what was in the box. Another part of a pack member, and I desperately didn't want to open it. Kaden stood next to me, practically vibrating with rage as Clayton cut it open.

I looked away as the stench of death hit the air. There was a collective gasp that went around the circle of gathered people. I had to look, even though I really didn't want to see the head in the box. As expected, it was from Tanner's mate, Lindsey, the one I'd fought for my place as female alpha. Her eyes were closed, but there was no mistaking the misery on her face.

Another one of the Ophiuchus pack members dead, and I felt sick to my stomach over it. It didn't matter that she had fought against me. She was, at the end of the day, still a pack member, and I never wanted to see her dead. But as long as we held Jordan, they would keep sending us pack members in a box—yet we couldn't give him up either. For better or worse, we needed him to break the mate bond, if nothing else.

Kaden let out a low growl and turned his back on Lindsey's head. His fists were clenched so hard I was afraid that his nails were cutting into the skin of his palms, and he looked downright murderous. "That's it. We're attacking the Leos at the full moon and getting our people back."

When he looked around and no one answered, he reached over and slammed his fist down on the table. It jostled the head, and bile rose up in my throat as Lindsey's head rolled to the side and fell off onto the plush conference room carpeting. No one moved to pick it up.

"Does anyone dare question this plan?" Kaden asked, staring at me, and then Ethan.

"No," Ethan said. "I think it's time."

"So you're going to give up your hope of making peace with the enemy?" Kaden asked.

Ethan spread his hands in defeat. "I've done what I can to convince the other alphas to help us. You have every right to try to save your pack members."

Kaden turned to me. "And you, Ayla? I need you to teleport us all to the Leo village."

I swallowed hard and reluctantly nodded. Did I like his plan? No, not at all. But I didn't see any other option either. Something had to be done—we couldn't keep getting our pack members' heads sent to us in boxes. I worried this action would only take the pack war to the next level, but there was no way I could convince Kaden to take another route. It was this way, or nothing, and maybe if I was there during the attack, I could stop him from going completely over the edge. We might even be able to find a Sun Witch to kidnap too.

"Yes, I'll do it," I said.

"Good. Begin preparations," Kaden said to Clayton. "We move at the next full moon."

————

WHEN THE DAY of the full moon came, I went to see Jordan again. I stopped in front of his door, and hesitated for the longest time yet. I was about to transport a group of fighters into the heart of his territory when they were at their most vulnerable, and let Kaden kill as many as he could in an attempt to save our rogue pack members. The last thing Jordan would want was to welcome me with open arms. I doubted he'd even talk to me. But he was also about to go into heat, and I couldn't let him suffer as I'd once suffered.

I finally opened the door and walked inside. Jordan was seated at the table, hands folded in front of him. He looked up at me, and there was no anger on his face. Not much of any emotion, in fact. He looked solemn and grim, as if waiting for a chat with death, as if he'd known I was coming.

I went to sit across from him. "We're going to attack the Leos tonight."

Jordan met my gaze levelly, and there wasn't a flicker of surprise across his face.

"You're not surprised?" I asked.

"No," Jordan said. "It's what I would do."

"Of course it is," I muttered.

He leaned back with a smug grin. "How does it feel to know your precious alpha isn't any better than I am?"

I'd once wanted to believe that Kaden would have never

stooped down to the Leos' level, but here we were. Jordan could gloat all he wanted, but it would be a hollow victory when he was paying in the lives of his pack members.

"I'm here to help you," I said. "The mating frenzy will start soon."

"I know. I can already feel it." He turned away, staring outside his window at the sun setting on the horizon, as if he couldn't stand to look at me any longer. "What are you going to do about it? You know I'll try to break the door down to get to you, no matter how much the thought disgusts me."

The fucking mating bond. I felt it too, much stronger than before, like the rising moon was taunting us with its pull. As an Ophiuchus, I wouldn't go into heat now, at least —but it would be sheer torture for Jordan. I had no idea what would happen to me either if I stayed near him. Maybe it was better I would be thousands of miles away tonight.

"I'm not going to let that happen," I said. I called out for Jack, and he came in with another guard, carrying a huge set of silver chains.

Jordan's gaze followed them as they approached, and he snorted. "Going to tie me up and leave me to suffer, then?" His eyes were hollow when they slid back to mine. "I suppose in your eyes, it's no less than what I deserve for all the wrongs I've committed against you and your precious alpha."

"No," I said. "*I'm* not as cruel as you think I am."

Lightning quick, before he could do so much as twitch, I grabbed his arm and yanked it toward me. My teeth turned to canines and my poison began to flow as I sank my fangs into his bare skin. Jordan jerked back just as quickly, trying to free himself, but I held on tight, releasing my poison as I counted to three. Then I let him go.

"What the fuck?" Jordan asked, but before he could ask me anything else, his face went slack, and he slumped down in his chair. I watched him for a few moments, trying to see how well I'd gotten the poison into his bloodstream, but he didn't so much as twitch. He was out cold.

Jack and the other guard quickly chained Jordan up and even attached him to the wall, strapping Jordan's arms flat against his sides, then repeated the process with his legs. By the time they were done, he was completely wrapped up. I hoped I'd dosed him with enough poison to keep him asleep for the night, but at least if he woke up it would be a lot harder for him to hurt himself—or get to me.

I got up to go, but Jordan suddenly twitched and groaned. I froze and glanced down at him. Was the frenzy starting already? Or had I not poisoned him enough?

"Thank you," he said, his words slurred as he somehow opened his eyes to look at me. "Be careful, Ayla."

I blinked at him as his eyes slipped shut again and his breathing went deep and even. The poison had fully taken effect, and in his sleep, he looked so young and innocent. He looked like my brother.

Be careful, he'd told me. He hadn't asked me to spare any of his people. He hadn't pleaded for their lives or told me not to go. But he'd told me to be careful.

I wasn't sure what to think of that.

A few hours later, when the full moon was high in the

sky, I felt itchy in my skin. Not exactly a pull back to Jordan, but a feeling of being uncomfortable and antsy. I couldn't tell if it was from Jordan going into heat, or anticipation for what we were about to do.

When it was time, I teleported to the garden behind the hotel, where Kaden and a group of shifters waited for my arrival. Dozens of them, mostly from the Ophiuchus pack, but with a few Libras too, I was surprised to see. I recognized many of them—Harper and Dane, of course, but also some who had come to the magic training to learn how to fight the Sun Witches. I could only pray we wouldn't face a lot of them tonight. I'd already pleaded with Larkin and Stella to stay behind in case something went horribly wrong —they would have to lead the pack in case that happened.

"Jordan's out?" Kaden asked, as soon as I appeared.

I nodded. "Like a light."

"And he won't wake up and escape?"

"Do you want to go check him yourself?" I asked, annoyed at being questioned like this. He should be able to trust that I could handle this, at least.

Kaden looked away, jaw clenching as he looked around the rest of the gathered shifters. The tension was running high and there wasn't a single cheerful face to be found. Harper caught my eye and gave me a short nod, always eager to rush into battle alongside her twin.

"Is everyone ready?" I asked.

A murmur of assent went through the group, and Kaden inclined his head slightly. The full moon was shining bright overhead, and when I drew on my magic, it came quickly and easily to me. I let the moonlight fill me and spread out to touch every one of the gathered shifters as I thought about the Leos and their village in Arizona, with the dry sand and rows of nearly identical sand-colored houses.

A second later, we were there under a full moon that was in a slightly different position in the sky. I'd teleported us just outside of the Leos' town, far enough away that they wouldn't be able to smell us the instant we arrived. We would have a bit of the element of surprise, but not for long.

Kaden started giving hand signals to split us into groups. I was in his group and we slinked toward the village, while the other groups circled around to enter through the back side. We'd have all the entrances and exits blocked, effectively stopping any shifters from escaping. Not that it mattered. They would likely be too wrapped up in their mating frenzy to even try to escape.

But as we approached, we all realized something was wrong.

After a moment, it hit me. There should have been the sounds of a pack in heat. I'd expected something along the lines of one of Mira's stories about the Cancer pack in heat, when groups of shifters gathered on the beach around bonfires, fucking their mates all night long until no one could move any longer. I'd experienced a similar thing when I'd gone into heat myself, and Kaden had done everything he could to satisfy me. So why was the village so quiet?

We sneaked into the town on high alert, some of us in human form and some in wolf, but after a moment, Kaden raised his nose and inhaled sharply.

"There's no one here," he said.

A strange mixture of both relief and despair rushed through me at his words. On one hand, no one would die tonight. On the other hand, there went our chance to save the missing pack members or capture a Sun Witch.

We continued forward, still cautious in case we were wrong, but it was obvious the town had been abandoned. The other groups of attackers joined us in the middle of the town, looking just as confused as we were.

"Go search the houses," Kaden said. "I want to know if they're hiding from us, or if they've been gone for a long time. If you pick up a trail, alert me instantly."

The other shifters nodded and broke away again to start their search. It was eerily quiet in the village, especially after the weeks we'd spent in the city, with noises around us at all times. Kaden stayed still for a few moments, his gaze pinned on something in the distance. When I turned to see what it was, my blood ran cold. *The gazebo.*

He stalked toward it through the Sun Witches' perfect garden, the one they'd created as a gift to the Leos. I followed him, at a loss for what else to do, though bile rose in my throat with every step. Memories flashed back of the last time I'd been in the gazebo, when Jordan had tried to force me to mate with him under another full moon. Had the Sun Witches controlled him, that night? I wasn't sure.

Kaden stopped in front of the structure and looked up at it. Then he stepped forward and punched one of the pillars as a look of pure fury crossed his face. The wood gave way under his shifter strength instantly, and the whole gazebo buckled. The structure groaned out a warning, but Kaden ignored it and ripped the broken piece from the rest of the gazebo and tossed it down.

Bit by bit he tore the structure down with his bare hands, and I couldn't tear my eyes away from his attack. It was oddly satisfying seeing him destroy the gazebo after all the pain the place had caused me. When it collapsed into a pile at his feet, I let out a sigh of relief, as if a huge weight had been lifted.

Finally, after the gazebo lay in pieces at his feet, Kaden began to glow. I watched mutely, trying to figure out what the hell he was doing. A strong wave of moonlight pulsed from Kaden's body, spreading over the surrounding garden. The plants withered and died on impact, leaving nothing but a bunch of husks.

"What are you doing?" I asked finally as Kaden set the remaining pieces of the gazebo on fire with his magic.

"I'm sending a warning," Kaden said, turning to look at me. His face was grim as he stepped away from the chaos he had created. "A reminder not to mess with me, or my people. Or my *woman*."

A shiver ran down my spine at his possessive words— and how much I liked them.

Maybe I didn't hate this villainous version of Kaden as much as I'd thought.

CHAPTER TWENTY-FOUR

WE SEARCHED the Leo village until well after dawn but found no sign of anyone nor any trace of where they'd gone. It seemed as though the place had been abandoned for some time, but Kaden wanted to wait 'til after dawn anyway in case they returned once the full moon was over. When no one showed up, we finally returned to the hotel with one very frustrated alpha.

Everyone was exhausted beyond measure, and like them, I was ready to sleep and forget about this entire night. But Kaden was wound tight with anger and restless energy, and I followed him as he headed straight for Jordan's cell and barreled through the door.

Jordan was still chained up and slumped over on the ground, but at least he'd survived the night. He raised his head and looked to be weak from the poison, but lucid enough. His eyes flicked to me, and that seemed to enrage Kaden even more.

"Where did the Leos go?" Kaden snarled at Jordan. "Your town was empty, and I know you had something to do with it."

Jordan gave Kaden a bored look. "How would I know?" he drawled. "I don't exactly have a phone in here, or any way to communicate with my pack."

Kaden moved in the blink of an eye and picked Jordan up by the throat, chains and all, too quick for me to do anything to stop him. He shoved Jordan against the wall, one hand wrapped around his neck. Jordan began struggling and sputtering, trying to get air, but Kaden was merciless. I stepped forward to stop him, but Jordan's eyes flicked to me, and he shook his head slightly.

"Tell me where the fuck your pack is, or I'll kill you," Kaden growled.

Jordan coughed, trying to get air. "I don't know," he wheezed out. "And even if I did, I would sooner die than lead you to my pack."

Kaden growled again and gripped Jordan's throat harder. The sound of Jordan choking was horrible, and I couldn't just stand by while Kaden did this, no matter how much I hated what Jordan had put me through in the past.

"No!" I said, trying to yank him off Jordan. "Don't kill him! He's more useful to us alive!"

For a second, I didn't think Kaden would listen. He bared his teeth at me and tightened his hold on Jordan's throat as if to prove a point. Jordan struggled against his chains, but he couldn't do anything to defend himself against the attack.

"Stop, Kaden!" I shouted, drawing moon magic into myself, ready to unleash a moonbeam bolt at Kaden if I had to. "Or I will make you stop!"

Kaden finally let go at those words and shoved Jordan back against the wall. He glowered at me. "You would fight me over him?" he asked, jerking his chin at Jordan.

"I will fight you when you're being a stubborn mule of an alpha who needs to go calm down before he does something he regrets," I snapped.

"Fine," Kaden said and stormed out without another word.

I let out a breath as I watched Kaden go. I had no doubt I'd have hell to pay for this later, but I needed Jordan alive. I crouched down in front of my brother and reached out to check his throat. His pulse was pounding with adrenaline against my fingers, and Jordan's eyes opened to look at me.

"Can you breathe?" I asked.

Jordan nodded slowly and swallowed. He coughed a few times, and I let out a sigh. He was going to be fine. The healing would go a bit slower because of the poison that still ran through his veins, but he would heal completely.

I called on the guards to unchain Jordan, then made sure he had a good breakfast sent up. He would need it for his shifter healing to kick in. Then I went after Kaden.

The angry trail of his scent was easy to follow and I caught up to him fairly quickly. He glanced back at me and then continued on his way. He didn't say anything, but the anger that poured from him was loud enough. He was *livid,* and there was no one to pin the blame on right now. No matter how much he'd wanted to kill Jordan, he had to know on some level that Jordan hadn't had anything to do with what happened tonight.

Kaden marched right up to Ethan's office and threw the door open. Ethan looked up, startled. I was surprised to see him in his office this early, but I supposed he'd been waiting for a report on the attack on the Leo village.

"How did it go?" Ethan asked, standing up to meet Kaden.

"Call the other alphas for a meeting," Kaden said. "Right now."

Ethan didn't cave under the pressure and simply gave Kaden a firm look. "They won't all be awake right now, but I'll schedule one for as soon as I can."

Kaden growled low in his chest, but Ethan didn't back down. Finally, Kaden let out a frustrated breath and shook his head. "Then set one up for this afternoon. Say it's an emergency. Make sure they all come."

"I'll do my best," Ethan said.

He went back to his desk and sat down, pointedly ignoring Kaden as he clicked a few things on his computer. Kaden left the room without saying anything else. I lingered, an apology on my lips. But what would I apologize for? Kaden being an utter asshole? Ethan should be used to that by now.

"I take it things didn't go well?" Ethan asked, without glancing up at me.

"There was no one there," I said, shaking my head. "Another dead end."

Ethan nodded grimly. "And now Kaden has a new plan."

"So it seems," I muttered, before leaving Ethan's office.

It was clear that we were wearing on Ethan's last nerve, and he would be a valuable ally to lose. I just hoped Kaden could reign it in in time for the meeting. I had no idea what he had planned, but there was a sinking feeling in my gut. Whatever it was, it wouldn't be good.

TRUE TO HIS WORD, Ethan managed to get all the alphas in our tenuous alliance together on Zoom by late afternoon. Once again, I was impressed by the sway he had over the other packs.

As soon as everyone was gathered, Kaden started talking. "I'm done waiting for you to decide on a course of action. You're fractured and weak, and you need someone to lead you." He crossed his arms, radiating his alpha energy throughout the room. "I'm taking over as leader of the Zodiac Wolves. You can either follow me or become my enemy. But know now that I won't show any mercy to my enemies."

The dread that had plagued me all morning while waiting for this meeting intensified. *How does it feel to know your precious alpha isn't any better than I am?* Jordan had asked. Kaden had once talked about taking over the rest of the packs or killing them if they got in his way, but I didn't think he would actually do it. I moved away, making sure I was off-screen in case I was unable to control the horror flickering across my face. The other alphas would be watching me, and if we didn't appear to be in sync, it could undermine what Kaden was trying to do. And even if I disagreed with this course of action, he was still my alpha— and I had to admit he was right, on some level. The other packs had taken far too long to do anything. Maybe this was the only way.

"Why should we follow you?" the Virgo alpha asked. She looked angry, much angrier than I'd seen her before. "How are you any better than Jordan and the Leos?"

"I have no interest in controlling you," Kaden said. He glanced over at me, and for the first time, I saw him soften a bit. "The Sun Witches are the real enemies, and I will destroy any pack allied with them." He turned back, and that brief flash of softness disappeared as quickly as it had appeared. "And if you're not allied with me, you might as well be allied with them."

"I agree with you," Ethan said, surprising me. "We've had enough time to deliberate and we need to come to a unanimous decision. But we are all equal here, as alphas of our respective packs, and I'm not sure we need one person to lead us. And if we do, I'm not so sure it should be you."

"We've tried it your way already, and waiting around and hoping for diplomacy isn't working," Kaden snapped. "Look at us, we've been going in circles over the same decision for weeks now, and the Leos continue to plot their revenge and get ready for their next attack. We can't waste any more time. They're holding members of my pack hostage, and the Leos have left their village and gone into hiding. They need to be found, and we need to prepare to launch an attack on them and on the Sun Witches. Since none of you are willing to make the tough decisions, I'll be the one to do it." He paused and glared at Ethan. "Unless you think you can lead us better?"

"Yes, actually," Ethan said coolly. "I think I can."

"Then I will fight you for it," Kaden said in a low, menacing tone. "To the death, if need be."

"Kaden," I whispered, horrified. I didn't care how my reaction looked to the rest of the alphas. He couldn't kill Ethan—he was our friend, and he'd taken in the Ophiuchus pack when no one else would. Who had Kaden become, making these blatant statements of violence against people who were our closest allies? I hardly recognized him.

Kaden and Ethan didn't break eye contact and the tension in the room ratcheted up, making it almost impossible to breathe. Were they going to fight right here, on the live stream with everyone watching?

Ethan finally looked away after a few more heartbeats. "Very well," he said. "We'll try it your way. You have the Libra pack's allegiance."

I let out a long breath I'd been holding, and the tension diffused noticeably. Kaden nodded, though he didn't look as pleased as I thought he would. Then he turned back to the computer screen and began unmuting the other alphas one by one. To my surprise, the other packs gave in more easily.

The Sagittarius, Pisces, and Capricorn packs all agreed to follow Kaden without question.

"If we're trading one asshole for another," the old Capricorn alpha muttered, "I'd rather have the one who's promised not to control us."

When Kaden unmuted Wesley, my brother hesitated. I was surprised, since of all the alphas, Wesley knew Kaden the best. "Ayla?" he asked.

I moved back into screen and gave him a tense nod. "I'm here."

Wesley searched my face for some time before his eyes darted back to Kaden. "Then you have the Cancer pack's allegiance, as long as Ayla is by your side, keeping you in line."

I swallowed hard. Could I keep Kaden in line? I wasn't sure anymore.

The Gemini alphas shared a glance when it was their turn to speak. "Before we agree, we want to know your plan," the female one said, and the male one nodded. For once, they seemed to agree on something. *Maybe Kaden was right,* I thought. *They needed someone to give them an ultimatum.*

"I'm taking the fight to the Sun Witches and their allies," Kaden said, to my surprise. "We'll do a series of targeted attacks against the packs who have allied with them, and then confront the Sun Witches at the winter equinox Convergence and demand they release us from the magic binding your wolves and controlling the mate bonds. If they refuse, the combined might of the allied Zodiac Wolves will take them down."

The Gemini twins shared another long look, and something seemed to pass between them telepathically, before they both nodded. "Then we will ally ourselves with you," the male said. "Like Capricorn, we'd rather be free and under someone's directive than enslaved."

The last one was the Virgo alpha, who had stubbornly refused to say anything thus far. She sighed and rubbed her temples. She looked much older suddenly, as if the weight of too many lifetimes rested on her shoulders. "I don't like this, not one bit, but we can't afford to become your enemies either. The Virgo pack will ally with the other Zodiac Packs to fight against the Sun Witches."

"Good," Kaden said, his shoulders relaxing slightly, though his tone stayed firm. "Now that we're all on the same page, each one of you will send some warriors and representatives to this hotel. It'll be easier than getting on Zoom calls every time we need to discuss something. We can coordinate attacks and make plans from here."

One by one, the other pack alphas agreed and got off the call to begin the arrangements. When it was done, Ethan got up and left the room without a word. I watched him go with a sigh.

Kaden glanced over at me once we were alone. "We need to start getting ready for their arrival. We're going to have a harder time getting these shifters to listen when they're used to listening to their own alphas. Are you going to stand with me as my alpha female?"

"I'll do what I must to keep us all safe," I reluctantly said, which wasn't exactly a yes, but it seemed to satisfy Kaden. For now, anyway. I feared I would be the only person who could stand up to Kaden if he crossed the line, and I was terrified of what it would do to us if I had to make that choice.

This was it. We were going to war...and I had no idea who Kaden was anymore.

CHAPTER TWENTY-FIVE

THE FOLLOWING DAY, I went to see Jordan at the usual time, sans my deck of cards. There was no need to pretend that I had to play games with him to see him. I just wanted to check up and see if he was all right and tell him what was happening. He might be able to give us a way to avoid going to war, though I doubted it.

I stepped up to the door, but to my surprise, Jack slammed his hand over the knob.

"You're no longer allowed to go inside," Jack said, and though he looked truly apologetic about it, I could tell he wasn't going to back down.

"You dare to stop me?" I asked as rage filled me.

"I'm sorry, Ayla," Jack said, and he sounded miserable. "Kaden gave me an alpha command. If you try to go in, I have to stop you—however I can."

I growled and nearly yelled at him to let me pass, but it wasn't Jack I was mad at. The fact that Kaden had used an alpha command on his own friend only proved how lost he'd truly become.

"Is Jordan okay at least?" I asked. "Healing?"

Jack nodded. "He's almost fully recovered from the other night."

That seemed to be the best I was going to get. I debated teleporting inside to see Jordan, but I didn't want Jack to get in trouble if Kaden found out. Instead, I walked away, simmering with anger. When I tried to find Kaden to give him a piece of my mind, he wasn't in the hotel and no one knew where he'd gone. Damn him.

My anger persisted throughout the day, and by the time I went to moon magic training that night, I was still upset. It must have been apparent on my face because Stella noticed immediately.

"What's going on?" she asked me. Mira looked over as well, frowning.

"It's Kaden," I muttered. "He's being especially insufferable."

"Does this have to do with him being the new leader of the Zodiac Wolves and sending them to war?" Mira asked. "Amos told me about that, and asked me to keep him updated, but I couldn't believe that the packs would agree to that."

"It's true," I said grimly. "We're going to war under the Ophiuchus pack's leadership."

"I'm glad Kaden is finally taking action," Harper said. "It's about time we tried to save our pack members and gave the Sun Witches some hell."

"Warriors from all the packs will be arriving in the next few days," I said. "Kaden's planning a series of attacks against the allies of the Leos at first since we can't find the Leos themselves, but then we're taking it to the Sun Witches at the Convergence."

"That means we'll need to step up training," Larkin said, tapping a finger against her lips as she thought. "We need everyone to be able to defend themselves against the Sun Witches."

She went ahead with Harper, as they discussed possible ways to train the new shifters, who might have never encountered magic before. Mira and Stella hung back with me, their faces worried.

Mira had one hand cupped under her growing belly as she asked, "You're not happy about this, are you?"

I shook my head. "I'm torn between feeling relieved we're finally doing something, and nervous about what will happen next. I'm worried about Kaden too."

"I'm concerned too," Stella said, biting her lip. "I've never seen him act like this. Yes, he often talked about taking over the Zodiac Wolves, but not with this same level of intensity. I'm going to talk to him later and try to see if there's anything I can do to help."

"Good luck," I said. "I've tried, and he won't listen to me. Maybe it'll be different since you're his sister."

"I doubt it," Stella said. "When Kaden makes his mind up about something, there's no stopping him. Even if I don't agree with him, he's still the alpha and I have to take his word as final say."

I thought about those words the whole time we trained, about how there was nothing anyone else could do to stop Kaden. I was the only one, as the tentative alpha female, who could even stand a chance of making Kaden see reason —but I didn't think I would have much luck there either.

When training was over, I returned to the penthouse alone. I needed time to think, to try to find anything that resembled inner peace. I felt so lost, like I was marooned on an island with no help in sight.

I walked over to the window and peered out at the sky. The moon was covered tonight, clouds completely obscuring the sky, and a light rain fell from them. I could always turn to the moon when I felt lost, but even it wasn't out to help me tonight.

I sighed and shook my head, and then reached for my phone. It had been forever since Wesley and I had talked one-on-one, and I wanted to just hear his voice. Maybe then I wouldn't feel so alone out here.

The phone rang a few times. *Pick up, please pick up,* I thought. I had no idea what he would be doing around this time, and he was a lot busier now that he was the pack alpha, but I just needed to hear his voice.

The phone clicked, and then— "Ayla?" Wesley asked.

I breathed out a huge sigh of relief. Just hearing his voice made something in me unwind, and I closed my eyes against a sudden press of tears. I had to wait for a few seconds, so my voice didn't shake in response. "Hi, Wesley."

"Are you okay?"

"I don't know." I was torn between wanting to eagerly

cheer Kaden on as he conquered our enemies, and worrying about what would happen to us if we became the very thing we were fighting against.

"I have to admit, I was surprised with your willingness to go along with Kaden's plan." He paused, and there was dead air on the other side of the phone for several long moments. "But it's good we're actually doing something instead of waiting for everyone to agree on something."

"I agree. I was going insane with the waiting." I chewed on my lip as I considered my next words.

"But?" Wesley asked.

"But...I've seen something dark in Kaden." Admitting it out loud felt like a betrayal and like getting a huge weight off my chest all at once. "I'm worried he's going to turn us all into something no better than the Leos."

"He won't do that," Wesley said. "Because he has you. Surely you can get through to him."

"I've tried, but he doesn't listen to me much anymore."

"Then keep trying. I know you, Ayla. You aren't one to ever give up, even when things get hard. But you'll find your way through this mess—you always do."

His words warmed me from the inside out. "Thanks, Wesley."

"Keep me updated. I've sent some Cancer warriors to help, and they should arrive tomorrow. Don't worry, I didn't send Brad."

I chuckled softly, remembering the bully I'd once been so afraid of. It seemed like a lifetime ago. "Good to know. Keep me updated as well."

"I will," Wesley said. "I'll see you soon, okay? The Convergence will be here before you realize it, and then this will be over, one way or another."

We said our goodbyes and hung up, just as the door opened and Kaden stepped into the penthouse. My breath caught at the sight of him, and all the anger returned in full force.

"Where have you been?" I asked.

Kaden shot me a hard look. "I was scouting the Aquarius pack lands to see if we can strike against the Leos there and free the pack from their control."

The Aquarius pack lands were right on Lake Michigan, which wasn't too far from Toronto, but I was still shocked by this. "And what did you find?"

"With a coordinated strike, I think we can take out the Leos there. Then we'll convince the Aquarius to join us."

"Just like that?"

Kaden pulled off his coat and hung it up. "It will take some more time before we're ready, but yeah. Just like that. And I want you to teleport us there."

"No." I crossed my arms. "I won't do it. I agreed to help get our pack members back from the people holding them hostage, but I'm not going on any raids in other packs' territory—especially when they haven't asked us for help."

He stalked toward me, crowding into my space. "I thought you would be on board with this. Shouldn't you want to free the Aquarius from Leo control?"

"Not if they don't want to be freed," I said. "Have you even asked them?"

"They haven't responded to any of our attempts to communicate with them," Kaden admitted. "But I meant what I said. They will either join us or stand against us."

I threw up my hands. "Yes, because everyone is either your ally or your enemy now. Including me, it seems."

"What's that supposed to mean?"

I poked his chest with my finger. "You won't let me see Jordan anymore. Do you really not trust me around him? Still?"

His face darkened at Jordan's name. "You've let your judgment become clouded when it comes to him. He's our enemy, and this is war now. He's lucky he's still alive."

"*My* judgment is clouded?" I clenched my fists, so infuriated by his words I was practically seething. "You're the one threatening to take out anyone in your way!"

"I'm doing what needs to be done." His voice was low, dangerous, and unbelievably sexy, despite the fact I was so angry with him I wanted to throttle him a little. "And you're going to help me as my alpha female."

"Fine." I trembled a little as I pushed him away from me. "Then I resign as your alpha female."

The words actually shocked him enough that he took a step back. "You can't do that."

"I can," I said, though the words broke my heart. "I'm not technically your mate, after all—and I won't stand by while you destroy everything we've worked so hard to build."

"Bullshit," Kaden growled. "You're still my woman. Always."

My heart caught in my throat at those words. *His*

woman. It was true. No matter how much we disagreed, I was still *his.*

"You'll have to use the alpha command on me if you're so desperate for my compliance," I said.

He stepped closer, backing me against the wall and putting his hands on either side of my head, caging me in. "We both know that won't work." His head lowered, his lips only inches from mine. "Although I think maybe you just want me to order you around."

"Don't be ridiculous." I dug my fingers into his chest, but I didn't push him away this time. He was so close that his scent filled my nose, spreading desire through my veins. I should be pushing him back, yelling at him to stop, but I couldn't help myself. I'd missed this closeness with him over the last few weeks. "You can't make me do anything I don't want."

"True." He nuzzled against my neck, brushing his teeth against the spot where he'd marked me before. "But I can remind you that you're mine."

I inhaled sharply as he captured my mouth with his and kissed me so thoroughly there was no doubt who I belonged to. I couldn't help but kiss him back, but it was an angry kiss, where I dug my fingers into his chest and snapped at him with my teeth.

When his strong hands began fondling my breasts, I knew I should push him away, to tell him that I wanted nothing to do with him unless he was done being an asshole, but I craved his touch even more. I was weak, when it came to Kaden. I *wanted.*

Kaden grasped my bottom lip between his teeth and bit down, just hard enough that it hurt. I stopped struggling and gasped at the sharp pain, and he pushed me back against the wall harder. Every inch of his body pressed against mine.

"Say it," he said, as his lips moved to my neck and upward.

"Say what?" I gasped out as he bit down on the lobe of my ear.

"That you're my woman."

"I—" I couldn't, not when I knew what that would mean. It would feel like giving in, and I refused to do that, even as he took control of my body.

He held me tight against the wall and then Kaden yanked open my jeans and slipped a hand down the front of them. His fingers slid to part my folds, instantly searching out my clit. He found it and circled, pulling the reactions straight out of my body. I was helpless against his masterful fingers, which were all too practiced in wringing pleasure out of me. He could tease me all night if he wanted. That wasn't his goal right now though. Right now, he was hell-bent on getting pleasure out of me as quickly as it could.

I gasped as he worked my clit with masterful strokes, making me rock back and forth against his hand to chase my pleasure. I moaned, reaching for Kaden and digging my hands into his shoulders. He didn't slow down, not even when my nails tore straight through the thin fabric of his t-shirt.

The pleasure screamed through my veins, tearing me open like one, big wound, and even when I opened my mouth and begged for Kaden to take mercy on me, he didn't so much as slow down. He brought me right to the edge and then pushed me right over it. I cried his name and pounded my fist against his chest. It almost hurt, the amount of pleasure he was putting me through, and I knew when it was done, I would want even more.

My legs gave way, and Kaden crowded me back against the wall, holding me up with his body. I felt the length of him, hard and hot against my stomach, but he didn't move against me. He leaned forward again, his voice low and dangerous once more.

"Still mine, little wolf," he said. "Always mine."

I was still coming down from the sudden, violent high he'd pushed me toward, and it took me a few moments to catch my breath and remember why exactly I was angry at him. It hit me suddenly, what this had been. Kaden was proving a point. He knew exactly how to get me to break, and he'd taken advantage of it.

I glared at him and shoved him away. "I'm your woman, but I'm not going to be your alpha female any longer."

Kaden's eyes flared, and for a moment, I thought he would do something to try to change my mind...or stop me in some other way. "Ayla—"

"Go," I yelled. "I don't want to be near you right now."

After a moment's hesitation, he stepped back and turned away. The door slammed on his way out, and I collapsed to the floor.

Whatever strength had let me say no to Kaden seeped out of me, and I closed my eyes and set my head against the wall. My heart still hammered in my chest, so hard that I was a bit worried for my health. The aftershocks of pleasure still ran through my body, a vivid reminder of what Kaden had just done.

I dropped my head into my hands and didn't try to stop the tears this time. There was no one to see them. The pain of the last few days washed over me, mixed in with the way my emotions were running high after that orgasm. I hardly recognized Kaden, or myself anymore. We were entirely different people, and I didn't like how much space had opened between us.

And worst of all, I knew he would be back—and when he did, I would be unable to resist him if he tried to claim me again.

CHAPTER TWENTY-SIX

I MOVED out of the penthouse that night. It was the only way I could think to get it through Kaden's thick skull that I wasn't his alpha female any longer.

The hotel was abuzz the next day with rumors about me moving into a different hotel room, because gossip spread like wildfire in a place full of bored, anxious shifters. Luckily they quickly turned to other topics as new shifters from the other packs began showing up in droves, filling the hotel to its capacity. Everyone became so busy trying to get the new arrivals settled that they didn't bother asking me what was going on with me and Kaden, which suited me just fine.

The days grew colder and rainier as we settled into December, and snow threatened to blanket the city as Ophiuchus season started. I felt it in my bones, an extra strength that made it easier to fight and to use my pack powers. We all took advantage of the extra strength and started upping our combat practice. I knew it wouldn't give us an advantage at the Convergence, since Ophiuchus season would be over by then, but we were all faster, better at learning, and able to practice stunts we wouldn't be able to otherwise. I just hoped we could learn them fast enough for muscle memory to kick in.

Harper, Stella, and I started training together out in one of the gardens behind the hotel. Since we were all shifters who also practiced moon magic, we were able to fight in ways that others couldn't, drawing upon our strengths to imagine what it would be like to fight both shifters and Sun Witches. None of them could use moon magic while shifted, so we'd started focusing on shifting between human form and blasting moonbeams, and then alternating with attacks in wolf form. It was slow going, but the more we practiced, the easier it became.

We were training together on one particularly brutal winter day, when it was so cold I thought we might turn to ice if we stayed out much longer. My breath fogged in front of me with every exhale, and when I wasn't moving around, my teeth started chattering. *This is just another part of training*, I told myself. The Convergence would be held in the California mountains this winter equinox, where it would no doubt be just as cold and likely covered in snow too. We needed to be able to fight in that kind of weather.

Larkin and Mira sat at the edge of the clearing, observing us and giving pointers as needed. Larkin, of course, was already adept at moon magic but couldn't shift, and Mira wasn't going to be fighting because she was way too pregnant now. They chatted while they watched, and I heard Larkin telling Mira, "There's a new app I found. It's called TikTok, and I've discovered a bunch of amazing romance novels from this hashtag #booktok."

"You'll have to send me some recommendations," Mira said. "Goddess knows I need something to keep me busy since no one will let me lift a finger while pregnant."

As they talked, I shifted from wolf form back to human and lobbed a blast of moonlight at Harper, who dodged it quickly as a wolf before racing forward to imitate a bite. I skittered away, shifting back as quickly as I could. We circled each other, growling and snapping, and then Stella launched her own attack against us.

Finally, Harper shifted back and held her hands up in truce, signaling it was time for a short break. "I think we're getting better at that. I even managed to throw a bit of moonlight during the Aquarius raid the other night."

I settled back into my human form with ease and raised an eyebrow. "How did it go?"

"We managed to sneak inside their lands and free them from the Leos' influence. The Aquarius alpha's daughter was being held hostage, and Kaden used his invisibility to rescue her and take out all her captors. After that, the alpha agreed to form an alliance with us, though he didn't seem as grateful to us as I'd have thought."

"Aquarius has always tried to remain neutral in the Cancer-Leo feud," Mira said. "They don't like conflict and generally prefer to keep to themselves."

"Did you take anyone alive?" I asked. "Or encounter any Sun Witches?"

"Did they know anything about our missing pack members or where the rest of their pack had gone?" Stella asked.

"No Sun Witches, sorry," Harper said. "We did manage to keep a few Leos alive at first, but if they knew anything, they weren't talking. Kaden slaughtered them all once he knew they wouldn't be of any use."

The shiver that ran through my body wasn't from the cold this time. No wonder the Aquarius alpha grudgingly agreed to follow Kaden after such a display. I was certain Kaden had made it clear that the Aquarius pack would be considered the enemy too if they didn't agree to his terms.

"We have more raids planned in the next few days," Harper added, glancing warily at me as if looking to see how I'd react. "Kaden wants to do as many as possible while the sun is in Ophiuchus."

A pang of something went through me when I realized I hadn't heard anything about these upcoming raids. Kaden never confided in me anymore, probably because he knew I'd disagree with his plans, or try to talk some sense into him.

As if my thoughts had summoned him, Kaden stalked into the garden, looking pissed. The atmosphere instantly changed, and the chatter died away as we all turned toward him.

"Everyone out," Kaden said after he'd stepped into the center of the garden and started observing all of us. Though

Harper, Stella, and I were all naked, his eyes only lingered over my bare skin. "I need to speak to Ayla alone."

The others hurried to comply, shooting worried glances at me before they scampered out of sight and headed back toward the hotel lobby. No one wanted to get in an argument between mates, especially not when one was an alpha.

"Show me what you've been practicing, little wolf," Kaden said. To my surprise, he settled into a fighting stance and motioned for me to do the same. I stepped into a hesitant starting position, wondering what Kaden was playing at. He nodded, and we began circling each other. He really was going to spar with me, like in the old days, when we were more enemies than anything else. Somehow here we were, almost back at the beginning. Were we enemies again now? I loved Kaden, but I wasn't sure anymore.

Kaden jabbed out first, and I ducked around him, retaliating by unleashing a blast of moonlight. He instantly put up a shield, showing me he'd been practicing his moon magic too, and making me oddly proud—and thankful Larkin was such a good teacher.

We went back to circling each other, prowling around with our eyes locked together. I didn't dare look away, in case I missed his indication of where he was planning to attack.

He shifted so fast I didn't notice it was happening until his huge black wolf was leaping toward me. I shifted in the next instant, barely managing to dodge out of the way in time. Then I did something I'd been working on in private, something I was sure only I could do, thanks to my half-blood heritage: I opened my wolf mouth and spewed moonlight like a fire-breathing dragon, spraying it at Kaden.

He jumped back before it hit him, and then shifted back to human form. "Impressive. But can you still fight without all of your fancy new tricks?"

"Naturally," I said, as I became human again.

We drew in closer to each other, both naked and sweaty now, and the tension rose the longer we went without any contact. There was a sort of danger here that felt thrilling like it could give way to passion at any moment. We were walking a fine line here, neither of us willing to acknowledge what lay between us, but neither willing to back down either.

I allowed myself to be drawn to him, almost like the mating bond pulling me closer. This went deeper though than any magic the Sun Witches could use on us. I wanted more than anything to bridge that gap between us, to pull him closer and say *fuck it, I'm yours.*

I couldn't do that though. Kaden jabbed out again, and I brought my hand up just in time to catch his forearm against mine, parrying the blow. I used the contact to whip my arm under his, and shove him bodily to the side. Kaden took a few steps back, and then the process began again.

"Move back into the penthouse with me," he said.

"I can't do that."

"I want you back," Kaden said, in that same no-nonsense tone that sounded like a demand. But then he added, "I miss you."

"I miss you too," I admitted, as a tiny part of my armor

softened to him. More than anything, I just wanted everything to be all right between us again.

"What's the issue then?" Kaden asked as he circled around me. "I'm finally getting things done and preparing the Zodiac Wolves to fight the Sun Witches. Isn't this what you wanted?"

"Yes," I said, drawing the word out. I went in for another attack, but Kaden parried me effortlessly.

"I hear a 'but' in there," Kaden said.

I aimed for his head, but Kaden blocked it. "But I'm worried you're going down a dark path and becoming the very thing we're trying to stop."

"I'm doing what I said I'd do." He grabbed my arm and pinned it behind me. "What I *always* said I'd do."

I used a move he'd taught me to escape his grasp and dart away. *Stubborn alpha male,* I thought, and kicked out at him. Kaden caught my foot and tried to drag me onto the ground, but I pulled it back with a heave and took a few steps back before settling back into the fighting stance.

But then Kaden managed to pin both my arms behind me, his grip so tight it was impossible for me to escape this time. His breath trailed across my ear as he held me from behind. "You know what I think? I think you enjoyed watching me destroy the gazebo, and I think you secretly enjoyed watching me kill all those Leos, even if you won't admit it. Tell me you wouldn't have done the same thing in my place, if those had been Sun Witches instead."

I opened my mouth to argue, but realized he might be right—there *was* darkness in my heart too. I condemned what he did, while secretly thrilling in his brutality. Gods, was I no better than him?

He spun me around before I could answer, still holding my wrists in place, and before I knew it, his lips were on mine. It felt like drinking water after being parched for days, even though this wasn't a nice kiss, not in the slightest. It was desperate, angry, rough, and full of emotions that flooded me.

"Tell me to stop," he said, as his fingers traced a trail down my neck, to circle my rock-hard nipples. "Tell me you don't want me."

I couldn't and he knew it. I wanted him so bad I was practically dripping for him. Heat simmered between my thighs, a pounding second pulse of desire. He released one of my wrists to slide two fingers into my pussy, and let out an appreciative noise.

"That's what I thought," he said.

I tilted my chin up and didn't say anything. I felt the hard line of his cock against my ass, so close to where I needed him, but I couldn't stand to answer him.

I still wanted him, despite everything that had happened between us, and there was nothing that would change that. No matter how dark Kaden went, he was still mine, and I was still his. We were too entangled, unable to resist the pull we had over each other. It was worse, in a way, than the mating bond, because it was completely us. There were no Sun Witches to blame, and nothing but our own desire fueling us into this frenzy.

Kaden released me and spun me around, and then his

hands were all over, his teeth caught in the soft skin below my neck. I tilted my head up, allowing him better access, and he growled. The sound was low, animalistic, and I shivered when I heard it. I loved it when he growled like that, like he couldn't control himself when it came to me.

Kaden circled one nipple with his hand, and then the other. I ran my fingers across the hot skin on his back, the strong muscles shifting under my hands as he continued his exploration downward along my belly and across my hips. It was like we were relearning each other's bodies, even though we knew every part of each other intimately at this point. We were in the middle of the garden, where anyone could walk by at any moment or watch us from the bushes, but neither of us cared. We were too wrapped up in each other.

Foreplay was out of the question this time—the need was too intense. Kaden gripped one of my thighs, and I lifted my leg to let him get easier access. His hands came up around my ass, and he pulled me onto his cock in one movement, sliding in and bottoming out.

I let out a sigh of relief as he paused. My eyes fluttered shut. *This is where he belongs,* my brain whispered. I shoved the thought back. It could say whatever it wanted, but I knew that there was a lot between us we had to figure out. But right now, I just wanted to feel Kaden. It had been too long since I'd had him like this, and I wanted nothing more than to lose myself in his body.

So I did.

Kaden thrust hard, and I met him. We built a rhythm together, our breaths coming quick and hard, the slap of flesh echoing around the empty garden. I found myself saying his name, over and over again, and he grunted as the pleasure built.

He kissed me again, his cock dragging against that perfect place inside of me. I shifted slightly to get a better angle and Kaden growled, tightening his hold around my ass, his fingers digging into my skin. The pleasure increased, but I didn't want to come yet. I was afraid that if we stopped, the real world would come crashing back in, and I wasn't ready for that.

But there was no holding it back, not when Kaden bounced me up and down on his cock with his strong arms, like I weighed nothing to him. He pumped into me relentlessly, his pace almost punishing, and I could barely catch my breath between each thrust. My eyes fluttered shut as waves of pleasure crashed over me, higher and higher until I was shuddering against Kaden, hands sliding against his skin, seeking more contact, a deeper connection.

"Yes," Kaden groaned, as his seed filled me. "You are mine. Now and forever."

When Kaden called me mine it always sent pleasure through me, but when he was thrusting into me, hands possessive on my skin, breathing those words while his cock was buried as deep inside of me as it could go, it made it all the more real. I truly believed that I *was* his, that I could be his forever, and that nothing could ever get in the way of that.

Our orgasms seemed to go on for an eternity, and I shuddered, still riding my own high, as Kaden claimed my lips again. The clear ownership in his kiss sent another ripple of pleasure through me, one that I never wanted to end.

But like all things, it did have to end. The echoes of pleasure faded away, leaving us both weak and boneless, and Kaden set me down on my feet again. No matter how good it was to touch Kaden again, to have his skin on mine the way it should be, it didn't change the fact that I was worried about him and about what he was doing. I shored myself up for what I had to do, even as my body and heart screamed at me to just *leave it,* to give in, to pretend everything was fine for a little while longer. But if I didn't do this now, Kaden would keep pushing, and he needed to know now that I wasn't going to give in, no matter how many times he brought me to orgasm.

"I love you, Kaden," I said, as I pulled away from him and shivered in the cold, finally feeling it now. "But this doesn't change anything between us."

His eyes flashed with darkness, but he bent down and tossed my clothes at me. "I didn't think it would. I just wanted to feel you come around my cock while crying my name, so I knew you were still mine."

He stalked away, and somehow I felt like I'd lost the battle between us again. I quickly got dressed, but even in my warm clothes, I shivered the whole way back to the hotel.

CHAPTER TWENTY-SEVEN

WE CONTINUED GETTING ready for battle over the next few days, as time slipped by at that strange pace of being too fast and too slow all at once. I wanted the Convergence to be here already so we could get it over with, but at the same time, I dreaded its arrival. I didn't know if an entire lifetime would make us ready to fight the Sun Witches and their allies.

At the next full moon in the middle of December, the Ophiuchus pack held its annual birthday celebration. Since most shifters in a pack had the same birth month, it was easier to just hold one big celebration rather than spreading it out. It was huge in most packs, with lots of food and fanfare, and the Ophiuchus pack was no different.

There were also no gifts exchanged, which made it focused on just being with each other. The only time that presents were given were between family members on rare occasions, usually for a milestone birthday. I'd never been a fan of attending the Cancer pack's annual celebration, simply because no one seemed to want me there—especially because my own birthday was in March. Not that my parents had deigned to celebrate it then either.

This was a new experience for me, to be surrounded by people I loved and cared about, and to be completely welcome. No one seemed to mind that my birthday was in another month—since I was part of the Ophiuchus pack, they celebrated me too.

We held it at the nearby nature reserve since the wolf noises would have been too much in the city and might have gotten some unwanted attention thrown on us. We didn't need any drunk shifters accidentally becoming wolves while a human was walking down the street.

We'd found a nice clearing in the park that the Libras often used for events, and all helped to decorate it with string lights and balloons. Someone had brought a speaker, and upbeat music filtered through the entire clearing, setting the mood. There were tables set up with food, so much that I had trouble choosing because I knew I wouldn't be able to try it all.

After I'd loaded up my plate, I began walking through the crowd. People called me by name, patting me on the back and grinning at me. No matter how much of a tumultuous start I'd had as part of the pack, I'd still been accepted. It was times like these that reminded me of how different my life was here from the Cancer pack—even if I was no longer alpha female.

It was also a much-needed break for everyone attending.

The weeks leading up to the big battle had taken a toll on everyone, as well as all the raids the fighters were going on. Everyone needed time to unwind and to remember how to smile. Even though everything was about to change for us at the Convergence, we could still take this time to have a little fun.

I caught sight of Mira, seated on the ground with her mate, Aiden. She waved at me but didn't get up. He had an arm around her, and her head was resting on his chest. I smiled at how happy they seemed. I still felt bad about pushing her toward Wesley when she seemed happy with Aiden, and now that she was pregnant, I felt even worse. Besides, who was I to tell anyone who or how to love, when I was a total mess when it came to Kaden?

I turned away and grinned as I caught sight of Harper and Stella dancing together. They each had a drink in hand, and I watched as Stella threw her head back and laughed. It was the most carefree I'd seen her in a long time. I smiled softly and started walking toward them, but before I could, my eyes were drawn to Kaden, easily finding him in the crowd like a second mate bond was pulling me toward him.

He looked at ease, not quite smiling but close to it. Jack stood next to him, grinning at something one of the other fighters was saying, and Dane nodded solemnly. They were sharing a story, from the rapt attention of the gathered crowd.

Kaden looked delicious tonight in a tight black t-shirt and dark jeans. I paused and let myself look him over. I'd thought about our time in the garden together every night since we'd parted ways. It had physically hurt me to push him away, and since I'd done so, I'd had a lot of time to regret it.

I watched as Kaden's muscles flexed as he raised a bottle of beer to his lips. Everything else faded away as I watched him. The music lowered to a thrum, and everyone else blurred around me. I only had eyes for Kaden.

Suddenly, nothing mattered except him. We were meant to be together, and I would make sure he stayed on the right path. The other alternative was to not have him at all, and in those days between him fucking me in the garden and now, I'd had plenty of time to think about how cold and empty my bed was without him in it. And maybe he was right—maybe I did like him a little too much as a villain.

I walked toward Kaden, and Jack nudged him. Kaden turned around and straightened, heat going through his eyes as he gave me a slow once-over. I blushed as I remembered him doing that many other times, usually when he'd been about to rip my clothes off with his claws.

Jack and the other shifters melted into the crowd to give us some privacy, leaving us with our own little secluded area of the clearing. I smiled at Kaden, and took my hand from behind my back, presenting him with a gift. I had struggled with the decision of whether or not to bring Kaden's present with me tonight, but figured it would be best to give it to him in public. If I waited, I wasn't sure I'd give it to him at all.

He frowned down at the bag and took it from me. "What's this?"

"Your birthday present."

Kaden took the book out of the bag and stared at it for a long moment. I'd agonized over what to get him for the longest time. Nothing seemed to fit until I found this book. Astronomy was Kaden's passion, the one thing he allowed himself to have that wasn't conducive to being an alpha. It was also one of the only things that linked him to his parents. The book of astronomy seemed to be the most thoughtful thing I could give him, an acknowledgment and an apology all in one.

"This is..." he trailed off and shook his head. I waited for him to say something else, but after a few moments of silence Kaden simply said, "Thank you."

Before I could respond, he pulled me in and kissed me. This was nothing like the garden, but was all soft, with no bite. There was still passion though, and I swooned into it, letting my eyes close and my body melt against his. *This is where you belong,* I thought. A key fitting into a perfect lock.

I drew back. "I don't want to be away from you any longer."

"It's about time you realized that," Kaden muttered, then pulled me close to kiss me again, deeper this time.

Suddenly, a shout cut through the festivities. I turned around to see what was going on and watched as the crowd parted to let through a harried-looking Clayton. He pushed his way through the last of the crowd and came to stand in front of Kaden. He was breathing hard and smelled of fear. I was instantly on high alert, whatever I'd been about to say to Kaden forgotten instantly in the face of danger.

"What is it?" Kaden asked, straightening up and going instantly into alpha mode. Clayton shook his head.

"Another package arrived," he said. "I'm sorry to interrupt, but I thought you'd want to know."

Kaden swore under his breath. "Where?"

"It's back at the hotel." Clayton swallowed. "It's...a big one."

"Show me."

The assembled crowd behind us began murmuring. The news was passed along, and the whispers became a discontented grumble. The festive mood was instantly gone, the poppy song a mockery more than anything else now. Kaden ordered everyone to carry on as we followed Clayton out of the clearing, but I had a feeling the celebration was already over.

CHAPTER TWENTY-EIGHT

BACK AT THE HOTEL, I didn't want to enter the room where the box was being held. Ethan stood outside of it, the door closed, his face resigned.

"You don't need to look at it," he told Kaden.

"I do." Kaden gestured for Ethan to step aside. "I have to know."

I supposed I had to know too, even though the dread made my footsteps slow as we stepped inside the room. The intense smell of death and decay hit me instantly, making me gag. The box was much bigger than any of the previous ones had been, and it reeked so badly I wanted to turn on my heel and run out of the room.

When Kaden touched the box, it fell open, as if it could barely contain the horrors inside of it. A dozen heads rolled out, and I covered my mouth to stop myself from throwing up at the sight. Old, young, and everything in between, all dead now. I wasn't sure, but I suspected it was every Ophiuchus member who'd left with Tanner. All our attempts to rescue them had been for nothing.

Kaden's face was grim as he picked out a card from the box and read out loud, "'You've ignored our warnings for far too long. Return Jordan now, or every single member of your pack will face the same fate.'"

"I'm sorry," Ethan said.

"Sorry?" Kaden trembled with rage, his fists clenching at his side. "If you'd let me go up against the Leos months ago when this started we wouldn't be in this position now!"

Ethan inclined his head but didn't have an answer to that.

"Fuck this," Kaden said, throwing the card down. "I'm done with this shit. It's time we sent them Jordan's head back in a box."

"No!" I called out, but it was too late, and Kaden was already gone.

I remembered all too well the last time he'd gone to Jordan and left him barely alive. Only my pleas had kept him from finishing the job, and Kaden hadn't been nearly as mad then. I clenched my jaw and considered my options. I'd only just tentatively reestablished the peace between us, and I knew that it wouldn't take much to shatter it. But I had to keep Jordan safe. He was family—and I still didn't know what would happen to the mate bond if he was killed.

I cast Ethan and Clayton a panicked look and then teleported into Jordan's room. It had been weeks since I'd seen him, and his hair had grown long and rugged, his face resigned as he looked over at me. Chains circled his wrists and ankles, tying him to the wall—a new addition I'd never have approved of. How long had we kept him in captivity now? Far longer than he'd once kept me.

"Ayla," he drawled from his spot on the bed. "Finally decided to come visit me again?"

"Get up," I said. "Kaden is coming and—"

Before I could finish my sentence, Kaden threw the door open. It thudded into the wall, cracking from the impact, as my alpha stormed inside. He picked Jordan up with both his hands and tossed him across the room.

Jordan shook himself but managed to stand slowly, rising to his full height. He grinned at Kaden, his eyes wild. "It's about time we fought again."

"For once we're on the same page," Kaden snarled back.

Jordan looked Kaden dead in the eye as he flexed his arms, breaking the chains around his wrists easily. He broke the chains around his ankles next, as if they were made of paper instead of metal, and faced Kaden down like a wild animal who'd finally broken free of his cage.

Shit. Was Jordan really that strong? If so, he'd been able to get free this whole time, but he hadn't. Why?

Before I could contemplate the meaning of that, Kaden lunged at Jordan, and the two alphas collided. Jordan smacked back into the wall, but then flipped Kaden over onto it, pummeling him into the stone.

The two shifters snarled and snapped at each other, fighting for dominance. I didn't think I'd ever seen Kaden act so brutal, so utterly unhinged. There was nothing human in the way he was fighting. This was pure shifter, and one aiming to kill. But Jordan was no better.

"Stop!" I shouted. Neither of them listened to me. I stepped closer as Kaden pushed Jordan into the kitchenette area. It toppled, the countertops breaking, the contents of the bar spilling from the wall. I flinched at the loud sound, as Kaden tried to bite down on Jordan's arm, who in turn rammed Kaden's head so hard into the wall it made a dull thud. I winced. If either of them came out alive after this, I'd be surprised.

"Please," I begged. "This isn't the answer! Have you ever stopped to think that this is exactly what the Sun Witches want?"

Still, they didn't listen. Jordan opened his mouth to let out a Leo roar, but Kaden punched him in the face, stopping the sound before we all began to flee in terror. They both grappled on the floor after that, somewhere between human and wolf, claws and fangs snapping at each other. It would only be a matter of time before someone got seriously injured. And then, death.

I couldn't stand to see either of them die. I needed to make a decision fast, but I wasn't strong enough to physically make them stop. Not with shifter might, anyway. But I had other gifts.

I gathered moonlight inside me and then unleashed it at the men, blasting them away from each other and halfway across the room. They fell back and I waited to see what would happen as they lay on the ground, panting and bleeding. Neither of them seemed interested in stopping. Jordan groaned and started pushing himself to his feet. Kaden got there first and lunged toward Jordan.

I didn't think, I just acted. There was no way that Kaden wasn't going to take advantage of Jordan being vulnerable. I threw myself in front of Jordan, arms held wide. Kaden stopped, his clawed hand outstretched. His face was drawn into a terrible snarl, so deep and twisted that I hardly recognized him—but I knew he wouldn't hurt me.

"Move," he spat at me. "I don't care if he's your brother. I'm going to rip his fucking head off and send it back to his pack in a nice little box."

"No," I said, shaking my head furiously. "We need to talk this out."

"You've tried that," Kaden said. "It didn't work. Now it's time for you to choose."

I blinked at him. "What?"

"*Choose.*" Kaden snarled at me, lips drawing back further. "Me or him. You can't play both sides forever, not when we're at war with each other."

"Please don't make me choose," I said, my heart breaking in two. "I love you, but Jordan is my brother, and no matter how much I hate it, the mate bond still hums between us. I can't let you kill him."

"It's okay, Ayla," Jordan said, sounding resigned again. "We all know who you're going to choose in the end. Let's just get it over with."

"Shut up," I told him. Did he really think I would stand by and let Kaden kill him?

"He's right, we both know what you're going to choose. And if you don't..."

"This is an impossible choice." I trailed off and searched Kaden's face for anything familiar. I didn't see a spark of sympathy. "This isn't you, Kaden. Please, just stop and listen to me for a minute."

"Choose!" Kaden roared.

I sobbed, the tears already flowing down my cheeks as my body caught up to my mind and pushed the shock out of the way. I couldn't believe it, but Kaden was right here in front of me, his claws extended toward Jordan, screaming at me to choose. I knew what I had to do...but I wasn't sure if I could do it.

"I won't let you kill Jordan."

"You've made your choice then." Kaden sounded hollow, as if every emotion had suddenly been cut out from him. Quicker than I could have thought to stop him, Kaden grabbed me and hauled me away from Jordan. I dug my heels in, expecting Kaden to toss me aside and try to attack Jordan again, but instead, he shoved me against a wall.

Kaden put his hand on my upper arm and closed his eyes. It took me a moment to realize that he was holding me right over my Ophiuchus pack symbol. A strange tingling sensation ran through my arm that quickly became pain. I sucked in a deep breath, and Kaden's eyes opened and met mine. There was nothing of the man I knew in them. He looked like someone else entirely, a stranger wearing my Kaden's skin. I sucked in a deep breath and gritted my teeth against the pain.

When he removed his hand, my skin was bare. I looked down at it in shock. The Ophiuchus pack symbol was just...gone. I shuddered, wondering what the hell Kaden thought he was doing, but it didn't take long for me to find out.

"I banish you from the Ophiuchus pack, Ayla Beros," Kaden said in a cold voice. "Take Jordan with you and leave. Immediately."

"Kaden, no," I whispered. I sagged against the wall, everything spinning around me. I could feel the lack of power in my limbs, the way my body ached around an empty space where the energy of the Ophiuchus pack should reside.

"Ayla?" Jordan asked, stepping toward me, his voice laced with concern. Kaden shot him a hard look, and I wondered if he would attack again.

I had no time to mourn. I pushed myself off the wall and launched myself at Jordan, teleporting us to my hotel room the second I grabbed his arm. He stumbled back, blinking at me as I let go of him, and I vaguely realized he'd never been conscious when I'd used that power on him before. I turned away before he could say anything and started gathering things from my room.

Here I am again, I thought bitterly as I decided what to take and what to leave. *Having to leave everything behind.*

"Are you sure this is the right decision?" Jordan asked as I stuffed some money and toiletries into my bag, along with my camera, the one Kaden had bought me. "We both know I'm not worth this."

"Shut up," I said again. I wasn't sure if he was worth it either, but I also knew I'd never forgive Kaden if he killed my brother. I had to stop him from doing it, not just to save Jordan, but to save the man I loved.

There was a frantic knock on my door, light and airy. I let out a breath. Not Kaden—he would never knock so softly. I strode over to open the door to a worried Larkin.

She wrung her hands together looking at me, and then at Jordan. "What's going on? I felt you use a lot of magic."

"I'm leaving with Jordan," I said, motioning to him over my shoulder. I didn't tell Larkin that I'd been expelled from the pack. It still didn't feel real. Maybe this was all a bad dream and I'd wake up in Kaden's arms tomorrow.

Larkin frowned and studied me closely. She wasn't stupid, and she could feel the tension zinging in the air. There was clearly more going on than I was letting her in on, but she didn't ask. "I want to come with you."

I shook my head. "You need to stay here and help the other packs prepare to face the Sun Witches."

Larkin chewed her lip, and then let out a sigh. "You're annoying when you're right."

I gave her a small smile, wishing that I could give her more. But my whole world was falling apart around me, and I didn't even begin to know what I could do to stop it. "Please take care of everyone here for me."

Larkin launched herself into my arms, and we hugged each other tightly. She knew this was a bad goodbye, even if she didn't have all the facts.

"Hey, it's okay," I said. "This isn't the end. I'll see you at the Convergence, okay?"

Larkin stepped back and nodded. She opened her mouth to say something else, but the sound of footsteps in the hall cut us both off.

"Ayla!" Kaden yelled, making my blood run cold.

Shit. Whatever he wanted now, it couldn't be good. I zipped up my bag and slung it over my shoulder, then grabbed Jordan's arm again. With my free hand, I raised a hand in farewell to Larkin, praying I would see her again soon.

Then I teleported us away, not knowing where we would possibly be safe.

CHAPTER TWENTY-NINE

WHEN THE WORLD shifted and reformed, I realized I'd teleported us to the Ophiuchus pack lands, right in front of Kaden's house. It was the last place Kaden would expect me to go, and also the last place he would check. It was also the place I'd instinctively gone to when I'd reached for safety. For home.

Jordan stepped away from me and held his hands up. "That had better be the last time you teleport me today."

I rolled my eyes and gazed around us. The Ophiuchus pack lands were beautiful, the already idyllic scenery turned into a winter wonderland at this time of year. But then a heavy sadness settled over me. This wasn't my home anymore, no matter how much it felt like that.

I wasn't Ophiuchus pack anymore.

I closed my eyes against the onslaught of memories tied to this place. There were too many of them, all including Kaden. I wouldn't be able to stay here for very long, because

I'd just break down. I needed to get out of here before that happened, but I didn't know where we could possibly go that would be safe. From the moment I'd left, I'd marked us as enemies of the Zodiac Wolves—or at least, the ones who followed under Kaden.

I reached down and touched my arm. I'd grown so used to the Ophiuchus pack symbol there. It had been an honor to receive it, especially after I'd grown up unworthy of the Cancer pack mark, and now it was gone. Tears sprung up in my eyes, and I was helpless to hold them back. I drew in a breath, and it sounded like a sob. The emotions welled up, too hard for me to push down any longer. They fought against my restraint and then broke free.

I pressed a hand against my mouth, but it didn't do any good. The sounds leaked through anyway, and the tears kept coming. A panic so intense, I could hardly stand it rose up in me, roaring through me like a fire.

I was packless again. Rejected by the man I loved. I took a staggering step back, needing something to lean against and finding nothing. How could Kaden have made me choose? It was an impossible choice, but I couldn't let Jordan die. Gods, what had I done? Now I had no home, no one to protect me, no one to call *pack*. And there was nothing I could do to change it.

A vicious part of my brain whispered that I'd made the wrong choice. I should have picked Kaden—at least then I would have a home still. I looked over at Jordan and instantly dismissed the thought. *How the hell was I supposed to choose?* I screamed silently.

Jordan sat down in the snow, his head turned away as I started hyperventilating. It wasn't the privacy I needed, but at least it provided the illusion of it.

I took a deep, shuddering breath in and reached up to wipe the tears off of my face. "Why didn't you escape all this time?" My voice was bitter and angry, but if Jordan was affected by any of that, he didn't show it. "I know you could have, and maybe then we would have avoided all of this."

It was easy to blame him, to turn it back around on him, when I was angry at myself for making a choice, or for not insisting that Kaden calmed down and talked this through with me like a proper adult.

Jordan stiffened, and slowly he turned to look at me. "You're a smart girl," he said. "Figure it out yourself."

I drew in a few more deep breaths, mind spinning as I thought back over the last few months. "You didn't want to escape. Did you?" But why would Jordan be so eager to be in enemy territory, where the threat of death was imminent?

Jordan didn't answer, which meant I was right. I went to sit beside him in the snow as the last of the raging inferno inside of me died. I'd have time to grieve later, but right now I needed to figure out the next step in our plan. *Ours.* It was weird to think of Jordan and I having a common goal, but he really was everything I had right now. I'd made my choice, and here were the consequences of my actions, sitting beside me. It would be easy to scream at Jordan, to place all of the blame on him, but I closed my eyes and reigned in my anger. It was all really directed toward myself and Kaden, and taking it out on Jordan wouldn't get me anywhere.

"Why didn't you want to escape?" I asked after a few moments, calmer this time.

Jordan looked over at me again. "When it came out that Harrison was my father, I was challenged daily for the role of alpha. I beat them all, but it made me start questioning whether or not I really should be the alpha. After you kidnapped me, I wasn't sure what would happen when I returned to the Leos. For all I knew, the beta had taken over, and he was nearly as bad as Dixon. I suspected they'd kill me on sight. And maybe, with my Cancer blood, I didn't deserve to be alpha anyway."

My mouth fell open at his admission. Where was the cocky, arrogant Jordan I knew so well? But I also sensed he wasn't telling me everything "That's all well and good," I said. "But you could have hidden out anywhere, or stepped down as alpha. There was another reason you didn't escape, did you?"

Jordan looked away from me, a muscle twitching in his jaw.

I tried again. "You stayed for me, didn't you?"

I thought he'd deny it, or just not say anything at all. "Fine," Jordan spat out. "It was nice to have a sister for once in my life, even if you are annoying as fuck." He glanced over at me with a scowl. "But don't think this means for a second that I care about you."

I smirked at him. "Too late. I already know you care."

He rolled his eyes and turned away again, but I'd seen something in his eyes, something that proved what I'd long suspected—that Jordan really did have a heart deep down in there somewhere, far beneath that arrogant smirk.

"I'm not sure where to go next," I said, after a few minutes of silence.

"Yeah, I can't imagine Kaden would like me sleeping in his house somehow," Jordan said with a dark chuckle.

"No, he definitely wouldn't, and I have a feeling I wouldn't be welcome anymore either." I shook my head, clearing those thoughts. Surely there was some way to mend what was between us. Surely I could fix this still. But right now I couldn't think about any of that until we had a safe place to stay.

I narrowed my eyes and looked out at the glittering forest as I considered my options. I could go to Wesley and seek shelter with the Cancer pack, but I had a feeling they wouldn't take kindly to me bringing Jordan there. Not to mention, I doubted Wesley would be able to forgive Jordan for his part in our parents' deaths, even if we were all technically blood related. And could I really trust Jordan with the secret location where the Cancer pack was hiding from the Leos? I wasn't sure.

I also considered taking Jordan with me to Lunatera, but again, I couldn't trust him not to reveal information about the place to the Sun Witches. Besides, I didn't truly understand how time worked there.

I wracked my brain, trying to think of somewhere else to go. "The Convergence is a little over a week away. We just need somewhere safe to stay until then."

Jordan looked over at me, his blue eyes wide and shocked. "There's no way you're going to the Convergence."

"Of course I'm going," I said, drawing myself up straight. "I might be packless now, but I'm still going to fight the Sun Witches. That's what I set out to do, and I won't rest until they're defeated. With or without the help of any of the other packs. Or you, for that matter."

"Just let it go and hide until it's over," he warned. "Stay out of it. For your safety."

I remembered what he'd said about the Sun Witches... and what he hadn't said. If they were controlling people's minds, including his own, that was even more reason for me to go to the Convergence. I had to protect the people I cared about who would be there—including Kaden. I still loved him, no matter what had happened.

"I can't," I said. "I'm not going to let my friends and family face this threat alone."

Jordan huffed out an exasperated breath. "Fine, but if you're going then I'm going with you."

I was oddly relieved to hear this. It was nice to have him on my side for whatever came next, even though I didn't fully understand his motivations.

"We can go back to the Leo village," Jordan said suddenly. "It's abandoned, right? But all my stuff will still be there, and we can stay there until it's time to go to the Convergence."

I hesitated, but couldn't think of anywhere else to go. "Do you know where the Leos are now?"

"No, I really don't. I haven't been in contact with my pack since you captured me."

"Damn."

"Maybe I'll find something while we're there, something Kaden missed." Jordan shrugged. "Either way, we should be safe there as long as they don't come back."

"If they do, I suppose we can just teleport away again." I stood up and brushed snow off my hands and my butt. "Let's go then."

Jordan stood a lot slower, narrowing his eyes. "I guess I don't have much of a choice, do I?"

I smiled grimly at him. "Not really, no."

In a flash, we were back in the Leo village, which looked exactly the same as it had last time I'd been here—still empty, except for a couple tumbleweeds rolling through town. Oh, and the destroyed gazebo of course.

Jordan's eyebrows lifted at the sight. "Kaden, I assume?"

"Yep."

"Can't say I blame him. I almost burned the place down myself after that night."

I gave him a sharp look, realizing once again how different Jordan was from the man I'd thought he was.

"You should stay with me," Jordan said, as he started walking. "Safer that way. Don't worry, I have a huge house. We don't even need to see each other if we don't want to."

"Okay," I said, relieved I wouldn't be stuck in that prison-turned-house I'd shared with Mira. Although I might have some clothes there, at least, along with that nice shampoo they'd gotten me. I'd have to take a little detour there later, once I'd had a chance to rest.

True to his word, Jordan's house was massive, the kind of grand mansion you'd expect the Leo alpha to own. There was even a fountain outside, along with lush green grass that must cost a fortune to water in this climate. Like the other buildings, it was done in a Southwestern style, but it was the biggest one I'd seen yet, with balconies that looked over the entire village.

"This was my father's—Dixon's—house," Jordan said, as we approached. "I should probably burn it down too, but my mom likes it."

"What happened to your mom after that night?" I asked.

"She wasn't the most popular woman, as you might guess." He reached down and grabbed a key from under the mat. "I have no idea where she is now though. Nor my brother, for that matter."

Griffin, I remembered, my brain supplying the name of Jordan's little brother, who was also my half-brother. I wanted to meet him someday.

As we stepped inside the huge entryway with big pillars and pale marble floors, Jordan staggered a little and almost tripped. I caught him with my arm, and when my hand came away bloody, I realized he was much worse off than I'd realized.

"Are you badly hurt?" I asked, trying to examine him, but then my heart sank. Even if he was, there was nothing I could do about it anymore. I no longer had Ophiuchus healing powers.

"I'm fine," he said, feebly pushing me away.

"Come on," I said, wrapping an arm around him to help him inside. "You need to rest up." I also wanted time to sit down and think about everything that happened, but I had to get Jordan to bed first. I needed to remain strong, just for this time.

He directed me to the many guest rooms, telling me I could have my choice of them, and then we made it to his room. The place looked like such a typical Leo bachelor pad that I rolled my eyes, with black sheets and gold everything. The only thing that stood out was a raggedy little lion that I guessed had belonged to him as a kid, along with a collage of him and his brother when they were younger, riding dirt bikes out in the desert. I studied their huge toothy smiles for a moment, before Jordan shooed me out of his room, assuring me he was totally fine.

I took the biggest guest room in the house, because why not? The bed had hunter-green sheets that made me think of the Ophiuchus forest and a little seating area with a couple of old books and some fake flowers on the table. I imagined Debra in here setting it up and wondered where she was now, and if she was worried about her oldest son.

Well, I'd done my best to keep him safe, even though it had cost me everything I loved. I only prayed I hadn't made the wrong choice.

CHAPTER THIRTY

IN THE MORNING, I went to the house where I'd been held prisoner in the Leo village and recovered everything I wanted from the place. Jordan and I raided as much food as we could find in the village, filling the freezer and pantry with things that had been left behind by the rest of the pack. Then we settled in to wait.

There wasn't much to do, and we found ourselves playing board games or watching TV to pass the time. I wanted to wallow, but that wasn't an option. I wondered how the Ophiuchus pack and our allies were doing as they prepared for the Convergence, and felt a pang of longing, wishing I was back in Toronto instead of here with Jordan.

After a few days, we got an unexpected visitor: my mother.

"What are you doing here?" I asked as I opened the door for her. When a knock had sounded on the door, Jordan and I had both launched into defensive positions, ready to defend against anything and anyone. The last person I'd expected to see on the other side of the door was my mother. "How did you find me?"

"That tattoo on your finger," she said, as she breezed into the mansion. "It allows me to find you whenever I need to. Did you really think I would miss your birthday?"

I stared at her. Surely she remembered the date of my real birthday—or was she just as confused by time in this world as I was in Lunatera? "My birthday is in March."

She blinked at me. "No, it's not. Who told you that? Harrison?" She blew out a breath and shook her head. "That fool. No, your actual birthday is December sixteenth."

Another thing he lied to me about. And for what purpose? Just to be horrible to me?

But then shock rolled through me, along with a pang in my chest. If my birthday was today, that would mean I was really and truly an Ophiuchus. The thought only brought back the sadness and made it even more intense. I bit my lip to hold back tears and forced a smile. "I had no idea, but I'm glad you're here."

She wrapped her arms around me and I closed my eyes tight against the sting of tears and just let her hold me for a moment, before she pulled back. She was looking over my shoulder at Jordan, and flashed him a smile.

"Hello," she said, then smiled at me again. "Is this Kaden? I'm so excited to meet him finally."

Heat filled my cheeks, and I exchanged a wary glance with Jordan. "No, this is my brother. Jordan."

Celeste opened and closed her mouth a few times, obviously shocked by this knowledge. "Are the two of you still mates?"

"Unfortunately, yes. We tried to break the mate bond, but it didn't work. We need a full Sun Witch, apparently. But at least Larkin was able to mute the bond, for the time being, so neither of us really feel it."

"I see." She studied Jordan for a few seconds. "You have Harrison's eyes," she pronounced eventually. "For better or for worse."

Jordan looked down, clearly uncomfortable with this statement. The look on his face was grim, but he didn't try to refute it.

Celeste shook her head and looked back at me. "How is Larkin doing? Is she settling into the human world well? I think about her every day."

"Yes, she's fine. She found a place in the pack very quickly as a teacher, something I'm sure you're not surprised about. She's been training the shifters with Moon Witch blood to fight, and is staying with the Ophiuchus pack." I paused and then added, "Don't worry. Larkin is more than able to take care of herself, she knows what she's doing."

"But what are you doing here? In this empty town?"

"It's a long story," I said. "Maybe we should discuss it over some tea."

"I'd like that," Celeste said.

The two of us sat down in the kitchen and I told her everything that had happened. It felt good to talk it out, and my mother listened without judgment to the entire story. Jordan stayed away the entire time, giving us some privacy.

When I was done, she opened her arms to me once more, and I let her fold me into a hug. The first one had been brief out of necessity, but this time she let me stay as long as I wanted.

"I'm sorry you had to go through that," she said. "You're always welcome in Lunatera, you know. We can keep you safe there. Even Jordan can come if he wants, as long as he doesn't cause any trouble."

I drew back from her embrace and gave her a weak smile. The offer had never been so tempting, but I couldn't take her up on it. "I know, and I'm grateful to you for the offer. But I'm a shifter, and so is Jordan, and we can't turn our backs on the problems with the Zodiac Wolves. They're still our family even if neither of us really has a pack right now."

Celeste smiled sadly. "I thought you'd say that, but I had to try and convince you anyway. You are my daughter, after all. I only want to see you safe and happy."

"I know," I said. "Thank you."

"On that note, I think it's time I gave you your birthday present." She removed a small box, no bigger than the palm of her hand, from inside a hidden pocket in her dark purple dress. "If you really are going to the Convergence, then it might be able to help you in your fight against the Sun Witches."

I opened the package carefully and discovered a small pendant, about the size of my thumb—a big chunk of moonstone set into silver. It was in the shape of the moon, and I tilted it in the light, admiring the play of iridescent colors, feeling the power leaking off of it. "What is this?" I asked. "It's gorgeous."

"It's imbued with the power of the moon," Celeste said. "I've been focusing on making it ever since you left. It holds as much power as I could physically fit into it. I almost went with a larger necklace, but it would have been too heavy."

"Thank you," I said, curling my hands around the pendant.

Celeste put her own hands over mine and smiled at me. "Wear it always. It will help protect you against the worst of the magic from the Sun Witches. I wish that I could go with you in person, but this is the next best thing I could think of."

I hugged her tight, closing my eyes. She really was doing her best to make up for lost time, and I couldn't fault her for that. She was doing everything she could to help, even if it wasn't to the extent that I wanted.

Celeste drew back and put her hands on my shoulders. "I know I have a lot to make up for," she said, echoing my thoughts. "I missed all of your birthdays up until now, and nothing pains me more. But now that we've been reunited, I'm going to spend the rest of my life making up for them. I hope that I can be there for all of your future birthdays."

"Thank you," I said around the lump in my throat as I slipped the chain over my head. The pendant rested between my breasts, winking in the light. It felt right, like it had been there all along, and I'd just been missing it. The power settled around me, filling in the space that the Ophiuchus pack's power had left. It wasn't quite the same, but I took a deep shuddering breath in and let it gentle the raging grief inside of me.

She finished the rest of her tea and stood. "I should get back, and leave you to your preparations. I'll be praying to Selene for you." She touched my cheek briefly and then strolled back into the entryway, where Jordan was passing through on his way upstairs. She rested her gaze on him but didn't give him a smile. "You take good care of Ayla for me," she said. "As a brother, and as a friend."

Was that what we were? Friends? We certainly weren't enemies anymore, but I wasn't sure what we had become either.

"I will," Jordan said.

She patted my cheeks with love in her eyes. "Happy birthday, my sweet girl. I hope to see you again soon."

Celeste raised her hands and created a portal, spinning pure moonlight into a doorway, then stepped inside it and vanished.

"Birthday?" Jordan asked, arching an eyebrow.

"I was just as surprised as you are," I said, fingering the pendant now resting on my chest. "Come on, let's finish our game of Clue."

"Why? We both know I'm going to win."

Jordan and I settled back around the living room, and I hated to admit it, but he was probably right. He had an annoying habit of winning most of the games we played.

I watched him as he took his next turn, and felt another vivid sense of loss. What would have happened, if we'd been raised together? Without the pack feuds, without the Sun

Witches interference? I could have had two brothers, not just one.

"What are you thinking about?" I asked when Jordan seemed to be taking an especially long time making his move.

He sat back and gave me a long look, before finally answering. "My entire life, I was taught that the Moon Witches were evil, along with the Ophiuchus pack. Even the Cancer pack, for that matter. But now you've introduced me to all of them, and I'm not sure what I believe anymore."

"I know how that feels, believe me. I went through the same thing at first. Contrary to popular belief, my first months spent with the Ophiuchus pack weren't all sunshine and rainbows. If you need anyone to talk to, I'm here for you."

"Yeah, sure, I'll definitely be taking you up on that offer," he said in a way that let me know that he definitely *wouldn't*.

I rolled my eyes at him and jabbed him in the ribs, a bit harder than I'd meant to.

"Hey now, I'm still recovering," Jordan said. "You're going to be mean to your own brother while he's wounded?"

"Oh please. I haven't forgotten all the times you said you were going to kill me. I think a little payback is what you deserve, don't you?"

Jordan shook his head, but he was grinning. "I might still kill you yet. At the very least, I'm going to beat your ass at this game."

"Bring it on."

He did beat me, fair and square, and I immediately

called for a rematch. *What would our lives have been like if we'd been siblings instead of enemies, with fathers who had cared for us?* It was hard not to imagine how much better life would have been, even if it was useless to think about these kinds of things in the face of everything we were still dealing with. It didn't do me any good to think about what could have been, but it didn't stop me from aching for a childhood in which we could easily rib each other like this.

"You know," Jordan said, as we packed up the game later. "You don't need to be packless. I could make you a member of the Leo pack right now."

It was a nice offer to make, even if the thought of being a Leo made my stomach turn. But then I realized Wesley could just as easily make me a part of the Cancer pack once again. I had bad memories of both of those packs, but I knew in my heart they weren't where I belonged.

"Thank you for your offer, but I don't think I can take you up on it," I said. "In my heart, I'm still an Ophiuchus, no matter what happened with Kaden. It's the only place I've ever felt at home."

Jordan shook his head, his mouth twisting in disgust. "How can you still be on the Ophiuchus pack's side, after Kaden treated you like that?"

"I'm not on the Ophiuchus pack's side. I'm still on the side that's against the Sun Witches, and that just happens to be the Ophiuchus pack's side right now." I frowned at him. "Whose side are *you* on?"

"I'm on my own side," Jordan said in a lazy drawl. "Same as always."

I blew out a frustrated breath. This felt a lot like when I'd interrogated him, when he'd given me the same non-answers. "How could you give your support to the Sun Witches when you knew everything that was going on with them?"

"It's not that easy, Ayla," Jordan said, and his voice was tight. "There are things you don't understand..."

"Okay, so explain it to me," I said and crossed my arms. There was clearly something more going on here, and I was sick of dealing with Jordan hedging around it. I could understand why he'd been hesitant to share this with me while he was still a captive, worried that I'd run back to Kaden and tell him everything, but there was no reason for him to continue with this secrecy. He knew that all I wanted was to go up against the Sun Witches, so why did he continue to hold information back from me? If he knew something that would help us take down the Sun Witches, why wouldn't he tell me?

Jordan frowned and opened his mouth, as if he wanted to say more. After a moment, he let out a sigh and ducked his head. "I can't say."

"You can't say?" I stood up, anger washing through me. "I've done *everything*, risked everything for you, and you won't tell me a simple thing like this?" I threw my hands up in the air. "You are completely unbelievable, Jordan," I snapped, and walked out of the room before he could spout more nonsense about how he couldn't tell me or that I wouldn't understand.

I was sick of playing these games with him.

CHAPTER THIRTY-ONE

WE LEFT Arizona in one of Jordan's cars two days later, knowing it would take some time to get to the location of the Convergence. This equinox was being held in the California mountains in the northern part of the state, which was quite a long drive from the Leo pack lands. We made lots of stops to rest and traded off driving, though things were still a bit tense between us ever since our argument, and made it there in three days with just a few hours to spare before the Convergence was set to begin.

Jordan parked miles away from where everyone else was meant to park, knowing stealth would be our ally here since neither side would be happy to see us. We hiked the rest of the way in wolf form, wearing our clothes and shoes in bags tied to our backs. I breathed in the intoxicating scents of the forest, happy to be back in one after all my time in Toronto and then in Arizona. Even though there was snow on the ground, the sun was bright, the sky was clear, and the forest smelled like *life*.

We stopped in a copse of trees a little ways away from where the main event would take place, facing the large clearing while remaining downwind, which was perfect if we wanted to make a surprise entrance. This Convergence looked wildly different from the last one. There were no festivities, no happy chatter of gathered packs catching up after a couple of seasons apart. It was quiet, without any interaction between the packs that looked like anything beyond curt nods and hasty words exchanged.

All of the enemy packs were already gathered—Leo, Scorpio, Taurus, and Aries. They had brought a lot of warriors, but I didn't see any kids among them this time. They must have hidden them away, knowing that this could turn into a war zone at any moment. After all of Kaden's raids over the last few weeks, they must know that the other Zodiac Wolves were planning to make their stand today.

"Look." Jordan pointed at something, and I followed his finger to a Leo pack member. "That's Austin Bates, the Leo beta. It looks like he's acting as alpha now."

"I'm assuming that's bad for us."

"Bates served under my father, and he's almost as cruel as Dixon was. I was hoping someone would challenge him for the position, but so far, no one has dared."

Behind the Leos, I saw a group of Sun Witches, and Evanora stood in the center of them holding a big golden staff that winked in the light, with a gaudy sculpture of a sun on top of it. Her daughter, Roxandra, stood next to her, looking proud and regal in red robes. I thought about the last Convergence, how I'd always wanted to get a closer look at the Sun Witches. Now I wanted nothing more than to take them all down.

As we settled into position, I looked over at Jordan and remembered the last time we'd been in a similar setting at the summer equinox, when he'd rejected me and watched his pack kill my family, and then hunted me down to finish the job of taking out every last one of my family members.

I could punch him, I thought. What had I been thinking? Friends? We were hardly even allies. But at the same time, things had significantly changed since that other Convergence six months ago, and I couldn't see Jordan as my enemy anymore either. But would he stand up to the Sun Witches with me, when the time came? That remained to be seen.

Jordan caught me staring at him and frowned. "What are you planning?"

"I'm going to use my moon magic to defend my friends and family as best I can. And you?"

"I'm just here to make sure you don't do anything stupid and get yourself killed," he said grudgingly.

There was a commotion from behind us, and Jordan and I quickly turned around to see who it was. Hundreds of shifters were approaching, and at the front of them was Kaden. My heart clenched so hard, I was fairly certain that someone was trying to rip it out.

I barely recognized the man I loved. Kaden looked like a hardened man, far older than his years, who had seen too much and gone through too many battles for his age. He was shirtless, standing tall and proud, flanked by Ethan and Wesley. My heart ached to go meet him, to stand beside him and take his hand in mine. We should be together, heading toward the battlefield as mates, willing to fight and die together.

I shook the thought away and took stock of the others who had come with him. Warriors from all of the allied clans walked behind Kaden and the other alphas, and I recognized many of them from the hotel. Stella and Clayton walked close with Kaden, and when I caught sight of Larkin, something eased in my chest. She looked so small and young among all the other shifters there, but I knew she would fight just as hard as any one of them today.

I spotted others I recognized too, including Harper, Dane, and Jack, and was relieved to see Mira and her mate weren't among the warriors here today. With only a couple months before Mira was due, I hoped they were back in Pisces lands getting some much-needed rest.

The overwhelming urge to join my pack washed through me as they approached. I'd spent my whole life being an outsider, and I was done with it. They were my home, my family, and they *needed* me. It didn't matter that I'd been kicked out of the pack because they were still my people. No matter what happened, they always would be my pack.

I couldn't bring myself to look away as they filtered through the forest and gathered in the clearing. Kaden said something in a low voice, and all of the alphas split up, fanning out to face the Sun Witches and enemy packs.

"Hey, do you think—" I turned to face Jordan, but he wasn't there. Something lurched through my gut, unpleasant and sudden. My body already realized what my mind was still struggling to catch up to. "Jordan?" I whispered, but there was no answer. I craned my neck to peer through the scrub as dread made my heart race faster.

Back at the Convergence, Evanora's eyes had started glowing, along with the staff in her hands. Then I caught sight of Jordan walking right up to her as if he'd never left her side. As if he'd been on her side this entire time.

"No..." Something twisted and broke deep inside me at his betrayal, even though I should have seen it coming. Kaden had been right all along. Jordan had never been on my side, and he'd never planned to help me, despite what he'd said to me. I should have never trusted him, brother or not. Fuck, I was such a damn fool.

A noise rustled behind me, raising my hackles, and then a hand closed around my shoulder, pulling me back. I spun around to face my attacker and then froze.

It was Kaden.

CHAPTER THIRTY-TWO

I BRACED MYSELF FOR A FIGHT, but Kaden yanked me closer, pulling me against his chest. His hands were gentle as they ran along my shoulders and arms. "Ayla," he said, and it sounded like he was relieved. I gasped, but before I could ask him what the hell he was playing at, he leaned down and captured my lips.

I froze, wondering if this was some sort of new attack, but Kaden just kissed me harder. The sounds of the shifters around us faded to nothing as Kaden slid his hands around my waist and pulled me even closer. I melted against him, my body so used to this that my mind didn't have time to catch up and warn me not to let him do this.

"Forgive me, Ayla," he said, pressing his forehead against mine. "I should have never made you choose, and never should have kicked you out of the pack. I'm sorry."

I could hardly believe my ears. Was Kaden...apologizing?

He kept talking, while I tried to find my voice to answer him. "I lost my temper that night, but as soon as I realized what I'd done, I regretted it. I went after you and tried to make it right, but you were already gone."

Was that what happened when he'd come to my hotel room, calling for me right before I teleported us away? I'd been so terrified for myself and for Jordan, I hadn't even stopped to consider he might be coming to apologize. I wasn't sure I could accept Kaden's apology so easily either. The man would have to do a lot of groveling to get me to take him back—but we would deal with that later. Right now we had more immediate problems.

"It's me who should be apologizing," I said, swallowing hard. "You were right. Jordan betrayed me." I jerked my head toward where Jordan stood beside Evanora, like her perfect little Leo pet. I'd sacrificed everything for him, and this was how I'd been repaid for it. "He's chosen his side, and it's with the Sun Witches, not us."

Kaden growled low in his throat at the sight. "I wish I could say I'm surprised, but I'm not." He turned back to me and caressed my cheek. "But I don't care about him. I'm just glad you're here."

"I would never miss this," I said, pressing my hand against his, savoring the warmth of his skin on mine.

"Ayla?" Wesley's voice called out, and then he was barreling through the brush to get to me. He wrapped me up in his arms, nearly lifting me off the ground. "I'm so relieved to see you here. But is it true you're no longer in the Ophiuchus pack?"

"A temporary misunderstanding," Kaden said. "One I intend to fix as soon as this battle is over."

I raised an eyebrow. "Assuming I even want to join your pack again." I did, of course. I just didn't want to make it so easy for him.

Ethan shook my hand with a smile. "It's about time you showed up. Kaden was pacing up a storm. I never thought he'd settle down."

Kaden shot Ethan a hard look, but that only made me smile wider. It was nice to know Kaden had been as miserable as me while I'd been away. I moved forward and embraced Larkin and Stella next. There wasn't much time for anything else, but I was overjoyed to see my friends and family once again. *This* was where I belonged.

Then we all charged forward to face the enemy.

"Welcome," Evanora called out, cutting into our reunion, her voice booming through the forest around us thanks to her magic. "Welcome to the Convergence. I'm pleased to see all twelve packs of the Zodiac Wolves were able to make it. I hope we can continue our rituals as we have always done in the past, despite recent circumstances."

Her eyes settled on Kaden and me, and then quickly looked around at the other Ophiuchus pack members. Kaden growled, low in his chest. I wasn't sure if Evanora could hear it, but it rattled through my rib cage, and the shifters nearest to us twitched.

"The Ophiuchus pack is not invited, nor welcome here," she said coolly.

"The Ophiuchus pack has joined the Zodiac Wolves,

and the twelve packs are no longer allied with the Sun Witches," Kaden said, raising his chin defiantly.

Evanora scoffed, and her lips curled up into a cruel smile. "Don't be silly. The Zodiac Wolves need us. Or have you forgotten we're the only ones who can release your wolves, find your mates, and protect you from the Moon Curse?"

Around us, the packs were staring at each other, tension rising with each passing minute. There would only be so much time before violence broke out, but we needed to keep the peace for a while longer. *This* would be the perfect moment to unveil how the Sun Witches had orchestrated the Zodiac Packs' reliance on them.

"All of that is bullshit." Ethan was the one who called out, surprising me. He didn't look angry, like Kaden did. He was perfectly poised and polished, never losing his temper in the time I'd known him. He really was a diplomat, no matter how many times that had gotten in our way in the past, but he was obviously done with diplomacy today. "We know you're locking our wolves away and controlling the mate bonds. The Moon Curse hasn't been around for centuries. Release us from your spells, or we'll be forced to retaliate against you."

Evanora's smile changed and became almost pitying. "I have no idea what you mean. You've been deceived by the Ophiuchus pack. They are notoriously good at using dark magic, and they've twisted your minds." She clicked her tongue and shook her head, and for all intents and purposes, looked genuinely remorseful. "It's really too bad."

Anger rose inside of me at Evanora's fake tone and the stricken look on her face. Even being directly accused, she continued to deny it. She was putting on a show that was good enough that it had confused and held the packs under her thrall for years, but we couldn't let that continue any longer.

"The only twisted ones are the Sun Witches," I called out.

Evanora's sharp gaze turned to me. "That's rich, coming from you, you Moon Witch half-breed."

A few mutters went up around the shifters at her words, but I ignored them. "You've been controlling us for centuries, turning the packs against each other and breeding us like dogs, all for your personal gain." I stood up straighter, and didn't look away. "It's time for this to end. *Now*."

Some of the enemy packs bristled and exchanged looks with their pack mates. It was clear that this was the first they were hearing of this, but I couldn't tell if any of them believed what we were saying, or if they would continue to follow the Sun Witches.

"No." Evanora's voice cracked like a whip. "We created you, and we made you what you are today. It's time for you to bow to us again."

"We'll never bow," Wesley said, glaring at Evanora. "We'd rather die fighting for our freedom."

Evanora let out a wicked laugh. "Oh, do try, little pup. Your might is nothing against our magic."

Kaden huffed out a breath. "Enough," he said under his breath. "This ends now." He looked over at Ethan, and then at Wesley, who both nodded. Finally, he turned his gaze on me, and I nodded as well. I was ready, my blood singing in my veins, eager for battle. We'd come here for this purpose, and I was going to see it through to the end.

Kaden raised his head and looked back at the rest of the shifters. "For freedom," he called out, and the shifters surged forward, echoing his war cry.

Some shifted as they ran, while others stayed in human form. I watched as the combined force of our allied packs charged into battle. On my right, Wesley became a huge wolf, his crab armor coming out to protect him, and several of the other packs began preemptively employing their pack abilities as well. The enemy packs rushed forward a heartbeat later, with a smaller surge of shifters. The two groups met with a clash of teeth and claws and shouts, and then it was utter chaos.

I followed Kaden, the thrill of battle running through me, and leaped at a Scorpio shifter. I avoided his poison tail and shot moon magic at him. He fell over with a whimper. Kaden, now a wolf, growled as he sank his teeth into a Leo's side. The Leo yelped and tried to get away, but Kaden shook him like a dog and the Leo went slack. I smiled grimly as I shot two more beams of moonlight out in quick succession, each finding their target.

Each side fought viciously, but we had a clear advantage, overwhelming the enemy packs in sheer manpower alone. For a moment, everything looked to be going our way. *This is easy,* I thought. *Almost too easy.*

As if Evanora herself had heard my words, she tapped

her staff against the ground again. It shouldn't have made a noise that cut through the thick of battle, but it did, and the resulting beam of light was overwhelming. I raised my hand against it, trying not to close my eyes in case someone tried to take advantage of the moment to attack me. But nothing came. Everyone seemed to be just as shocked by the beam of light.

When I lowered my hand, the first thing I noticed was the utter stillness. The fighting had paused, and shifters were looking around at each other as if confused.

I turned to Kaden with a question in my eyes. *What the fuck is going on?* I planned to ask, but before I could, the shifters collectively shook themselves out of it. To my horror, a Libra pack member turned and started attacking Stella. She moved away reflexively, looking around as if to make sure everyone was seeing what was happening, as if she couldn't believe it with her own eyes.

As quickly as she'd been attacked, our allies all started fighting with each other. Those who were still in human form shifted, and friends began turning on one another, trying to take each other down like they were worst enemies. Only the Ophiuchus pack seemed to be spared from the frenzy that had taken over all the other shifters around us.

Ethan suddenly charged at Kaden, who dodged out of the way and shouted, "What the hell are you doing?"

A growl sounded to my left, and potent fear made my hackles rise. Wesley snarled at me, preparing to lunge for my throat at any moment. His wolf eyes were wild, staring at me like he'd never seen me before.

"Wesley?" I asked, holding my hands out in front of me. "It's *me*, it's your sister."

There was no flicker of recognition in his blue eyes. He surged forward and I rolled out of the way, unwilling to try and defend myself against Wesley. He had never so much as raised a hand to me in jest. Why was he attacking me now?

"*Stop*," I begged, but it didn't do any good. Wesley whipped around and attacked me again. There was no hesitation. If I let him catch me, I knew he wouldn't hesitate to kill me.

"Please," I said, dodging another attack. "Don't do this! Fight against whatever it is the Sun Witches have done to you! This isn't you!"

But Wesley either didn't hear me or didn't care. My heart broke as he attacked again. This wasn't supposed to be happening. He'd promised to have my back always.

The Sun Witches must be using their mind control magic, I realized. The same kind of command that Celeste had done to me must now be gripping all these shifters' minds. But how could Evanora do it on such a huge scale, spreading her magic across so many shifters?

CHAPTER THIRTY-THREE

THE OPHIUCHUS PACK all gathered together, our backs to each other, trying to stay alive as our friends and allies attacked us. Even though we were immune, there were so many more of them than there were of us. Each shifter would be overwhelmed in minutes.

"Wesley!" I tried again, but he didn't so much as twitch at the sound of his name or the obvious pain in my voice. He moved, lightning-fast, and the breath was knocked from me. He loomed over me, lips drawn back in a snarl, and snapped at my neck. I tried to roll out from under him, but before I could, Wesley pinned me in place with one giant paw.

Shit, I thought, feeling a cold rush go through me. *This really isn't the way I thought I'd die.*

Before Wesley could lower his teeth to my neck, a blur of reddish fur crashed into him. I blinked and looked on in awe as Jordan knocked Wesley out and turned back to me.

He snarled, as if he wanted to attack as well, but he didn't move any closer.

I held my hands up. "Jordan, if you give even half a fuck about me, stop!"

Jordan's teeth snapped, and I could imagine him saying, *yeah right*, as he slowly advanced toward me. I gritted my teeth. My other brother attacking me too now. This one wasn't quite as much of a shock, at least. Jordan trying to kill me was nothing new, after all.

But then he paused, about a foot away from me, and shook his head. He looked confused, as if he was listening to some tiny voice inside him that told me to stop.

He can't kill me because of the mate bond, I thought, and an idea quickly formed in my head. It was stupid, half-cocked, and it might not even work, but I had to try at least before Jordan could break through whatever was holding him back. *Idiots,* I thought about the Sun Witches. *Your magic is conflicting.*

I reached for the invisible cord that existed between me and Jordan at all times. I hadn't thought about the mate bond in weeks. It was hardly noticeable anymore, but when I turned my attention to it, it thrummed to life. I brushed past Larkin's dampener spell, delving into it and tugging *hard* on the bond between us.

Jordan shook his head harder, letting out a whine. I paused and looked down at my chest. My mother had given me this gift to help protect against the Sun Witches' spells. *Could it work?*

I slowly took the necklace off, the battle still raging on

around us, but it seemed no one wanted to mess with Jordan enough to attack me. I crossed the last bit of space between us, and Jordan snarled a warning, but he didn't move. I held the necklace out in front of me like an offering. His eyes caught on it, and something flashed through him, something strangely human.

I put a hand on top of his head and rubbed his fur a little. He whined as if he wanted to pull away but couldn't. I felt him fighting it, his powerful muscles trembling with the effort not to attack me. I'd have to act quickly if I wanted him to break free of whatever this was. I slipped the necklace over his head, and he jerked violently like he'd been stuck. The struggle left his eyes, and when he looked at me, I saw recognition in them.

Jordan shifted back immediately and touched the moonstone necklace around his neck with obvious relief. "Thank you."

Something in my heart eased. "Something tells me you've been controlled by the Sun Witches before, haven't you?"

Jordan nodded silently, getting that same, pained look in his eyes as I'd seen not long ago when I'd questioned him about the Sun Witches. "Many times," he finally said. "But now your moonstone necklace has broken their hold over me. I'm finally free."

But I wasn't. Evanora's seductive voice suddenly attacked my mind, telling me to *fight, kill, main, destroy.* I immediately threw up a mental shield woven of moonlight, blocking her out, though it took almost all my strength to do so. Damn, she was strong. And without my necklace, I was vulnerable to her magic now too.

Somehow I fought her off and stood up straight again, while Jordan remained by my side this time, making sure none of the other wolves got near me. The battle raged on around us, and I quickly stepped to the side as an Aries shifter got past Jordan and nearly rammed into me. All around us, packs who had sworn their alliance were ripping each other apart like it was nothing. This was nothing short of a bloodbath, worse than even the last Convergence. I let out a horrified sound as I watched a Cancer shifter tear into his brother from the same pack. *They can even turn shifters of the same pack against each other.*

"We have to do something," I said, turning back to Jordan.

"I have an idea," he said and shifted back into wolf form before I could ask him what it was. He let loose a massive Leo roar that caused every shifter in the vicinity to cower or flee. It was enough to stop the bloodshed for a few moments, the clearing going almost eerily quiet. How could anyone doubt that he was the Leo alpha after a display like that? I hadn't heard a Leo roar that potent in quite some time. Since Dixon was alive.

Then Jordan let out another roar, different in pitch and tone, and clearly for a different purpose. As if compelled, all of the Leos quickly shifted back to human form and began picking up fellow pack members. One by one, they fled the clearing, taking as many downed shifters as they could.

"What did you do?" I asked.

Jordan shifted back and smiled at me, a ghost of his usual cocky grin. "I used the alpha command to make them all stand down. I wasn't sure if it would work against the Sun Witches' power, but it did. If we can get the other alphas to do the same thing, we'll be able to stop this bloodbath."

"Smart." But there was one problem. I only had one moonstone necklace, and there were a lot of alphas. "We need to find Larkin."

I hadn't seen her since the battle had started, and I feared she might have fallen in the chaos. But Jordan became a wolf again and raised his nose before barreling through the shifters who continued fighting, including Kaden and Ethan. I hurried after him as quickly as I could and caught sight of Larkin's slim frame in the crowd. She looked over at me wildly before lobbing another beam of magic at a Virgo shifter.

"The Sun Witches are controlling them," I told her, as Jordan took down a Taurus who tried to get in our way.

"No shit," Larkin said, before shooting off more moonlight.

"Celeste gave me a moonstone necklace and it freed Jordan," I told her. "Is there something we can do for the other alphas so we can free them from the Sun Witches' magic too?"

Larkin grunted and wiped at her brow as she considered. "I might be able to shield a few of the alphas from the Sun Witch magic for a bit and break their control."

"Do it. Once they're free, they can control the rest of their packs and make this madness stop."

Ethan was the closest to us, still going after Kaden, who looked pained, as if he was trying to hold himself back from hurting his friend. Larkin raised her hands and chanted a few words, while Jordan kept all the other shifters at bay around us. A brilliant burst of moon energy encased Ethan in his wolf form, and his ears twitched. It didn't seem to be enough. I poured my own magic into the spell, copying her words after a few more iterations. The magic seemed to shimmer in the air, unstable against the onslaught of the Sun Witches' immense power, but we kept pushing.

Then Ethan staggered back and shook his head. He shifted back immediately and looked around, horrified.

"What is happening?" He looked at Kaden, the horror deepening on his face. "Why was I attacking you?"

"Use your alpha command to make your pack stop fighting," Jordan ordered. "Tell them to get out of here, and take as many of the injured with them as they can."

We didn't have time to explain everything, and luckily Ethan seemed to understand that. He didn't question it, just shifted and let out an earsplitting howl. It worked and the Libras all stopped fighting, most of them shifting back to their human forms and looking around confused. Then they left the clearing, many of them carrying other shifters, just as the Leo pack had done.

A low growl sounded behind me, and I turned back to Wesley, who was just now stirring. His eyes snapped open and he snarled. I quickly cast moon magic over him, pouring all of my frustration and urgency into the spell to make it stronger. Larkin joined me a second later, and then Stella and Harper and a few others joined in too, copying the words of the spell as best as they could.

When Wesley's eyes cleared, I rushed forward immediately, wrapping my arms around his neck. He shifted with me still holding onto him, and I almost cried when his arms came up to reciprocate the hug.

"Ayla?" he asked as if he'd been woken from a deep sleep. "What's going on? Why was I trying to kill you?"

"I'll explain later," I said. "Just use your alpha command to make the Cancer pack stop fighting and flee the area."

Wesley pulled back and looked around, as if shocked to see his pack fighting, but he did what I asked, and soon the Cancer pack had also fled the battlefield.

But even with three packs gone, it barely made any difference. There were still too many packs fighting and not enough time to reach all of them. The killing continued, brutal and relentless, and I knew it wasn't going to stop unless we did something. But how was Evanora controlling everyone?

The staff, I realized. It must be similar to my moonstone necklace but on a much bigger scale, allowing her to amplify her own magic.

"We don't have enough time to help everyone," I said. "We need to get that staff."

Kaden jerked his chin toward where Evanora was standing, watching everything unfold with unbridled glee. "Let's go."

"We'll maintain the shields over Wesley and Ethan, and try to expand it to any more alphas we can reach," Larkin said, motioning to Stella and Harper. I was suddenly incredibly thankful for all the time we'd spent practicing magic together with Larkin.

"Be careful," I told her, praying we would all see each other again soon. They were all competent fighters, but it didn't matter in the face of this level of brutality. I couldn't focus on them though. I had to trust that they would make it out alive. Right now, my focus needed to be on Evanora, and on getting that staff.

"I'm coming with you," Jordan said. "I will never let them control me again."

I nodded at Jordan and took his hand, then grabbed Kaden's too. The three of us were always linked together somehow, it seemed.

I teleported us right into the middle of the Sun Witches. There was no use fighting our way through the masses, and this would give us the element of surprise. The moment I let go of Kaden and Jordan's hands, I shot a beam of moonlight right at Evanora's chest. I didn't expect it to hit, but it did. It didn't do much more than make her stumble, but it was enough. Kaden leaped forward, hands shifted into claws, and slashed at her arm. Blood welled up, and she dropped her staff with a scream.

Kaden pounced on her, following her all the way down, and slashed at her chest. Blood welled up there, and for a moment, I thought we had her.

Then a blast of sun magic hit all three of us, knocking

Kaden completely off of Evanora and making Jordan and I stumble. I swung around, ready to fight. Roxandra's enraged face charged toward us, but then her eyes settled on Jordan and began to glow with bright sunlight.

"Jordan," she called out. "Come to me."

I felt the immense power in her words, and though Jordan began to tremble, he managed to hold his ground. The moonstone necklace seemed to be warding off her magic, though I wasn't sure how long it would last.

I wove tendrils of moon magic around Jordan, shielding him from her power, and she let out a sound of angry protest. With her magic no longer lashing at him, he launched himself at Roxandra, who let out a yelp and disappeared in a puff of smoke. She reappeared behind us and blasted me with more sunbeams, but this time I was ready and I managed to block them.

While Roxandra had us distracted, Evanora slowly sat up and met my eyes. I had enough time to see the utter hatred and spite contained in them, and then she reached for her staff. I opened my mouth to scream for Kaden to kick it away from her, but her fingers closed around it before I could even make a sound. Then she disappeared in a burst of light and smoke.

The other Sun Witches began vanishing as well, teleporting away much like I could. Dammit, they were getting away again!

Then Kaden suddenly appeared out of nowhere next to Roxandra, his invisibility dropping just before he sank his teeth into her arm, injecting her with Ophiuchus pack poison. She looked over at him, infuriated, and then the light left her eyes. She slumped forward, and he let her go, letting her fall to the ground in a slump.

The other Sun Witches had all disappeared, but a flicker of hope rose up in my chest. We finally had a Sun Witch.

CHAPTER THIRTY-FOUR

WITH THE SUN WITCHES GONE, the control over the fighting shifters was broken. It went from a loud, messy battle to absolute silence in just a few heartbeats. It was incredible, how quickly the control was broken, and then the assembled shifters remembered themselves.

A howl went up, followed by a few human screams, murmurs of confusion, and many pained cries. I looked at the carnage, at the number of both wolf and human bodies that lay on the ground, unmoving and covered in blood. There were too many dead, and even more were injured. I didn't know how many more of the living shifters would die from their wounds alone. I closed my eyes against the grisly scene, trying to reconcile it with the plan we'd had in our heads. Even closing my eyes, there was nothing I could do to block out the pained cries of the shifters as they realized what they'd done, and how they'd attacked their own pack members, friends, and family.

The Virgo alpha's voice cut through the panic and pain that was welling up in me. "Virgos!" she called, and I opened my eyes to see her pack gathering around her. She looked worn, tired, and completely horrified, but still fierce as hell. "Start healing whoever you can. Start with our pack members first so they can help us, and then take care of the other packs. Friends and enemies alike," she added, giving them all a meaningful look.

The Virgo pack members all dispersed quickly and started picking their way through the blood-drenched clearing, crouching over shifters to check if they were breathing or not. Their movements were slowed a bit by the snow on the ground, but they didn't let it stop them.

"Join them," Kaden ordered, looking around at the Ophiuchus pack members closest to him. They nodded and moved forward to help the Virgos with their own healing powers.

Kaden then moved to my side, and together we gazed across the clearing at the aftermath of the battle. Everyone was bloody and exhausted, and there was a sense of defeat permeating the air. We hadn't won anything, and we'd lost a lot. Too much, really. Wolves had been made to fight and kill each other, all because of the Sun Witches' control. There was no way we could have foreseen this or prepared for it, and I wasn't sure if the survivors would be able to deal with the guilt over what they'd done.

"How are we ever going to defeat the Sun Witches when they can control us so easily?" Ethan asked. His gaze was fixed on Stella, who was tending to one of his pack members. The fallen shifter looked on the verge of death, and Stella's eyes flicked up, bright with tears.

I didn't have an answer, and from the resounding silence from everyone else, they didn't either. I was still reeling from the amount of violence we'd all just been subjected to. The Sun Witches really did see us as nothing more than animals. To them, we were completely disposable, just pawns to be moved about and tossed aside when we'd served our purpose.

But at least now we knew what they were capable of, and so did all of the other Zodiac Wolves. Maybe we'd be able to change the minds of the other packs and convince them to join us too, to help make a truly united stand against the Sun Witches for once. It wouldn't be easy, but we'd have to try—and we had Jordan on our side now. Of that, I was sure. If he could change, then anything was possible.

Besides, we had a Sun Witch in our captivity too. We would finally be able to break the mate bond between me and Jordan, and hopefully, Roxandra would have some answers for us as well. We would interrogate her about ways to break the spells that locked away our wolves and our mates, and figure out how to stop Evanora from controlling everyone too.

"We'll find a way," I told Ethan, finally answering his question, and the words resonated through my bones like a promise. I wouldn't let the Sun Witches win. Not after what they'd done to me, to all the shifters, and to the Moon Witches too.

I looked around for Larkin, remembering my promise to

keep an eye out on her. She was with Wesley and looked as pale as a ghost, but they both appeared unharmed. I let out a relieved sigh.

Kaden wrapped his arms around me and I leaned into him, grateful for his touch, even if a part of me was still mad at him. I couldn't face that yet though, not when I was relieved to just be alive. Someday soon we would have a reckoning, and I wasn't sure where we would end up after that, but for now, I just wanted him to hold me.

The sun cast a grim glow over the already grisly scene, but as I watched, it brightened just a bit. Shifters stood up, brushed off the death that hung over them, and walked together side by side as they left the clearing. Among all the pain and suffering, there was a small glimmer of hope for the future. It was barely enough to light a fire by, but it was still there.

And I was going to cling to it with everything I had.

ABOUT THE AUTHOR

Elizabeth Briggs is the *New York Times* bestselling author of paranormal and fantasy romance. She graduated from UCLA with a degree in Sociology and has worked for an international law firm, mentored teens in writing, and volunteered with dog rescue groups. Now she's a full-time geek who lives in Los Angeles with her family and a pack of fluffy dogs.

Visit Elizabeth's website: www.elizabethbriggs.com

Join Elizabeth's Facebook group for fun book chat and early sneak peeks!

Made in the USA
Las Vegas, NV
07 June 2022

49938063R00185